Crypt of Souls

Book Two of the "Stolen" Series

a novel by

K. A. Krisko

Tulk Tales

"Yet man dies not whilst the world, at once his mother and his monument, remains. His name is lost, indeed, but the breath he breathed still stirs the pine-tops on the mountains, the sound of the words he spoke yet echoes on through space; the thoughts his brain gave birth to we have inherited to-day; his passions are our cause of life; the joys and sorrows that he knew are our familiar friends--the end from which he fled aghast will surely overtake us also!

Truly the universe is full of ghosts, not sheeted churchyard spectres, but the inextinguishable elements of individual life, which having once been, can never die, though they blend and change, and change again for ever."

— H. Rider Haggard, King Solomon's Mines

For maps, support documents, .gifs, trailers, and other extras, visit

kakrisko.com
and click on the 'Stolenworld' link

Table of Contents

Chapter One...1
Chapter Two..9
Chapter Three..21
Chapter Four..31
Chapter Five...43
Chapter Six...57
Chapter Seven..69
Chapter Eight...85
Chapter Nine..97
Chapter Ten..109
Chapter Eleven...127
Chapter Twelve..143
Chapter Thirteen..155
Chapter Fourteen...167
Chapter Fifteen..179
Chapter Sixteen...195
Chapter Seventeen...207
Chapter Eighteen...221
Chapter Nineteen...231
Chapter Twenty...245
About the author:..251
Other works by K.A. Krisko: 252

Chapter One

A thin spiral of black greasy smoke curled out of the stone chimney of Rioletta Eris' house. A few feet above the roof, it bent, swooped down to where Rioletta was weeding the potted kitchen garden, and drove purposefully at her eyes.

"Go on, get out of here," she growled, swatting it away. The smoke reared back, then twisted away towards the woods, poking and searching. It broke into undulating snake-length segments before it disappeared between the trees.

A thin, blond-haired girl darted out of the house. "More, Aunt Rio?"

"Yes, Justah, this is the last pile. Take them quick, they're trying to crawl back in the pot."

Justah grabbed a large handful of sneakweed that was slowly inching itself across the stone floor of Rioletta's portico and ran back inside to stuff it in the stove. Burning was the only way to get rid of sneakweed; if you left it lying around after pulling, it would re-plant itself in the very pots you'd just pulled it out of. As it was, the smoke would make its way to the woods to fertilize other sneakweed plants, after, of course, trying to get in their eyes as a final revenge.

1

Rioletta stood and wiped the dirt from her hands on her trousers. "I guess that'll keep them weed-free until we get back," she said as the smoke tapered away and Justah joined her again.

"When are we going?" Justah asked impatiently.

"A few days. Some folks are leaving already. The rest of us will go all together in a big group. We'll have to travel four days to get to the Polebray. But once we're there it'll be a lot of fun. The celebration will be big this year."

Rioletta was almost as anxious as five-year-old Justah to leave for the Polebray. It was the one-hundredth anniversary of the Dispersal, and the planned festivities would attract thousands of people from all over the region. There would be opportunities for trade and many social events. It had been a hard winter, and she was looking forward to a break.

The Younger Council, short one member since the expulsion of Cardon, had taken on a lot of responsibility over the winter. With Mosse and Tereret gone, the three remaining members of the Elder Council needed their help, especially as Ladon, the Council's leader, had traveled a great deal. The Sydian settlements had entered into a new cooperative agreement to facilitate trade with Dobor and the Tadian region following the overthrow of Tabor by the First Chosen. Ladon had been tapped to head the Trade Council, and the responsibility had taken him out of Andolith frequently. In addition, there had been discussions with the deposed Elder Council of Tabor regarding the make-up of their government-in-exile, and tense meetings in West Ford with members of the First Chosen and the Council of Tane.

"Come on, now, Justah, it's time to go home," Rioletta told the little girl. "Thank you for your help; it's much more difficult by myself."

"How come I can't stay at your place anymore?" Justah asked as she poked along behind Rioletta towards the center of town and the house of her grandmother, Lida.

"Because I'm very busy with the Council. Your father has more time for you now that he's not on the Council anymore. And when he's busy, Lida is there."

As they approached Lida's house, Rioletta saw Cardon's wagon parked alongside, set up and ready to go. He'd shown her how he'd attached lead ropes for his horses to the back with break-

2

away connections in case something happened. He planned to bring his racehorses to the Polebray, with the hopes of interesting others in them as well as showing them off. Over the winter he had acquired both Mahquant horses, the taller, slimmer horses of the plains, and some of the local horses, which were shorter but more agile in the trees, mostly on credit, to start his breeding program. One of the local mares was at Rioletta's disposal, and she would ride it to the Polebray.

Cardon had agreed to take the few pieces of woodwork and the paper she'd manufactured over the winter in his wagon. She was hoping to sell it and use the extra money to buy small goods which would undoubtedly be for sale at the Polebray, but which had been in short supply since the overthrow of Tabor. Many luxury and useful items came from the Tadian region. Tabor produced wine and mustard, but they also produced some of the most efficient medicines, anesthetics and antibiotics. There were orchards south and east of Dobor, and around the south side of Hyolon there were other small settlements that salvaged and recycled goods from the Ruined City. These were the items in short supply, the ones Rioletta looked forward to obtaining.

As Rioletta turned back from Lida's house, she heard someone shout her name. Andor Acaladon waved at her from a few houses away.

"Hey, Rio, come take a walk with me!" Andor called. "I'm sick to death of packing and arranging things, and I need a break."

The two of them wandered through the middle of the plaza where the giant decorative sundial gleamed in the afternoon sun. Most people had mechanical clocks, courtesy of Pateret's family, but the sundial served as a check. It lay on a raised platform about waist-high, and was some ten feet across, with a huge triangular shadow-maker. Rioletta had used it as a Viewing talisman before, and she ran a hand over its polished rim as they passed by.

"When are you planning on leaving?" Rioletta asked as they walked north towards the path to the Contemplation.

"Tomorrow. We're about ready. Creed wants to get there early, he's impatient to start the party," Andor laughed. "We'll meet you when you get there. We'll have an assigned campsite. Let's hope it's to the west; the ones to the east will be swampy and they'll have mosquitoes. Are you travelling with Cardon?"

3

"I'm riding by myself," Rioletta said. "Cardon agreed to take my trade goods in his wagon, though."

Their conversation slacked as they began to climb along the dirt track that led out of the village and up the side of the ridge upon which the Contemplation sat. There was a good view from up there, and as Sorcerers they were free to use it as they wished. The hike was short, only a little more than half a mile, but it was a good way to stretch their legs without wandering off into the forest. They scrambled up the steep side of the hill and then hand-over-hand up the final rock face of the Contemplation to where the circle of rocks stood on top. There was an easier way to the east, but Andor and Rioletta preferred the direct route.

Rioletta turned to look over the village, then scanned to the southwest, as was her habit when she wished to contact Nikal of Dobor via her Viewing talisman. She fingered the black talisman absently. But Andor bumped her on the arm; Rioletta glanced at her and then followed her gaze to the north across the back of the Contemplation.

A boot stuck out from behind one of the upright rocks. Someone was sitting or dozing behind the rock. Andor and Rioletta met each other's eyes, and Rioletta could read Andor's unspoken intent to startle whomever the boot belonged to.

As they snuck quietly around the rock, Rioletta saw that it was Cardon. He sat with his shoulders against the rock, slumped, his legs stretched out, head lolling, mouth slightly open as if asleep, and she could see his eyes flickering under his eyelids as though he dreamed. But there was something odd about his posture.

Andor reached down and grabbed Cardon by the shoulder, her joke forgotten. "Hey, Cardon, are you all right?"

But Cardon did not respond. Alarmed, Rioletta knelt and took one of his hands while Andor shook him again more forcefully and shouted his name. Rioletta concentrated hard; she had occasionally been able to contact Cardon's mind before, and she hoped she might be able to wake him. She felt only a fleeting sensation of confusion, but in a few seconds she felt his limp hand move and then his eyes opened. He looked around in confusion for a moment, then pushed himself up from his slumped position and stared at them.

"Cardon, are you alright?" Rioletta demanded.

4

"I was only dozing," he said uncertainly.

"No," Andor said, "don't try to fool us. That was no sleep I've ever seen."

Cardon flushed and climbed to his feet. He seemed a little unsteady, and his eyes were haunted and distressed. She had seen that look too often over the last few months.

"What were you doing, Cardon?" Andor demanded, studying him, hands on hips.

"Nothing," Cardon said more decisively. "I came to get away from everybody for a few minutes. I've been here long enough, I've got to get back and finish packing. Did you bring Justah home, Rioletta?"

"Yes," Rioletta said, "but…"

Cardon did not wait for her to form her question. Rioletta and Andor watched as he hurriedly jumped down the side of the Contemplation and rushed down the path.

Andor turned to Rioletta. "You should talk to him, find out what's going on. That was no sleep I've seen. It was more like the end of a fit or a trance."

"I don't talk to him so much anymore," Rioletta admitted. "Since he's not on the Council, I've mostly seen him this winter when I went to pick up Justah or drop her off."

"And there's Nikal. Still, you're the best friend he's got, and someone should figure out what's going on with him. You know he's forbidden to practice any of the Skills he learned at Hyolon. I suppose I could tell Ladon what we saw. Or Charnia."

"No," Rioletta sighed. "Let me talk to him first. Ladon's busy, and you know Cardon still avoids him, although he's been more than fair. And he dislikes Charnia."

Although Cardon had been relieved of his Council duties, Ladon had not relieved him of his apprenticeship with Charnia, the village's most senior Healer. There were very few with that skill in Andolith, and although he disliked it, Cardon had shown great promise, particularly in the treatment of injuries. Thus Ladon had decided he should continue with his education and help Charnia as she required it, and Cardon's arguments to the contrary had fallen on deaf ears. Ladon was his father's cousin, and as his senior relative as well as Leader of the Council, he had a great deal of control over Cardon's activities. Of course, Ladon had also made it clear that

Cardon was not to practice any of the Forbidden Skills he'd learned, or even any of the Restricted Skills taught only to the Sorcerers. If Ladon suspected Cardon of practicing either, Rioletta knew Cardon would certainly pay for it in one way or another, and although Rioletta and Cardon were no longer as close as they had once been, she still felt protective of him.

The two women climbed back down the Contemplation. Where the trail merged with the village clearing, Andor split off towards Creed's house. Rioletta went back the way she'd come.

The back door of Lida's house was open, and Cardon worked a piece of leather at the counter just inside.

"Cardon, we need to talk," Rioletta said from the doorway.

Cardon glanced up and back down quickly. "I'm busy."

"Cardon, if you don't talk to me, I'll tell Ladon I suspect you of practicing the Forbidden Skills."

Cardon threw the leatherwork down and stalked wordlessly out the door. Rioletta kept up beside him as they headed for the edge of the pines on the northwest side of the village. Just inside the shelter of the forest, where it was cooler, Cardon stopped and leaned back against a tree, his arms crossed, one knee up defensively.

"Cardon, what was going on up there on the Contemplation?" Rioletta pressed him. "Was it something you did on purpose? Don't try to tell me you were napping; I took your hand, and you know our connection is strong enough for me to feel some of what you feel, even from a distance."

"And what did you feel?" Cardon asked, meeting her eyes for a fleet second.

Rioletta paused. "Fear, perhaps. Grief. But nothing specific."

There was a long silence. Rioletta let the pressure of expectation do her work for her, and finally Cardon relented.

"It comes without warning. I promise you it's nothing I'm doing on purpose, and there's no need to tell Ladon I'm practicing the Forbidden Skills. They come to me unbidden."

"Who comes to you?" Rioletta pressed.

Cardon shook his head. "Voices. Not that I'm hearing them in my ears. They're in my mind. I've tried to dismiss them as manifestations of the damage I did to myself by taking the transformation draught, but I can't. The thing is, it's very similar to the feeling I had when you and I communicated, when you were

6

camping in the woods and I was in Tabor. And I trusted that then and came to you, and it was real."

"Perhaps this is real, too, then," Rioletta suggested. "Perhaps someone is trying to talk to you."

"No." Cardon shook his head again. "It's not possible, much as I wish it were."

"Why not?"

"Because one of the voices is Marsavrina."

For a moment, Rioletta could not form words. Marsavrina was the Tabor Sorcerer inductee who had led Cardon along the Path of Transformation, with whom he had Mind-shared, and she was the mother of Cardon's child Justah. But she had been struck down by a Skill of her own making, a Forbidden Skill, when she and the rest of the Younger Council had transformed the Elder Council and imprisoned them in tapestries. Her body lay in a stone crypt somewhere near the Ruined City of Hyolon, and no dead person could pass a thought, for nothing of a person survived the body in death.

"This worries me," Rioletta finally said. "How long have you been hearing this voice?"

"This voice and one other," Cardon corrected. "I've been hearing Marsavrina since not long after I found them dead. The other voice I hear is Skadar Vrinal, the youngest of the Younger Council. I can understand hearing Marsavrina's voice as hallucination, for I knew her well. But I knew Skadar little, and it strikes me as odd that my mind would choose him, instead of, say, Malbec or Chasandahl, whom I knew better."

"Do they say anything specific? And do you always fall into a trance like that?"

Cardon nodded. "I can feel it coming on, so I seek a private place. And always it's the same thing. Marsavrina calls my name: '*Cardon, Cardon, we lie in the crypt of souls!*' And Skadar says, "*'Deep in Hyolon, but we have no key.'*" Always it's the same. It's disturbing, and it haunts me. I've thought that perhaps if I returned and found where they lie and assured a proper cremation for them, the voices would go away."

"There's no way you or any of us can go there now," Rioletta said. "We have no idea what our reception would be should we run into any of the First Chosen in their own territory, but we can guess they aren't pleased with us for rescuing and removing the Elders. It's too dangerous. Perhaps we should tell Charnia; she has some expertise at calming the mind."

"No!" Cardon said vehemently. "I beg you, do not tell Charnia, or Ladon either. I don't want it getting about that I'm completely insane. I'm not in a decision-making position; Charnia reviews everything I do, so it's no matter to anyone what goes on in my own mind."

"I wouldn't have told Ladon anyway, I only threatened that to get you to talk to me," Rioletta said. "But I won't tell anyone if you don't want help, except perhaps Andor, who saw you on the Contemplation."

Cardon smiled for the first time as Rioletta revealed her hollow threat. "I should have known better," he said. "And most likely I should have told you before now. But it's as if I thought if I told no one, it would be less real. Don't worry about me; perhaps it will pass with time."

"Perhaps. Adla Kathreftis of Dobor will be at the Polebray, I'm sure," Rioletta said. "If you don't want to get a calming potion from Charnia and haven't anything you can use yourself, perhaps Adla will have something for you. She's very Skilled."

"Yes, I look forward to seeing her," Cardon said thoughtfully. "Now I have to continue preparing. I have my own leatherwork to pack, as well as a large amount of stuff Charnia wants to trade. And my mother will be wondering where I've got off to, leaving Justah with her when I promised I'd be around this afternoon."

"I have a few more reams of paper for you to take," Rioletta said. "You can come pick them up at my house and take them back with you, and that will give you an excuse for your absence."

Chapter Two

Two days later, Rioletta and most of the population of Andolith left for the Polebray. They didn't get started until mid-morning, and at first the going was slow as they sorted themselves out along the road to Matbor. The entire village had been reduced to a jumble of wagons, carts, and horses. Summer dust rose around them, and some of the younger travelers escaped it by riding through the open oak woods on either side, their agile mounts darting through the trees. Rioletta could spot them easily even through the trunks; they wore brightly colored shirts, and in the hot weather of late June, no one was wearing a tunic or jacket.

Very few were left in Andolith to keep watch over the town. This was the one-hundredth celebration of the Dispersal, the time when their ancestors left the cities and moved to the scattered settlements in which they now lived. It was worth celebrating, and a good excuse to trade and interact with others they didn't often see or with whom contact was usually restricted.

Even Stolen and Justah were along. After some thought, Ladon had put it out to the Trade Council that they were sheltering two people born of Sorcerers who had practiced the Forbidden Skills, and their appearance was due to the transgressions of their parents. There was no need, he said, to punish the offspring for the deeds of their parents, and they had been adopted into the community. It was expected that Stolen and Justah would garner

9

some attention at the Polebray, but the promise to the Lefollah would be kept without imprisoning the two in their own village.

Rioletta could see them both ahead. Justah rode with Cardon and Lida in their wagon, ignoring her father's orders and scrambling dangerously over the goods piled in the bed to shout and wave at the children of Alaxas in a nearby wagon. Stolen rode his own horse. He had become quite adept at riding over the winter, primarily because of his ability to communicate directly with the horses, and he rode with only a saddle blanket and a lead rope on a halter. He wore the long-sleeved green shirt and the high-waisted brown trousers common in the Sydian, and the clothing disguised his appearance. At first he might be mistaken for a man with untrimmed hair; only when Rioletta came closer could she see that the hair intermingled with leaves, and he went barefoot rather than booted.

The Andolith travelers made it only as far as Matbor that evening, near the intersection where the Tabor Ford road branched to the west and the Rhamphor Road toward the south. Usually this was a trip that could be accomplished in little more than half a day, but the large group traveled slowly, and it took a lot of time to set up camp and then break it down. Rioletta found it frustrating; she'd traveled the same route once before with Andor, and the trip had gone much more quickly.

Matbor itself was nearly deserted, but travelers heading south from Tabor Ford crowded the road, and the dust settled in Rioletta's hair and left a coating of grit on her face and even in her ears. They camped twice more, once south of the Sydian and once just north of West Ford, and came into West Ford itself early in the morning on the fourth day. It took several hours to get the wagons ferried across the Rhamphor and regrouped on the south side. Rioletta took the opportunity to wash up in the shallows upstream of the crossing. By midday they were finally traveling again, heading west along the river, and they approached the Polebray in early evening.

The Polebray was a huge spreading flat of cottonwoods, box elders, and willows along the southern side of a huge bend in the River Rhamphor. Usually the gathering was a spontaneous affair, and those who had goods to trade arrived now and then during the ten days around the Solstice, with a loosely-organized event held on the Solstice eve. But this was a special celebration, and a company had been engaged to organize the event. Campsites were assigned, areas had been laid out for vendors, food, and competitions, horse corrals had been erected, first aid and security provided, and sanitary facilities had been brought in.

The main entrances to the Polebray were fenced and gated, and tables had been set up to check travelers in to their sites. The Andolith group stopped near the eastern gate and Ladon went to get information. Rioletta noticed a large water-clock set up on a dais; it was the time-check for the events, and all who entered the Polebray used it to set their own timepieces.

Ladon came back with a handful of maps, which he passed out to the group. "We've got a nice spot in the cottonwoods, about halfway along to the other gate and a quarter-mile south. Andor and Creed and a few others have checked in already; their tents should be there. Find a spot, set up your camp, and then take your horses to the corrals. We're not to have horses in the camps except for packing and unpacking or for moving wagons around. That'll help keep things clean and the flies down. Use the facilities they've provided, too; no stumbling off in the dark behind the bushes. Trade fair, have fun, and if anyone gets arrested, don't send to me looking for bail money!"

There was laughing and cheering, and Ladon swung up on his horse and led the group through the gate and onto the grounds of the Polebray itself. Rioletta stared from side to side as they passed many tables, wagons, and tents set up with goods for sale or trade, organized into alleys by category and set up almost like a town. Unskilled villagers mingled freely with the Skilled. The smells of cooking wafted through the cottonwoods to greet them. Far away to the west, dust rose in the area of the horseracing track; many people were trying their hand at the competitions already. Painted signs with arrows had been attached to posts where rows of vendors crossed, showing the way to the archery trials, dance floor, small animal judging, and other locations. Tents had been set up for treatment of illness and injury and marked with bright yellow flags, and there were several sub-stations for security. Guards wandered the crowd in uniforms with bright yellow sashes, lightly armed, looking relaxed and slightly overwhelmed. Children ran along the stalls at full speed and occasionally fell headlong into the dirt. Some of them had their faces painted like animals; others carried elaborate foods on sticks.

Their camp was well away from the cacophony of the stalls in amongst huge cottonwoods. Soon everyone was unloading their personal gear and setting up sleeping areas. Rioletta unloaded her own gear from Cardon's wagon and helped him set up a tent and chairs for Lida and Charnia. Justah would stay with Creed's older sister Alaxas and her children, which would free Cardon to attend to his horses. Cardon set up his own bedding near Rioletta's, which she had laid down near several cots and tents that were already in place.

She rummaged in the bed of the wagon for a bag of tent stakes that had sorted itself down into the bottom just behind the wagon seat. The bag was tantalizingly close to her fingertips, but just out of reach. Then someone clapped her on the shoulder, and she turned to see Creed.

"Let me help you, there," he grinned, and reached easily into the bed to remove the bag. He was a full head taller than her.

Andor came up behind them. "Well met! You've made it! Cardon, do you need help moving the horses?"

"Yes, if you don't mind," Cardon said. "I need to get those six out to the tracks over there to the west and the two cart-horses to the main corrals after we set the wagon. Rio, have you got a map?"

Rioletta grabbed the map off the seat of the wagon and poked at a spot on it. "Furniture and woodwork, here. We can take the wagon and I'll offload my stuff. The area for craft and writing supplies is near the furniture area, so I can sell both together if we can get a good spot. Then you can take the wagon to the leatherwork area and set it up as you like. If I'm lucky, I'll have very little for you to take back."

"Except, of course, for all the stuff you're going to buy!" Andor laughed. "Meet us back here afterwards, then. There's time later to sell. You should walk through and see where everything is and get some food. You won't believe how much stuff there is. Let's get Morcah and Pateret, too."

Creed and Andor each jumped onto one of Cardon's Mahquant horses bareback and trotted away towards the special corrals at the racetrack. Before she put the map back on Cardon's wagon seat, Rioletta studied it until she found the Dobor camp area. She fingered the black teardrop amulet that hung at her neck. She didn't think Nikal had arrived; but she would be able to find him whenever she wanted once he did.

Over the winter, Rioletta had become more adept at contacting Nikal through the talisman, and in the spring, as Ladon had promised, she and Andor had been allowed to make a trip to Dobor. Before they left, Ladon took her aside.

"You're permitted to continue your education in the Restricted Skills of Monitoring and Viewing," he had said. "They don't directly change the lives of others, and I see little problem with them. However, I have a bigger issue with the Distance Communication you engaged in, albeit unwittingly, with Cardon. It's too much like Mind-sharing, and that is Forbidden. You are not to receive training in that, and any other Restricted Skills will require my permission first."

Rioletta had agreed and promised, although she hadn't reminded him about her communication with Nikal via talisman; she was not positive he knew about it. That was not Mind-sharing, she reasoned, but was facilitated through the talisman itself. It was specifically authorized in the Charter as a Restricted Skill, although it was not one of the Skills chosen for Andolith in their City Charter. But neither were Monitoring and Viewing.

She and Andor had traveled together to Dobor, crossing the new Dobor Bridge, and they had spent several days mostly in the company of Nikal and Adla. Nikal had taken her around the village and showed her the glass recycling yards that belonged to the Kathreftis family. His house was very different from those in Andolith, with an open courtyard in the back and a view over the rest of the town; and of course there was lots of glass, so it was open and light inside. It had been an enjoyable time, and she looked forward to finding him again at the Polebray.

An hour after they arrived, with the wagon set up for trading and the horses corralled, Rioletta, Cardon, Andor, Pateret, Creed, Morcah, and several other young people from the village strolled through the crowds in the cool of early evening. Pateret was still recovering from her burns of nearly a year before, and she wore tight leather gloves on her hands and a high collar. She often tired quickly, but Rioletta had noticed that she had not lost her interest in explosives, and knew she would help with a demonstration of fireworks on the Solstice eve.

13

As darkness fell, lights began to glow at each corner and the vendors lighted many more lamps and torches at the fronts of their stalls. Rioletta strolled with Andor and they stopped frequently to examine wares that caught their eyes.

"This soap is nice," Rioletta said, handing a bar to Andor for inspection.

"You could make that at home," Andor said, sniffing the bar.

"But I don't want to make it," Rioletta said. "I'm willing to pay for the convenience. These little luxuries are what I miss."

"I miss some of the stuff we used to get from Tabor, too. Hopefully we'll hammer out a good set of agreements with the First Chosen pretty soon and they'll start sending more goods to Matbor. They're pretty disagreeable though."

"Bitter that they were passed over, and maybe insecure about their standing in the community," Rioletta agreed. "I'm not convinced how soon things will stabilize, so I'm planning on stocking up here."

There were booths upon booths of food, and soon all of them had handfuls of stacked paper baskets and loaded satchels, and several of them carried wineskins they had brought and filled from casks loaded on wagons from Tabor. Creed had brought a metal flask that he kept in his satchel, filled with harder stuff. They wandered near the competition clearing, where targets had been set up on bales of hay for the following day's archery contests. A number of young children, with the supervision of their parents, were practicing by the light of torches.

"Are you going to enter?" Rioletta asked Andor as they leaned on the fence between the sales and competition areas.

Andor snorted. "I haven't shot a bow in more than a year. I'm no hunter, and never will be. But Creed and Tannon will enter."

Tannon and Creed were the champion archers in the Sydian region, but this would test them against all manner of folks, from near and far. The competitions were broken into women and men, which had sparked an outcry until the organizers had agreed to rotate the top female archers into the men's competition. The women used lighter bows, but otherwise there was no reason to separate them, except for the large numbers of entrants.

"I hear Rath of Luth will compete," Andor said.

14

"Who's that?" Rioletta had not heard the name, but Luth was a dairy area south of the Sydian, one of the communities beholden to Andolith for their Sorcerer's Council.

"Her family owns property in Luth, but she's been gone for many years, employed elsewhere as some kind of guard on the Western Trade Routes. I hear she came back to her parents' house in Luth after her father passed away. Supposedly she has some skill with a bow, so let's hope she does well in the competition. I'd like to see a woman come out on top."

"There are a few other women from Andolith who'll compete," Rioletta said.

"Well, I'll cheer them on from the sidelines," Andor said. "But my money's on Tannon to win overall, and I wouldn't be surprised if Creed places high. There's money prizes for the first five positions."

"And there will be horse races tomorrow evening," Rioletta said.

"And a lot of other things," Andor replied. "The hard part will be deciding what to watch."

"Cardon and Stolen will both ride." Rioletta knew she would be watching the races, even if Andor was undecided.

They strolled along at the back of their group behind Morcah and Creed, who walked shoulder-to-shoulder, mock scuffling over the flask. The crowd was so heavy that two opposing lanes of foot traffic had formed, and they shuffled along more slowly than they might otherwise have walked. Music began from somewhere to the north; there was a stage set up near the river, and nightly acts were scheduled.

Rioletta saw Creed's back stiffen ahead of her. He turned to the side, staring at someone deep in the crowd passing the opposite direction. Morcah caught his glance and stiffened, too. Rioletta scanned the crowd, and a face seemed to catch her eye: familiar, but not identifiable.

"Durigon Cautes!" Andor hissed in her ear, and with the name came the memory. Durigon had once lived in Andolith; indeed he had grown up there, and his family still lived there. But he had been gone for twelve years; this was the first Rioletta had seen or heard of him since. She had been only thirteen when he left.

15

With the push of the crowd, their group was shuttled along uncontrollably, and they soon lost sight of Duri.

"Do you remember him?" Andor asked.

"Yes, but I never knew him well," Rioletta said. "He was several years older than me, a big kid in my eyes."

There had been a fistfight, she recalled, and the village children had gone running to see. Rioletta had gone as well, and when she arrived, she'd been surprised to see that Creed was one of the combatants. She thought of Creed as slow to anger, good-natured in general. But he rolled in the grip of another boy, and the punches flew. "I saw the fight, right before he disappeared. But I never knew what happened afterwards."

"Creed got the upper hand pretty quickly. He was a lot bigger than Duri, even though they're the same age," Andor said.

"I'd say that still holds," Rioletta said, glancing over her shoulder at Duri in the crowd. Creed was tall and powerfully built, but Duri didn't look much taller than her, and he was thin. "I remember Tannon and Ladon showing up. I was afraid of them that day, they both looked so angry."

Tannon had taken Creed to the ground to restrain him from continuing the beating, she remembered; even then, Creed had screamed epithets and accusations at Duri, blood running from his nose.

"They were angry," Andor affirmed. "It sure looked like Creed was picking on somebody smaller than he was. But afterwards they found out why the whole thing happened."

"I only heard rumors," Rioletta said. "I heard Duri took some liberties with some of the younger girls."

"Yes, and one of them was my sister Lystra," Andor said curtly. "She was eleven. Duri bragged about it and Creed got wind of what he'd said. Creed may have a mischievous streak, but he's got a strong sense of what's right and what's wrong. I'm not saying it was a good thing to do; he nearly beat Duri to death. He should have gone to Tannon or Ladon with what he'd heard. But I'd be untruthful if I said I was sorry."

Duri had eventually healed. Soon after, he had disappeared from the village, and Rioletta had not thought about him since. "Creed was protecting the younger kids. Perhaps he let his emotions get the better of him, but it's understandable. So is your reaction; it was your little sister. I don't blame you. I hope Creed didn't get in too much trouble."

Andor shrugged. "It didn't go badly. He wasn't hurt much in the fight, a bloody nose and split knuckles. Tannon confined him to the house for a month, but he walked away from that several times with no consequences. I know, because that was when we were becoming better acquainted, you might say." She grinned at Rioletta.

"Ah, I didn't realize you two had been together that long," Rioletta smiled. "Now I'm getting the bigger picture."

"Yes, probably that was part of what set him off, Lystra being my sister. You're lucky you didn't find out more about Duri than you wanted to; but I think you were off-limits, being promised as a Sorcerer. Mosse strongly suggested that Duri go somewhere else to seek his future, and I think his parents felt that was best as well. No one blamed Creed, and no one would have stopped him if he'd beaten Duri again. I haven't heard about or seen Duri since."

"Surely they couldn't still bear each other a grudge," Rioletta said. "And surely Duri's grown up by now."

"You never know," Andor replied. "After all, they never had to deal with each other again. If Duri had stayed in Andolith, I suppose they would have had to learn how to ignore each other, but they never had that opportunity. But there are a lot of people here, and the chances of them running into each other face-to-face are fairly slim, I think. I have to admit, I'm curious about where's he's been. He looked well enough, strong, in a wiry kind of way."

It had been a long day, and Rioletta tired during the dramatic reenactment of the Dispersal Sorcerers sending everyone out of the cities and made her way back to the camp alone. There it was quieter, although she could still hear the crowd and the music, and, during the night, people making their way back to their beds. She occasionally woke to lights and once heard Andor laughing.

It was light when she awoke. They had built a big fire in the middle of the camp, surrounded by cottonwood logs, and there was a grill over it with several kettles on to heat water. Ladon and Pateret were there; Cardon and Stolen sat nearby, talking seriously about the races that evening in which both of them would ride. Stolen was nervous; he hadn't come with them the night before. He had excused himself, saying he was unused to the number of people and disliked the looks he got, although no one had been rude or even questioned him.

Rioletta intended to work most of the day selling paper and woodwork, at least until the archery contests. After a cup of tea at the fire ring, she dressed in a clean shirt from her baggage, took her satchel, which she had unloaded of the previous evening's loot, and made her way into the Polebray to find some breakfast.

The choices were almost overwhelming. She passed the demonstrations of livestock and crops, the contestants for the largest, finest, smallest of everything; there were leatherwork and horse equipment booths, furniture and woodwork from Andolith and other woodland communities, and compound, recurve, and crossbows and arrows; cases of antique firearms; wool, thread, and fabric; huge spools of rope; recipes, dishes and housewares, clothing, and knickknacks. In the food court, she found beer already being served alongside the casks of wine from Tabor, and a wide variety of breads and fruit compotes, several of which she sampled.

Just beyond the food was a kind of alcove, in a thick grove of trees, and there she saw painted and unusual enclosed wagons, with drop-down sides. A faint musty odor emanated from the area, and she was drawn towards it.

As she stepped into the heavy shade, she found herself fingering the glass teardrop at her neck. It prickled at her mind, but she ignored it while she looked around. This was an area where she could spend a great deal of time, and a great deal of money if she wasn't careful. These people were largely salvagers, dealers in antiques and artifacts gathered from the Ruined Cities. Their wagons were crammed with small items: hinges, jewelry, small pots and glasswares, buttons, tiny bits and pieces unknown, and--most interesting of all to Rioletta--books.

Many were damaged, and many were in languages she could not read, but some were at least partly intelligible. As a Loremaster, she had an affinity for books and collected them as she could, regardless of topic. Printing presses were not Forbidden Technology, and modern books were created regularly and distributed widely, but Rioletta preferred the intrigue of the old, the connection to the past and the days before the Dispersal. Partly she wondered what it had been like and how it had been to make the final decision; it had been Sorcerers like herself who had brought

18

about the conclusion of the Era. Recently she had sought more information, not only because of her own curiosity, but also because she felt an obligation to make the most informed decisions she could to lead her community into the future, and those decisions required deep knowledge and understanding of events past and present. At the same time, she knew all documents brought in to Andolith were supposed to be vetted by the Elder Council, who had final say as to what information was necessary and useful to know.

She flipped idly through a small tome, dusty and moldy, but even that she could not truly afford, at least not until she sold some paper.

"Expensive, but pretty," said a voice in her ear. "Were you ignoring me?"

Rioletta looked up with a smile. Nikal Kathreftis stood close by her shoulder, his eyes sparkling under his dark brows.

"I'm sorry, now that I think of it, I did feel you. But I was too absorbed in the books to pay attention."

"And yet we found each other," Nikal said. "Perhaps a part of you paid attention after all."

"Could be," Rioletta said. "When did you arrive?"

"Late last night. I got little sleep. But I'll be free today; there's little for me to do, I'm not a craftsman of any kind. The rest of my family will sell glass. I'd help, but I find that sales go better when I'm not around." Nikal laughed.

Rioletta thought that might be true; he had an intense look, with a thick shock of dark hair, and a tendency to look out from under his brows with his head slightly lowered, as if scowling. Even when he smiled, his black eyes stayed sharp, and he made some uncomfortable. Rioletta had learned in Dobor that he had a reputation as the best Viewer around, and some thought he could see something of what they were thinking as well.

"Well, I'll spend at least part of the day selling the paper and woodworks I managed to create over the winter, but I don't intend to spend all my time selling. I'd like to look around more and I want to watch the archery contests and the horse races this evening."

"Fair enough. Will you meet me for lunch, then?"

"I will. Did Adla come? I think Cardon would like to talk to her," Rioletta said, suddenly remembering her conversation with Cardon in the Syrola.

"Yes, she's here. Come, I'll walk you to your table."

Chapter Three

A group of Andolith residents sat bunched together in the crowd in the shade of the cottonwood trees surrounding the archery grounds in mid-afternoon. Rioletta was paying little attention to the contests; instead, she thumbed carefully through a small book with a curiously heavy cover, written in a slightly archaic form of the Tadian dialect and in excellent shape. It was a gift from Nikal, who had found it in the antiques wagons while she was working her table. She was extremely pleased with it, both as an artifact and because it showed that Nikal had paid attention to her tastes.

The inscription on the inside cover showed it had been written in Hyolon before the Dispersal. It was about gardening for spices and healing herbs in small spaces, intended for use in a city plot but also useful for kitchen gardens. Its usefulness made it even more desirable.

Rioletta and the others, including Nikal, Andor, and Ladon, were seated in short folding seats of wood and canvas, which could be slung over the shoulder once collapsed. The purveyor of the seats had been doing a brisk business, and a good sum of Andolith money had gone into his pockets. Ladon had not entered any of the contests; he rarely hunted and had little time for sport. But he had come to watch his brother Tannon and Tannon's children as well as

21

the other Andolith residents, and any other contestants from the Sydian who could be cheered on if none from Andolith advanced.

The adult recurve contests were divided into women's and men's divisions, with the best of the women, who started first, working into the men's competition partway through. The contestants had signed up beforehand and drew lots to determine starting position. A later position was preferable because a good shooter who started early would have to advance through all the ranks and might become tired by the end, putting him or her at a disadvantage.

They were about halfway through the men's competition and the women were beginning to work in by the time Rioletta placed the book carefully in her satchel and began to pay attention.

"There's Rath, she must have done well in the women's," Andor said, nudging her and nodding at a woman stepping up to the line next to one of the men.

Rath of Luth did not look particularly imposing. She was of an indeterminate age from that distance, anywhere from her late thirties to her early fifties. She was of average height, fit appearing, but not exceptionally muscular, and she wore the garb of a traveler and a short leather vest common among those employed as guards. She appeared to be enjoying herself as she smiled most of the time and nodded at her adversary at the line.

The contest was a combination of speed and accuracy. There were two line judges, one on either side. Two contestants stood side by side, feet planted, bows down, arrows in a quiver in a location chosen by the shooter. At a whistle, each contestant brought his bow up on target, took an arrow, nocked it and released it, followed by two more for a total of three. One point was awarded to the fastest shooter; the rest of the points were determined by a concentric-ring target, with the center ring about the size of Rioletta's palm.

At the whistle, Rath easily bested the young man next to her in speed; she was also more accurate, and the man bowed and stepped out. Rath was joined by another man, whom she also bested. The contest continued, and soon the times began to narrow as the best competitors were set against each other. With each round, Rath continued to stand her place.

"Watch how Rath does it," Andor said, leaning over towards Rioletta. "She's not always the first to get her shot off. If it were a

22

single-shot speed contest, she'd have lost by now. But she makes it up in the second and third shot. See, a lot of the men are hunters; they're pausing and breaking their vision just a bit to look where their shot went. Good practice in hunting, with a moving target. But this is a stationary target, and it's not going to move. Rath keeps her bow at exactly the same position as it was for the first shot and nocks an arrow with the bow up, rather than bringing it down again."

"But you have to have a light pull to do that," said Rioletta. "If it was a heavy pull, she'd have to move it to set the string."

Andor glanced at her. "Nothing says you have to have a heavy pull for the competition. She's shooting the way the guards do, rather than the hunters. I'd heard she's been working as a guard, and they're trained for battle shooting."

The interest in the competition was heating up now, with a woman so far up in the ranks. All of the other women had been bested and the second queue had been closed down, so all the shooters competed in the same line-up. There were only a few remaining, and these were the best.

Finally Creed stepped up to the line beside Rath. He grinned and nodded at her; he was in second standing, and he was fast and accurate. The whistle sounded, and both contestants loosed their arrows. There was a pause, and the line judges looked at each other, then both spread their hands.

"A tie!" people in the audience shouted.

It would have to be judged on accuracy. The judges, Rath, and Creed walked up to the targets and looked carefully. All three of each contestant's arrows sat in the middle ring. The judges would have to draw a still smaller ring and score the hits that way, as specified in the rules for tie-breaking. If that did not break the tie, they would shoot again.

The judges huddled over the targets, then stood upright again. One of them shook his head.

"Sorry, Creed," he said. A look of surprise crossed Creed's face, but in an instant he broke into a grin, turned to Rath, and clasped her hand.

Creed pulled his arrows; the judges put up new targets, and Tannon stepped up to the line.

This was the last round; Tannon was in first standing among the men. The whistle blew once more, and this time the judges agreed quickly: the speed went to Tannon. The accuracy was very close, but in the end, Tannon came out ahead. He clasped hands with Rath, then raised his bow in the air. The main part of the purse was his, but Rath, Creed, and two others would collect a good sum as well.

Ladon had been watching the contest attentively. "That's the closest I've seen a woman get to winning this contest in a long time."

"She drew well and shot well," Morcah said. "Usually the women are bumped because their upper body strength is taxed by too much shooting, not because of accuracy or speed. Pateret's a good shot for a few rounds, but she can't hold her strength long enough for a contest."

Ladon pushed himself up out of his chair and went over to the targets, where a crowd of people congratulated the winners. Rioletta saw him clasp hands with Tannon and Creed; he turned to Rath, and after clasping hands, he bent to talk to her. A few minutes later, as the Andolith group gathered their chairs and belongings, Rioletta looked back to see that Ladon was still deep in conversation with Rath. Andor caught her glance and grinned.

"Think Ladon's got an interest?" she asked teasingly. "There are some young women in Andolith who'd happily take some of Ladon's attention, but he's too aware of his position to take advantage of that. And most of the women his own age in Andolith are married or have dependent children. But Luth isn't far away, and I'll bet they knew each other when they were younger."

"Do you want to wait for Creed?" Rioletta asked.

Andor stood on tiptoe to peer over the crowd. "No, he's in the thick of it. He'll have to collect his money, and I think there's a traditional toast. Not that he'll want any of that; he had enough last night to last him for a while. We'll find each other later. Look, there's Durigon Cautes."

Rioletta saw Duri at the fence that separated the spectator area from the archery grounds. He was staring intently in their direction. Andor stared back purposefully for a moment, then turned on her heel.

The group wandered off to find dinner and drinks and to listen to the music at the stage before the evening horse races. Cardon and Stolen were not with them; they were checking and readying the horses at the race corrals. Both of them would ride, but Cardon had told Rioletta he did not expect them to win anything. The horses were young and unused to racing alongside others, although they were fast enough. His main purpose, he said, was to introduce them to racing and to show them off with the idea of increasing interest in them and advertising his leatherworks.

After dinner there was still time before the races, and Rioletta and Andor returned to their campsite for respite from the crowds. The grove of cottonwoods was cool and the noise and dust reduced, and the two of them unfolded their new chairs and sat in the shade looking towards the Polebray. Andor emptied her satchel of the items she'd picked up during the day and examined each one, showing them to Rioletta. Rioletta pulled her book out and flipped through it once again.

The back cover was definitely oddly thick and hard, with an indentation around the rim. The front cover was not as thick, which made it stranger. Rioletta ran her hand over the inside of the back, pressing gently; she was a paper-maker and had made book-bindings and covers before, so the make-up of the cover interested her. She noticed tiny, faint writing, repeated again and again in a kind of design on the paper that covered the inside of the back, and brought it close to her face to try and read it in a shaft of light falling between the cottonwoods.

It was still difficult, so she reached in her satchel and brought out a gift she'd purchased for Justah, a real glass magnifying glass in a leather case. Using that, she was able to distinguish individual marks. It took a Reading Skill to cause the marks to rearrange themselves into a legible order, and it was difficult and took a lot of concentration; certainly only a Loremaster used to such Skills could accomplish it. Although the sentences that eventually resolved were somewhat archaic in composition, Rioletta was able to make out that the back cover could be used as a flower press or herb press for small plants. Following the instructions, she slid her nail into a thin slot along the bottom edge of the cover, and the inner layer popped up with a small snap.

"Look at this!" she exclaimed, and showed Andor, who scooted her chair closer. "It says you can use the cover as a plant press." She pulled the inside cover off the backing to find an indentation within. There was a small tab sticking up from the indentation, and when she pulled it, it turned out to be a strap under a thin, palm-sized card that popped out. She took the card and examined it.

"What do you think this is made of?" she asked Andor. "It's not wood or metal."

Andor took it. "Is it part of the press? I guess you put a small flower in the hole and cover it with this card, then put the cover back together. It must be some material they used to make in the Ruined City; most of that technology is Forbidden now. It would have to be absorbent but not given to mildew if it's intended to be in contact with a flower during pressing."

Andor turned the card over in her hand several times while Rioletta studied the instructions on the inside cover again.

"Hey, look at this!" Andor pulled the card apart lengthwise; a paper-thin blade, with a handle made of part of the card and a sheath of the other part, slid out. Rioletta took the blade and examined it; it sparkled in the sun, dust-free even after all the years it had lain hidden in the book cover, and a faint blue light seemed to play upon the edge.

In a moment, she realized that the card came apart further. The handle of the knife parted to reveal a saw-toothed piece, and a toothpick-sized wrench with an irregular shape pulled out of the side.

Andor's half, which made up the sheath, came apart flat side to flat side to reveal an open round piece like a washer and a piece shaped like a key. Finally, they realized that each edge where the handle and sheath met and each edge of the card was made in a subtle carved pattern.

"What in the world is this intended to be?" Andor wondered as she held a handful of the tiny tools.

"A toolkit for flower-pressing, perhaps?" Rioletta said. "I'm not sure what you'd use all these parts for. The blade is handy enough. But I'll tell you one thing: had the seller of the book realized this was in here, the price would have been far beyond what Nikal could have paid for it. I was flattered enough with the book as a gift; this makes it truly special, even if he didn't know what it contained."

"And a little weird," Andor said, returning the handful of tools to Rioletta for reassembly. "You should read that thing word for word and see if you can figure out what those all are for."

"Definitely," Rioletta agreed. "I can't wait to show Nikal."

Rioletta put everything back together and stowed the book carefully among her things at the campsite. They left their chairs and headed towards the racetracks, where bleachers had been built and crowds were already gathering.

The first of the races had already begun by the time they arrived, and they spent some time wandering the crowd, looking for people they knew. Finally Rioletta spotted Creed and Nikal near the top of one of the bleachers, and they wound their way up through the lower seats to squeeze in with the Andolith group.

"Cardon's going to run a couple races from now," Morcah said, leaning over towards Rioletta. "Stolen can't run the same races because there are equipment requirements, and he won't ride with a saddle, so he has to wait for the bareback races. He'll be easy enough to pick out, though."

"Cardon's harder to tell apart, he looks just like the Mahquant," Creed put in.

"Or any other *quant*, for that matter," said Andor. The word "quant" meant clan or group, and there were five such clans among the horse-breeders of the eastern Region of Ankara, including the Kirquant of Cardon's mother and the Mahquant. The *quant* were heavily represented in the horse races, and Cardon's friend Skyros was there. Cardon had taken up the Mahquant manner of dress while he stayed with them and reverted to it now, although while in Andolith he usually wore their styles.

There were more of the shorter races, intended for the small, fast-start ponies, and then the races turned to longer courses designed for distance runners. Cardon had brought six horses. He intended to ride three races and have Stolen ride three.

Cardon's first horse ran well, although she was not in the top five; she stayed steady on the course and in the front bunch. Rioletta could see that Cardon was pleased, and when the contestants were lined up for the second race he received a good round of applause. Although he had never regained his health completely after his

27

experimentation in Tabor and remained on the thin side, he was still good-looking enough to capture the crowd. He smiled and waved in response, and glanced up into the stands as if looking for the Andolith group. Rioletta waved back. She was happy for him; he seemed to be enjoying himself, and that was rare enough lately.

He ran the next two races on different horses, and although the third horse took fright and skittered around a bit, they all ran well enough to attract the attention of breeders and buyers. Cardon was obviously in control of his mounts; several of the other riders fell off during the races, or in some cases before or afterwards, and in some instances the horses started too soon or could not be pulled to a stop afterwards.

Then the races turned to more exclusive events, including bareback. Cardon walked with Stolen as the horses were lined out; there was a murmur in the crowd, but the riders were too far away for most people to be able to see clearly, and Stolen had chosen to remain clothed in a long-sleeved shirt, although he rode barefoot as usual.

As the race began, Stolen's horse leapt forward with a great surge, and Stolen held her back. She settled in to the middle of the pack quickly, and as they passed the halfway mark she began to gain ground. Rioletta found herself clenching her hands in her lap and she could hear Andor urging him on. Stolen rode easily and gracefully, and at the end of the race he was in third place and stood to earn some money. Now the crowd paid more attention. In the second race, in which he rode a second horse, a young stallion, he garnered applause, although he did not acknowledge it as Cardon had.

Stolen also took third this time, letting the horse run into the front of the pack earlier in the race. He apparently thought better of that strategy, and during the third race he once again held his mount until the final half. Then the horse, a powerful dark bay, surged forward with no apparent urging and edged ahead of the leaders. Stolen came out in front by a head, and ended his evening with a more successful set of runs than Cardon, and his first money in his pocket.

The Andolith group cheered noisily and wound their way down to the track to offer congratulations. Cardon was busy caring for the horses and nodded only briefly before disappearing; but

Stolen was cornered by several young women. Rioletta thought he looked both worried and pleased; the women were curious and flirtatious, and she found herself thinking that if Stolen played it right, he might have an opportunity to spend some time with one of them. After all, despite his odd appearance, he was not unattractive, with his deep black eyes, olive skin, and chestnut hair mostly overwhelming the leaves. Polebray romances were not uncommon, and the stuff of stories later.

As they walked back towards the entertainment and food, Rioletta told Nikal about the book. "I left it at my campsite, but I'll go get it and show you. It's quite a piece of work!"

"I wish I could tell you I noticed that and drove a hard bargain to get you something so valuable, but it's not true," Nikal said. "I got the book because it was in good shape and readable, and seemed to be on a subject you'd find useful."

"And I love it for those reasons," Rioletta replied. "This makes it all the more intriguing, whether you knew it was there or not. Remember how we found each other at the antiques wagons? Perhaps you found the book on purpose, too."

Nikal frowned. Rioletta wondered for a minute if she'd said something wrong, but she couldn't fathom what it might be.

"You're not necessarily wrong. I did feel some sort of pull," Nikal said finally, "but maybe I'm just reading into it now that I know there's something special about the book. Anyway, go and get it; I'll buy us some drinks and meet you near the stage."

Rioletta went off towards the campsite at a fast walk. There was no one else there, or at least she did not initially see anyone. Then she heard a sound, and saw a figure in the brush back of the campsite.

Curious, she walked a bit closer and saw it was Cardon, bent over and vomiting in the weeds. Perhaps the stress of the races was too much, she thought; or he had had too much to drink over the last two days, or eaten strange food that disagreed with him. Whatever it was, it would be unkind to leave him in distress without at least checking that he would be all right. Rioletta called out to him and made her way into the bushes.

"Are you all right?" she asked, touching his back as he bent, hands on knees, breathing heavily. "Let me get you some water."

Cardon nodded, gripped her shoulder, and followed her back to the campsite, where he collapsed heavily on a log near the fire pit. Rioletta found a keg of water and a cup and brought it back to him. He swished some in his mouth and spit, then drank a little bit.

"Did you eat something that disagreed with you, or was it just the stress of the races?" Rioletta asked as he regained a bit of color in his cheeks.

"Neither." He shook his head and sipped again. "Rio, the voices are much worse here. Much worse."

Rioletta had forgotten about Cardon's voices. "What do you mean they're worse? More frequent?"

"More frequent and louder, much louder. It's as if they're screaming at me. Always the same thing, '*Cardon, Cardon, we lie in the crypt of souls!*' And then, '*Deep in Hyolon, but we have no key!*' I haven't got much sleep since we arrived. It got worse as we traveled, worse the closer to Tabor we got; now it's worse than it's ever been!"

"Do you want me to find Adla? I'm sure she can do something for you, let you sleep at the very least."

"Yes, yes! Please! Can you bring her here? I don't think I can walk around; I don't want the crowd near me."

"I'll bring her here," Rioletta promised. "But Cardon, I think we're going to have to tell someone else as well. This is getting too serious. You can't go on like this."

"Yes, later. I don't want to think now. I'm exhausted. Just please bring Adla."

Rioletta grabbed a map that was sitting near the fire, but she had no idea if Adla was in the Dobor camp or not. She hadn't seen much of Adla, having spent most of her time either with Nikal alone or with the Andolith crowd. It would be best to find Nikal, and together they could find Adla. She would tell Nikal what was happening, too; Cardon wanted privacy, but Rioletta needed advice, and it was clear Cardon wasn't thinking clearly. She would have to make the decision for him.

Chapter Four

Rioletta ran back to the Polebray and wound her way through the alleys of stalls and wagons, which were now becoming familiar to her. Finally she arrived at the stage and searched for Nikal along the edge of the crowd. He was leaning against a tree with a drink for each of them.

Rioletta ran up out of breath. "Nikal, do you know where Adla is?"

"Yes, probably, why?"

"Cardon is very ill and is asking for Adla," Rioletta explained. "It's like when he arrived at the camp after the death of the Younger Council. She helped him then. Can we find her and bring her to him?"

"Of course," Nikal said, though not without some impatience. "She's probably in the main tent of the Healers, where she's been sharing techniques. But why is it you who end up taking care of Cardon? Get Charnia to care for him. I want you to be able to enjoy the Polebray, and I haven't much time to spend with you."

"We'll get him medicine to make him sleep, and then there'll be no point in my sitting with him," Rioletta promised as they hastened towards the medical headquarters near the racetrack. "I want to show you that book you bought me, anyway."

Adla was, as Nikal had suggested, in the main medical tent with many other Healers. As the three of them hurried back to the

31

Andolith camp, Rioletta explained what Cardon had told her after the day on the Contemplation.

"The voices have been getting much stronger lately, particularly after he arrived here," she said. "I have to assume they're some manifestation of the damage he did to his mind, since he's quite sure Marsavrina and Skadar are dead."

"Perhaps," Nikal said, "but he and the Younger Council were in contact with the Outcasts, and they practiced the Forbidden Skills. There are other Forbidden Skills besides Shape-shifting and Mind-sharing."

"Yes, but what are you getting at?" Rioletta asked.

"He's thinking of the creation of a template, I assume," Adla said. "You know that nothing remains of the consciousness after the death of the body, at least under normal conditions. If a person dies of old age, or illness, or injury, then that which was once them returns to the universe, to whence it came before birth. But the Outcasts, or so we've been taught, believe it's possible to create a mind template that can survive death, if and only if that death is caused by the casting of a Skill."

"But that's nonsense," Rioletta said. "How would such a thing survive, with no body for it to take form within?"

"No one believes it can survive on its own," Nikal said, "but the Outcasts think the consciousness can be captured, or written, within a few minutes of bodily death, by the actions of a Mind-sharer. It can then be kept in one's own mind for a short period of time, until it can be transferred into a new body or otherwise stored."

"Of course, something similar is in the Charter, enumerated as a Forbidden Skill," Rioletta said, "but the Charter says it requires 'deadly preparation resulting in damage to the mind and body' and that it can cause death. I've never heard it seriously discussed."

"Well, the Dobor Sorcerers are exposed to most of the Forbidden Skills, as are the Tabor Sorcerers, so we know of their existence and actions, although of course we don't practice them. But just because the Outcasts believe some of the Forbidden Skills are possible doesn't mean that they actually are. No one has accomplished most of them, and many die trying. I only mention it because of Cardon's voices and the mention of a 'crypt of souls,' which seems in line with Outcast beliefs...but it could be he heard

32

about these things while he was with the Younger Council, and now his own memories are playing tricks on him. In fact, that's much more likely."

They reached the Andolith camp and found Cardon at the fire pit. He sat quite still while Adla took his hand to feel his illness. She spent several minutes with him, then withdrew and began to prepare her medications.

"Did Rioletta tell you?" Cardon asked hoarsely.

"Yes," Adla said. "It seems to me you need sleep now. I'll give you what I gave you at the camp in the Riola outside Tabor; it worked well for you, didn't it? That will calm your mind and give you focus; and then we'll follow with a sleep aid and you can get some rest."

"Thank you," Cardon said. He took what Adla gave him mechanically. Within a few minutes he appeared to relax, and Rioletta led him to his bedding. She waited a few minutes until he was asleep, then returned to Adla and Nikal at the fire ring.

"He'll sleep for at least twelve hours," Adla said. "Getting some rest should help him, but there's something deeper going on. I'm not sure I have the Skill to fix an issue of this magnitude. At some point he will need to consult with an experienced Healer."

"I agree, but convincing him will be more difficult," Rioletta said. "Perhaps he can talk to someone outside Andolith, someone besides Charnia."

"Cardon may not care for Charnia, but she has quite a reputation among the Healers," Adla said. "Like it or not, she's probably the one who can do the most for him. But there's nothing else we can do right now. We might as well leave him alone to sleep."

Rioletta sat down and reached into her satchel. "Here's what I wanted to show you, Nikal," she said. She opened the book and slid her thumb into the slot on the rim of the back, pulled up the inside cover, pulled the tab, and handed him the card. Adla leaned in to see.

"The characters on the back cover can be unscrambled to say that the back can be used as a plant press. It took the full extent of my Reading Skill to decipher it. Andor thinks you would put a small plant in the depression, cover it with the card, and then close the back cover. But there's more. See if you can figure it out."

33

Nikal examined the card, turning it over several times. "Each edge is cut differently," he said. "There are little notches and waves." He shuddered suddenly. "But there's something else, I don't know what. The book draws me, I feel something from it. That's unusual with an object. Perhaps it was used as a talisman by someone at some point. But it would have been long ago."

He handed the card to Adla, who also turned it a few times. "Ah," she said. "The card slides apart. See, Nikal, there's a blade inside."

Rioletta showed them the remaining tools hidden in the card. "I think there's more to it, but I haven't figured it out. Why is the card notched on the sides, for example?"

Adla was leafing through the book, looking at the illustrations of flowers and herbs. "Many of these are medicinal, but some we would no longer use for any purpose," she said. "There seems to be a notation convention, but I can't find any key to explain what the markings mean."

"How so?" Rioletta leaned over Adla's arm.

"See, the identification of each plant is here on the bottom of the plate, although the names are different than those I would use. In some cases, the name is written in slanting letters; in other cases it's underlined. In a few cases, such as this one here, the underline is broken."

"Or jagged," Nikal said. The light was getting poor, and the lines were hard to see. "Rioletta, where's the card?"

Rioletta handed him the card, and Nikal turned it several times, then laid it on the page. The notches cut in one side of the card lined up perfectly with the jagged line beneath the name of the plant.

"That's interesting. Are there others?" Rioletta asked.

Adla turned several pages and found another plate with an underlined name. Nikal turned the card again, and another side fit the slightly different line. They found six such plates in the book, and each time, a different side of the card, or the inside where the sheath and handle of the knife-blade parted, fit the line.

"Obviously the card is meant to be used to identify specific plants," Nikal said. "Perhaps the sides are numbered somehow, and you can use a formula to create mixtures for specific uses."

"All of these are plants I'd consider dangerous," Adla said. "Only two are plants we use as medicinals anymore. Some of them cause hallucinations, and several can cause death if not used very carefully. There's truly no reason I can see for them to be featured in a book about kitchen herbs and spices."

"Another interesting thing," Rioletta said, "if I'm not mistaken, Adla. One would use a different part of each of these six plants: bark, root, leaves, seeds, flowers, or sap."

"Correct," Adla said. "That is interesting, although I don't know if it's significant."

"I see I'm going to have to read this book very carefully, cover to cover and word for word," Rioletta said. "Now I want to solve this little mystery! This is quite a gift you've given me, Nikal! I suspect it'll keep me busy for a while."

Nikal sat back and handed her the card. "Be careful. There's something about this book I truly don't like. Maybe it's only the poisonous plants, but I'm beginning to regret having bought it for you."

"I don't regret it," Rioletta said. "I think it's fascinating."

Just then there were hurried footsteps through the dark, and Jakal, Tannon's youngest son, ran up. "Have you seen my father?" he gasped, out of breath.

"No, not lately. Nor Ladon. What's going on?" Rioletta asked.

"Creed's in a fight," Jakal said. "With that man he used to know when they were kids."

Rioletta, Nikal, and Adla jumped up. "Where?" Nikal shouted as Jakal ran on.

"By the corner of furniture and yarn-spinning!" Jakal yelled back.

A crowd had gathered by the time they arrived. They pushed through to the front. A circle had formed, and Creed and Duri faced off in the middle. Creed had removed his shirt, either to avoid being grabbed or to challenge Duri by showing off his musculature. To Rioletta's surprise, Tannon and Ladon were there, at the front of the circle. Tannon held a security guard back with one arm.

"Aren't you going to stop them, Tannon?" Rioletta asked.

Tannon snorted. "No. They're not children anymore. If they want to beat each other bloody, let them go at it. Maybe they'll get it over with and we can leave this be."

Andor also stood near the front, arms crossed in obvious disgust. Morcah and many others from Andolith were there as well.

Creed and Duri circled each other warily. Duri was much shorter than Creed, lithe and wiry, but without the reach or strength. He moved carefully and quickly, his hands slightly raised and loose rather than fisted, a tight smile on his face.

"Creed better watch it," Andor muttered to Rioletta. "I think Duri's learned something since he left Andolith."

Creed made a move to grab Duri, but Duri darted quickly out of the way. Seeing that Duri wasn't going to allow himself to be taken to the ground easily, Creed charged him full-bore. Duri sidestepped again, but he was hemmed in by the crowd, and Creed reached out, grabbed his shirt, and threw him down. In an instant Creed was on top of Duri on the ground, just as he had been during the fight twelve years before.

But Duri wrapped his arms around Creed, set his feet, and made a sudden twisting thrust with his hips. Creed flew off sideways, and Duri took the opportunity to scramble to his feet. Creed jumped up quickly, but it was obvious he had been taken by surprise.

Rioletta put her hands over her ears as the crowd around her yelled louder. Creed grabbed Duri again and threw him to the ground almost at her feet. She scrambled back, pushing into the crowd. Duri was on his feet immediately, and the crowd surged forward again.

Duri threw no punches, but defended himself against Creed's swings, blocking them and stepping off to the side. Rioletta saw that he was still grinning as though he was enjoying the fight, in contrast with Creed's anger. Then Duri darted forward and threw a roundhouse kick, his shinbone making solid contact with Creed's thigh.

Creed staggered for a moment, his face contorted in pain. Duri had hit him in a nerve bundle on the side of the leg. The crowd roared again and Creed, encouraged by the yells, pressed Duri backwards with a new volley of punches.

36

Suddenly, someone from the crowd gave Duri a hard shove in the back. It hurled him forward into Creed, who landed several hard punches. Duri leaped back into a clear area of the circle, but blood ran from his eyebrow and the side of his face. He looked around quickly, as if expecting to be set upon by others in the crowd as well. Rioletta saw that the grin had vanished, replaced by a hunted look.

As Creed approached him again, Duri made a sudden motion with his hand to the side, and a knife appeared. Creed sucked his stomach in and rounded his back as he jumped off to the side. The knife flashed near his gut and up towards his left arm. The crowd surged forward, and Duri was quickly thrown to the ground on his back, with Rath of Luth's knee on his wrist. The knife was wrenched from his grip, and Duri yanked to his feet. Rioletta was shuffled around in the crowd, but she could see Creed with others around him, their numbers holding him back from continuing any fight.

Duri was hauled off by the security guards, and in a few minutes the crowd trickled away, leaving the Andolith group with Creed, who stood with hands on knees, catching his breath. He rubbed his leg with the heel of his hand and wiped sweat off his forehead.

"Little creep learned something while he's been gone," Creed said with some surprise.

"I could have told you that in the beginning," Andor said, handing Creed his shirt. "The Sydian may be a safe area, but those who leave it probably discover that much of the rest of the world is not so safe. Many practice fighting arts, and Duri has gotten quite good at it. I've seen exhibitions while I've traveled. That knife didn't come out until someone else got involved; he must've figured it was him against a bunch of other people, not just you. The shove was unfair, and he's hardly to blame for defending himself."

"How did it start, anyway?" Rioletta asked.

Creed shrugged. "Don't really know. All of a sudden we were face to face, and then it just happened. Kind of like picking up where we left off."

"Well, you can leave off for good, now," Tannon said. "Duri will probably be thrown out of the Polebray for pulling that knife.

Maybe they should throw you out, too. You're bleeding, you should go to one of the aid tents and get bandaged."

Creed examined his arm, but it was only a small nick. "I'm fine. If Security wants me, they can find me at the stage. I'm not going to miss the celebration tonight if I can help it."

"Come on," Andor said, "let's go get something to cover that, and something to drink, then we'll find a good spot at the stage. You're lucky. I don't doubt Duri could have truly sliced you open had he wished to. Rio, Nikal, Adla, are you coming?"

"Sorry, but I'll decline," Adla said. "I've got some friends in the medical tent I'd like to spend some time with." She smiled at Andor, but grabbed Rioletta by the arm and pulled her to the side.

"I'll check on Cardon a few times over the evening. I'm sure he'll sleep through the rest of the celebration, but I'll make sure he isn't too heavily sedated for safety," Adla said.

"Thanks," Rioletta said. "That makes me feel better, but I'm sorry you won't get to relax."

"It's all right. Go enjoy the rest of the night. I'm not one for big parties, anyway."

It was the last night of formal celebration, and many would leave the following day after a final push to sell trade items. Music and performances went well into the night, and Rioletta, Nikal, and the Andolith crowd staked out a spot near the stage with chairs and blankets. People came and went, bringing food and drink, including the Tabor wines, brews, and harder liquor. Those who had made purchases brought the smaller items to the group to be admired. A few traders worked the crowd with satchels and pocketed vests, selling small items. One of them offered a variety of smokes, and Morcah and Creed called him over.

"Not tobacco," he assured them with a smile. "I guarantee satisfaction."

"Oh, come on, Creed!" Andor exclaimed when Creed pulled out his money. "You don't even know what's in those smokes!"

Nikal examined a couple, sniffing them cautiously. "I'm familiar with some of these. They won't cause anyone any harm, if they've been properly prepared."

"And what if they haven't?" Andor argued. Creed tucked his money away to placate her, but later Rioletta noticed Morcah with the vendor at the side of the crowd. She knew Morcah liked to smoke, and she figured Creed might get a taste of one of them later.

Rioletta spent the night at the Dobor camp with Nikal. He had set up a large tent for privacy, back in the woods away from the main fire ring.

"Well, what do you think?" Nikal asked as he showed Rioletta in, holding the tent flap aside.

"It's luxurious for a tent! That's a nice, comfy bed you've set up there. I can't wait to try it out!" Rioletta laughed.

"In that case, let's try it out right away," Nikal said, pulling her to him. "I'm suddenly not interested in a nightcap!"

The two were up early the next morning. They wandered the stalls for a final time and found some breakfast, then made their way to the Andolith camp. Rioletta went to Cardon's spot immediately; he was awake, but still groggy, and sitting near his bedding.

"Well, how do you feel?" Rioletta asked.

Cardon glanced at Nikal, who stood a short distance away; other than their short contact the previous evening, they had not spent time around each other since the previous year's journey to Tabor. Rioletta could feel a prickle of conflict between them. She knew Nikal didn't think much of Cardon and his decisions, and he'd dropped enough hints that Cardon had begun to pick up on those feelings.

"It's not much better," Cardon admitted. "I feel better, because I slept, and Adla's medicine allows me to concentrate a little more and ignore what I choose to ignore; but the voices still come frequently, kind of in surges. I really don't think they'll go away until I provide for the proper disposal of the bodies. I think that's the source, along with my own guilt."

"I've been thinking about this myself for some time now," Nikal said. "The Younger Council were Vrinac and they had many family members who at this time have no idea besides rumor what happened to them. The First Chosen are no friends of Andolith at this point, but I think you do not bear a grudge against the Vrinac family in general, and you could perhaps garner some trust and thanks if you were to return the bodies of the Younger Council, or at least point out where they lie."

"I would have to return to the area to do that," Cardon said. "I can't describe it well enough."

"Then perhaps that's what we should do," Nikal said. "I'm willing to go along as a liaison. Dobor has retained reasonable enough relations with Tabor, and I'm well known to the First Chosen."

"We'll need to go to Ladon," Rioletta said. "I know you don't want to do that, Cardon, but perhaps the time has come. You could run off by yourself, but if you want anybody else from Andolith to go with you, you'll need Ladon's permission."

Cardon sighed. "I suppose you're right, and I guess more than just Nikal and I should go. Have you seen Ladon this morning?"

"No, but I think I heard his voice as we came in to the camp," Rioletta said. "He's likely near the fire pit. Let's catch him now before he goes off into the Polebray."

Ladon and Rath were at Ladon's campsite, preparing to head into the Polebray for a last round of shopping before beginning to reorganize and pack.

"Good morning, Ladon," Rioletta began. "I'm afraid I need to talk to you about Cardon."

Ladon sighed. "Now? I suppose it can't wait."

"I don't think so," Rioletta said. "You know I wouldn't bother you if it wasn't important. You should probably hear it directly from Cardon. He's at the fire pit."

"Well, Rath, you might as well hear some of what's been going on around here since you left," Ladon said. "It's not really a secret, but you might be shocked at a few things."

"I'm interested," Rath said. "I've seen quite a bit in my travels. I doubt I'll be too shocked." She followed Ladon to the fire pit, where Morcah was pouring coffee for Andor and Creed.

Cardon told Ladon about the voices, how he had been hearing them since leaving Tabor, and how he thought returning the bodies of the Younger Council, hidden now for almost a year, to their families, might quiet his mind.

Ladon was obviously uncomfortable with the idea of sending Cardon back to Tabor. "You've had nothing but bad experiences there, and it's not safe for a Sorcerer, even an ex-Sorcerer, of Andolith, at this point," he argued.

"We won't go through Tabor," Nikal said. "We can ford the Rhamphor to the west of here and head up through the orchards south of Hyolon to Dobor. The ford isn't good for wagons, but horses will make it, at least this late in the season. We can keep out of the public eye. From Dobor we'd bypass Tabor to the west on the old East Road along the edge of the Ruined City. There won't be much traffic on it since everyone will have done all their trading here. We can find the place where Cardon was sheltering and backtrack to where he found the Younger Council from there. Once we know exactly where their bodies are, I can go to Tabor and approach the Vrinac."

"We should take Stolen, too," Cardon said. "He's the only other person who knows where the bodies are, and if I can't find my way, perhaps he'll be able to."

"Where is Stolen, anyway?" Ladon asked.

Cardon shrugged. "I haven't seen him since after the races last night."

"Didn't see him last evening, either," Creed said with a grin. "But if there'd been any trouble, I expect we'd have heard. He's probably fine. We can ask for him this morning."

"Who else will go?" Andor asked. "Creed and I can spare time. It's best to go with some kind of protection, and I'm known in Tabor too, and I'm a Negotiator. And Rioletta, of course, and Morcah and Pateret would be good."

"No!" Ladon exclaimed. "You're not going to wipe out the whole Younger Council for this venture! Pateret can't travel that far, anyway; she has not fully recovered, and the Polebray will be enough for her for a while. And you don't need a Wayfinder; Morcah is needed in Andolith, especially if I allow Andor to go, which I see has some merit. Rioletta, I see no need for you to go, either."

"Except that she's the only one both Cardon and I can distance communicate with," Nikal said. "I think that might be important, especially if we need to split up at any point. We can do it using talismans, not Mind-sharing," he added quickly as Ladon frowned.

"All right, I accept that," Ladon sighed. "Cardon, Nikal, and Stolen for sure; I'll think about Creed, Andor, and Rioletta. No more."

"Don't think too long," Nikal said. "If we're going to go, we should go while people are traveling from the Polebray so we won't be conspicuous."

Rioletta glanced at Ladon's face to see how he was taking being spoken to in that tone, but Nikal was of the Elder Council of Dobor and thus Ladon's peer, despite his youth. Ladon merely nodded. "Give me some time. We'll have to arrange for someone to drive Cardon's wagon back and take Justah and Lida, and for someone to take the horses, too. Anything you've bought that you don't want to take with you will have to be packed. Rath, perhaps you could help us out?"

"I expect I could at least lead a couple of horses," Rath said. "I haven't been to Andolith in years, and I'd like to visit anyway. Then it'll be a short hop over the Sydian to Luth."

Rioletta went to where her gear was stashed to sort and pack. After some hesitation, she placed the book in her satchel, which she would take with her, rather than in with the rest of her purchases, which she would send back. She had no real reason for doing so, other than a desire to work on the mysteries within it.

Chapter Five

Most of the residents of Andolith left the Polebray that day, along with other residents of the Sydian. The Polebray was much quieter, with no more organized events. There were large gaps in the alleys of stalls, although a good number of vendors stayed until the last minute to sell as much as possible. Some cleanup was already beginning: the stage was being torn down, and garbage collected by crews.

Rioletta, Andor, Creed, and Nikal cruised the stalls for the last time. There were better bargains to be had now, but the most desirable items had been purchased early. Rioletta did manage to find an acceptable cover to protect her plant book. Most of the food was free or minimally priced since the vendors wanted to dispose of it before it went bad. All of them ate their fill and purchased some supplies for the upcoming trip.

They found Stolen at the race corrals, tending to Cardon's horses. He was smug and noncommittal about where he had been, despite Creed's cajoling. Andor told him about Cardon's voices and their plans to find the grave of the Younger Council, and asked if he would consider accompanying them.

Stolen turned to one of the horses and busied himself with some small task. "I have known of Cardon's voices for some time," he said, surprising them. "Of course, I work with him often, and for

43

long times. I have seen his spells, and he did tell me he was bothered by the memories of his friends. If he wishes me to go, I'll go. I'm sure I can find the place, and if it bothers him to be near it, I will show you where it is and how I closed it up."

"We'll spend one more night here, then, and leave tomorrow morning," Andor said. "Rath and Ladon will bring the wagon and horses back and care for them until we return. Pack what you need to travel and leave the rest with Cardon's wagon."

"But there's no rush. Come with us and walk around the vendors," Rioletta urged.

Stolen hesitated, then agreed, smiling. He put away the tools he'd been using and hopped over the corral fence to join them.

After lunch the group returned to the Andolith camp to finish their arrangements. Cardon had remained in camp, and Adla was there visiting him when they arrived. Nikal and Adla went back to the Dobor camp to prepare; Adla would ride with them as far as Dobor and provide Cardon with whatever aid she could.

Rioletta had little to do, so she settled herself in the shade of a cottonwood with her back to the trunk; her folding chair had already been loaded. She took out the book and installed it in its new cover, then began to read it carefully, word for word, looking for anything that jumped out at her. She read the title page and printing data first. Since she knew next to nothing about Hyolon, those sections meant little to her. She examined the inside cover page and first few pages with the magnifying glass as well, but found nothing.

Next she began to read the body of the text. The wording and form of the characters was slightly archaic, but the years had not been long enough to make it unintelligible. She read very carefully, making sure she understood each passage before going on; it was not difficult, as she knew most of the principles already, and the topic was not esoteric. She made sure to refer to each plate as it was referenced and examined each with the magnifying glass. She also took out the card and re-compared the cut edges to the lines beneath the plant identifications.

She was done with the little book within three hours and had examined it physically as closely as she could with little result, except that she was now familiar with its contents. But the card was not explained in the text, and the plant press was only referenced in the tiny characters spiraling over the back inside cover.

She got up to stretch and take a break from her study. She was sure there was something more, but it was not accessible via normal physical means. Her next move would be to examine it with other means; but that could wait until later.

She wandered to the front of the camp, where Ladon, Rath, and Morcah were finishing up with Cardon's wagon, securing all the belongings and making sure the bedding and camp gear was accessible for the travel home. Creed and Andor were just returning from the Polebray, having scrounged the last of the bread from several of the vendors who were on their way out. Andor handed Rioletta a loaf to keep with her on the journey.

"How's that cut on your arm today, Creed?" Rath asked. "You did a good job avoiding that blade, though I'm not sure he intended to make contact anyway."

"I didn't even really see it. I think I avoided it by instinct," Creed shrugged, turning his arm over to examine the slice on the inside of his forearm. "The cut'll heal fine, it's minor."

"What do you know about Duri, anything about where he's been since he left Andolith? Ladon has told me the story of his departure."

"I know as much as anyone else, which is nothing," Creed said. "I hadn't seen him or even thought about him until I ran into him here."

"Well, he's been somewhere where they teach the physical arts, perhaps working as a guard for a trading company," Rath said. "I don't recall running into him on the Western Trade Routes, but I recognized many of his moves and know them myself."

"You know those moves?" Andor asked with some interest. "I saw how you took Duri down when that knife came out. What would you think about teaching them in Andolith?"

Rath shrugged. "I don't know, would anyone be interested?"

"I think some of the women would be, right, Rioletta?" Andor said. "Those of us who travel a lot could always use new techniques to protect ourselves. I imagine some of those can be used defensively, as well as offensively."

"Quite right," Rath said. "Perhaps this winter would be a good time, if Ladon will have me in Andolith."

Ladon smiled and looked at her. "I'm hoping we'll see quite a bit of you there. I'm sure there are a few who'd be interested in learning your bow technique, as well."

Creed nodded. "I would be. It would only take a little bit more speed to beat my father."

"And me, of course," Rath pointed out. "What will I do for money if I'm out of the running in the archery contests?"

Creed laughed. "I'll let you come in third."

"And I thought I was retiring to my parents' dairy," Rath sighed. "But that wouldn't suit me. I'll have more fun teaching what I know."

"And I'll bet you have some stories to tell, as well, about guard duty on the trading lines," Andor said. "Good! We'll have something to look forward to this winter!"

The Polebray was quiet that evening, and they made their own meal over the fire at the camp, then sat around and talked until it was too dark to see. Rioletta took a little time with the book while it was still light; her first attempt was Illustrative Animation, a Restricted Skill taught to Loremasters. The form of animation she knew allowed illustrations to move on the page and act out the part of the story they were intended to show.

Rioletta checked every illustration, but got nothing except some minor movement that made it appear that the plants were growing, budding, or moving in the wind; in a few cases there was a zoom effect that allowed her to better visualize specific plant parts, such as sepals and pistil attachments. She put the book away and joined the group at the fire again.

Ladon awakened Rioletta before dawn the next morning. She got up and rolled her bedding, then went with the rest of the group to the corrals to fetch the horses. Wagons were hitched as the sun rose, horses were saddled and lead harnesses checked. Rioletta stowed her bedding and saddlebags behind her saddle on the gray mare, checked her cinch, and led the horse to where Cardon, Stolen, Creed, and Andor were checking their own mounts. Nikal and Adla arrived within a few minutes, and the small group mounted and waved to the rest of the Andolith camp. They would leave by the eastern gate, as if they were heading back home; Ladon thought it unnecessary that the entirety of Andolith know where they were going or what they were doing, and Cardon preferred it that way as well.

Once they had passed through the eastern gate, they turned south and followed the fence surrounding the Polebray all the way around to the western side. They came back to the river exactly opposite where they had left the fairgrounds, but out of sight behind a rise.

The Rhamphor here was wide and muddy-banked, surrounded by rolling hills of grass punctuated by groves of cottonwoods in the hollows.

"The ford we're heading to is west of the southernmost finger of Hyolon," Nikal told the party. 'There's a ridge of rock there, and the river hasn't been able to dig as deep a channel. Instead there's a cascade, and below that it spreads out and is shallower, with a rock bottom. We'll cross there, and then make our way through the orchards to Dobor."

The day was warm and sunny, and Rioletta, Andor, Nikal, Adla, and Stolen were all in good moods. They moved along at a brisk walk, chatting and joking and reviewing their days at the Polebray. Cardon was quiet, which was not unexpected; but Creed was on edge and distracted. On several occasions, Rioletta saw him pull up and stand in the stirrups on top of one rise or another and look behind them as though he thought they were being followed.

By midday, Rioletta could see a high, steep-sided rise ahead of them. It sloped off to the south, but the Rhamphor cut through it.

"There's the ford," Nikal said. "We'll cross just this side of that rise. It's still an hour or so to the ford; let's stop and have lunch here. Then we'll cross and ride a few hours north through the plains. We should be near the first orchards by the time we're ready to make camp."

They dismounted on a rise and made lunch, looking out over the grasslands. It was much more open here, and fewer cottonwoods grew along the river. There were no settlements, but herds of animals ranged in the distance.

"How are you feeling, Cardon?" Adla asked. "Do you need something with your lunch?"

"I'm all right. I want to be alert enough to ride safely," Cardon said. "I'm just looking forward to getting this over with."

It was getting quite hot, and they continued at a slower pace so as not to overheat the horses. In little more than an hour, they came to the ford near the ridge of rock. The trail continued close to the face of the ridge, and there were many patterns chipped into the wall there, some resembling people, some animals, with many designs of unknown meaning.

Nikal led the way and Adla followed in the rear of the group, since both had crossed there before. Rioletta disliked water crossings, but all went well, and the horses climbed the opposite bank.

By late afternoon they were riding through brush and scattered oaks, and eventually they came to an orchard, the first they had seen. Nikal suggested they stop for the night, and rode off to find the grower's house to see if they could take some fresh fruit and camp beneath his trees.

Cardon immediately stretched out on his back, hands behind his head, after removing his gear from his horse. He closed his eyes, although he didn't seem relaxed. He refused any of Adla's medicines until he was sure they wouldn't have to ride anymore that day.

Creed sat watchful, his crossbow slung across his back. He had brought the crossbow, a compound, and a recurve for competition to the Polebray, and after leaving the celebration he had switched to the crossbow. Rioletta thought perhaps he was taking his duties as guard too seriously. But after all, there had been reports of robbers in the Tadian, and now would be a good time for them to strike. Travelers returning from the Polebray were apt to be carrying cash, and they were a small group in an isolated area, with good cover for those wanting to remain unseen in the orchard and tall scrub brush.

When Nikal returned, they built a small fire and prepared dinner from the leftovers from the Polebray and some of the fruits from the orchard. The trees in this section were old and little tended, but they bore some fruits just becoming ripe. As the evening cooled, Cardon slept, now drugged, and with Creed sitting slightly apart, the others talked around the fire.

"You know, there are other Lefollah besides the groves you have seen," Stolen volunteered. It was unusual for him to start a conversation, and Andor quickly followed up with a question.

48

"What are these other Lefollah like? Where do they dwell?" she asked.

"Well, there might be some around here," Stolen said, looking around in the gathering shadows. "I feel as though there are, but I might not be able to speak to them. Like humans, Lefollah have different dialects and take different forms depending on where they live."

The thought of Lefollah in the area made Rioletta's nerves prickle.

"There are different races, then," Andor said, looking around as well. "They must look more different from each other than people do, if they resemble the trees near which they live."

"No," Stolen disagreed. "The main form of each Lefollah is much the same, but it is hidden inside a shell grown to resemble the trees. The shell is more like clothing. Branches and twigs and leaves are grown that can be thrown down to make mobile bodies and to use sunlight, and roots are made to drill into the soil for water. These are part of the shell, although there is a close connection between the shell and the body. The Lefollah can go about in these shells if necessary, but in some situations, they will shed the shells and move about in their internal forms."

"I didn't know that," Rioletta said. "You mean the Lefollah I've spoken to are disguised by an outer shell, and I haven't seen a true one?"

"No more have I seen many humans in their true form, without clothing. Although lately I have seen a few more," Stolen answered.

Andor laughed. "And what is your true form, Stolen? Is your skin only an outer shell, or do we see the real you?"

Stolen smiled and spread his arms. "I am not Lefollah, only changed. I am a human being, born if not raised, and what you see is what I truly am. I have no outer skin or shell, only leaves and twigs and clothing to disguise me."

"Can you grow and shed leaves and twigs when you want, like the Lefollah, or is it beyond your control?" Nikal asked.

Stolen paused. "I have some small control over it," he said. "I'm not like a true Lefollah, and I have been unsuccessful at shedding all my leaves, obviously. But I've improved; I grow fewer and retain fewer than I used to. I don't want to grow more, so I've never tried to do that purposefully. When I do shed a leaf, I remain in contact with it for some short time. It must be like when the Lefollah shed their leaves to send them about as spies. I can feel them, but not for long. After a while they shrivel and die."

"But are there truly other Lefollah around here, or are you only guessing?" Rioletta asked uncomfortably. If there were Lefollah nearby…

Stolen looked at her. "Not close, I think. If there are, they are old, maybe part of abandoned orchards, and not mobile. More like the Twisted Trees than the ones of the grove of the Syrola. They will not bother us."

As it became dark and the fire burned down, the group fell asleep one by one. Rioletta remained awake for a while, lying on her bedding. She could see Creed's silhouette where he sat near the embers, looking out into the dark, and she felt safer for that.

The following day they rode through orchards, first old and scattered, then newer ones, then well-established and well-cared for ones. They entered Dobor in mid-afternoon and rode directly to Nikal's house.

Dobor was considerably larger than Andolith, although not as big as Tabor. It was directly south of Hyolon, with a spur of old buildings, almost covered in vines and hidden by domestic plants gone feral, to the west. Although Dobor was much closer to the outskirts of the Ruined City than Tabor, Hyolon did not seem to loom over it as much. The buildings were shorter on the south side of Hyolon, which, as Nikal explained, had been the industrial section. There was a rise to the west, and the main paved street of Dobor was laid out north-south along the base of the rise, and there were large trees throughout, not cottonwoods but elms and other domesticated varieties. This layout served to block the view of Hyolon, except for glimpses here and there.

Nikal's house was set upon the western hill. It was a spreading, open place uncrowded by other residences, which were widely scattered along the rise. The group rode up a winding, paved trail to Nikal's stable. The house itself had a brick-paved front entrance, huge windows throughout, gardens, a number of large trees, and a back terrace enclosed on three sides by the main part of the house and two wings. The open side was to the west, and it had been planted with flowering shrubs to form a low wall of vegetation, punctuated by several small multi-stemmed trees. The terrace was set with tables and chairs, and from there the view of Hyolon was much more pronounced.

The front rooms looked out over the main part of Dobor, a view much more to Rioletta's liking; but Nikal preferred the terrace with its comfortable furnishings. She had learned that Hyolon did not bother him as it did her and many others who visited. Nikal, like the rest of his family, had grown accustomed to its presence, and the glass salvagers regularly entered the city itself. Rioletta had always heard that the Ruined City was dangerous in many ways, but Nikal's family dealt with that as they had for generations, taking well-armed guards with them on their foraging journeys.

Once the horses were unpacked and stabled, Nikal showed the group to their bedrooms in the house wings. He put Rioletta's things in his own room. Adla remained with them for the time being; she intended to prepare a stock of medicines for Cardon to take with him as they traveled north.

The evening was warm, with a slight breeze bringing the fragrance of the flowering shrubs. Nikal lit a fire in a pit in the terrace, and they took their meal outside.

Creed seemed to have relaxed now that they were in the city, and with a couple of Nikal's beers on board, he became more talkative than he had been since they left the Polebray. "Hey, Morcah, did you save any of those smokes from the Polebray?"

Morcah shook his head. "Sorry, Creed. What did you think of that last band on the final night?"

Andor snorted. "Do you even remember the last band?"

Morcah and Creed launched into an animated discussion of the band and their favorite songs. Rioletta scooted her chair back a bit underneath one of the lamps and pulled out her book. She had not had a chance to examine it since she had animated the illustrations, and she was impatient to get back to figuring out what it had to say, if anything.

Her next move, she decided, would be to have it read itself to her. Sometimes authors would add words and phrases to the spoken version that could only be discovered by those with Loremaster's Skills. In that way, books distributed to the general public could also hold special messages for Sorcerers and members of specific groups.

Nikal stopped next to her on his way back from his cellar. "Any progress?"

"No." Rioletta explained her plan, as well as the animation technique.

"You should be careful with that," Cardon put in from the fire pit. "Books can hold all sorts of information, some of which we might prefer not to read."

"Cardon, I'm a Loremaster, books are my thing," Rioletta said somewhat curtly. "I know what I'm doing, at least so far."

Cardon glanced at Nikal and shrugged, but Nikal only smiled. "Let me know what you find out," he said. "I'm sure you can figure it out."

Rioletta said nothing, although she noticed that Nikal had suddenly become less worried and more accepting of her interaction with the book now that Cardon was expressing his concerns. With the rest of the group engaged around the fire pit, she settled back in her chair and opened the book to the first page. She applied her Narrate Skill to it, with a dampening Skill to keep it quiet and not disturb the others. The book began to read itself aloud in a sonorous male voice, and Rioletta followed along. She kept a pen and paper handy, to note what and where extra words or changed phrases were inserted or deleted.

Everything seemed word for word until they arrived at the first plant identification, one of the plants with a jagged underline matching a card side. The voice identified the illustration as "Plate Two," although it was the first plate. The voice also gave a third identification for the plant, having first used the common name, then the scientific genus and species designation. Rioletta knew the flower, a pretty ornamental with poisonous blooms.

It seemed odd that the Narrator had misidentified the plate, but Rioletta knew the Narrate Skill was sometimes used to pass on information that wasn't meant to be available to everyone. She wasn't sure what the intent was, but she kept listening. The next couple of plates were correctly numbered, but then she came to another one that the Narrator identified differently from the text. When she discovered a third and then a fourth, she knew the misidentifications were not a mistake. She couldn't figure out the purpose. It was frustrating, but an interesting mystery. She was even more entranced with Nikal's gift by the time she put it aside for the evening.

She rejoined the group for a last drink before bed. Nikal smiled and gestured to her, and she curled up next to him on a large settee.

They decided to spend the following day and night at Nikal's house before leaving for Tabor. Andor, Adla, and Creed shopped for food and supplies in the village, while Cardon, Stolen, Nikal, and Rioletta relaxed at the house. Rioletta took the time to continue with the book; when she was done, as she had suspected, she had a new number and name for each of the six plants that matched the card.

She tried a few more Loremaster Skills, including reading it backwards; but that produced nothing but garbled sounds. She Scanned it, which caused it to flip to important passages and read those aloud, and Riffled it, which caused it to flip through to specific pages and stop for her to read those sections herself. Neither of those produced anything, and nor did Sorting, Ordering, and Outlining.

Nikal joined her on the terrace with cool drinks; the day was sunny and hot. Rioletta explained what she had found out and showed him the re-numbered plant plates.

"I'm running out of book-related Skills to use now," Rioletta said. "But somehow I suspect there's more to be discovered."

"Yes," Nikal mused. "Perhaps we need to use Skills on it that aren't book-related."

Rioletta raised her eyebrows. "My only other true Skills are the Andolith Skills: Stealth, Misdirection, and Concealment. I don't think any of those will work on a book."

"No, but you also know Monitoring and Viewing," Nikal pointed out. "I've never Monitored or Viewed a book; those Skills are intended for open areas, not for objects. But I suppose it might be possible."

"We also know Distance Communication," Rioletta said.

"No, I wouldn't use that," Nikal said. "It involves opening the mind to the intrusion of others, a type of Mind-sharing, and that's dangerous enough when it's with someone you know. I don't even know if it would work with an object, but I don't think it's wise to try."

"Agreed," Rioletta said. "But you're a much better Monitor than I am. Perhaps you should try."

Nikal settled himself into a chair and put out his hand. "All right, give it to me. But stay here next to me and watch; if something happens, I may need your help."

"What?" Rioletta asked. What did he mean, *if something happens?*

Nikal did not reply; he had opened the book on his lap and closed his eyes, one hand holding the pages down.

"Huh," he said after a few moments. "What do you know? It's working. Someone must have designed this book to be Monitored, although that seems odd. Have you got pen and paper?"

"Yes," Rioletta said. "Do you want to write or dictate?"

"I'll dictate it to you," Nikal said. "It's a recipe. Let me get back to the beginning."

Rioletta wrote as Nikal reeled off the directions for the creation of a potion, one that sounded dangerous and horrible to Rioletta. It included normal ingredients, such as water, but also six ingredients not specified except by number and ratio.

Nikal fell silent, and in a few moments opened his eyes. "Read it back to me."

"Take six parts of the first to twenty parts of the second," Rioletta read, and continued through the recipe to the end. "The ingredients must be added in order from first to sixth. This is the preparation for the Receiver. The Receiver must be Healer or Mind-Sharer and prepared in advance via the Transformative Path, or this concoction will be deadly and the task will not be accomplished. This preparation will also allow the Receiver to use the Index to choose."

"Well, what do you think that means?" Nikal mused.

"I'm not sure," Rioletta said, "but it mentions the Transformative Path, which would be the set of drugs and concoctions used to bring someone to the Forbidden Skills, the path Cardon started down with the Younger Council."

"But of course they wouldn't have been Forbidden a hundred years ago when this was written," Nikal said, "although someone took great pain to make sure this recipe was hidden. So far it has taken Loremaster and Monitor Skills and specifies that the concoction is to be used by a Transformative Healer or Mind-Sharer, with an Index of some sort. At least we know why the plants were re-numbered in the vocal text; they have to be added in order in this recipe."

"But that doesn't explain the card," Rioletta said. "It is certainly keyed to the plant plates. I originally thought it would be used to find the order of the plants, but that doesn't seem to be true."

"No, it seems to be the other way," Nikal said. "The order of the plants can be used to number the sides of the card."

Rioletta sat silent for a minute. "But for what purpose?"

Nikal shrugged. "I don't know. I don't know what a Receiver is, but I do know the concoction made from this recipe would be extremely dangerous if not deadly."

"Perhaps less deadly if someone had developed a tolerance to some of the ingredients," Rioletta suggested. "Maybe that's why only one who has started on the Path of Transformation can take it."

"Maybe," Nikal said, rising. "It's just strange all around. But I hear the others returning. Let's make lunch; Monitoring makes me hungry."

Chapter Six

Andor and Creed returned with a good supply of easily-packable food. Andor sorted it and portioned it out for the saddlebags. Creed displayed a machete he'd picked up, much like the *quant* one Cardon wore, to add to his bows and belt knife, and a second, somewhat slimmer version for Stolen. He had also purchased a couple of heavy canvas saddle-sheaths for the machetes; they were not the type of tool one wore on one's belt, nor could they be drawn easily, like a sword. But once wielded, they were excellent for clearing paths of overhanging branches and vines while on horseback, and could be used as a weapon if necessary.

They rose early the following morning and ate breakfast for the last time at Nikal's house. While everyone was involved in packing the horses, Adla pulled Rioletta aside.

"I've given Cardon a store of medicine to keep his mind calm and focused and to help him sleep at night, with instructions as to how much to use. I went over the instructions quite carefully, and I know he's a Healer and should understand. But he's very disturbed and distracted. I have some fear that he might take too much of one or the other in an effort to maintain control."

"Perhaps I should take the medicine and portion it out to him," Rioletta said.

"I think it's best to allow him some control," Adla said. "It's humiliating to have to beg for relief; let him portion it out to himself as he sees fit. But I have some other items to give to you, just in case."

Adla held out two packages. "If you should find him impossible to wake in the morning or if he slips into unconsciousness at any other time, use these to revive him; otherwise his breathing could become so slow that he dies. The first one is a paste; if he's unconscious, he won't be able to swallow. You'll need to rub this inside his mouth; it will be absorbed from there. Once he's awake enough to take a little water, give him a tablet from the second package. Those are stronger and will last longer. You may need to give him several doses of each, for the sleeping medicine acts for a long time and these stimulants are short-lived. Of course, if this happens, you may need to take the sleeping medicine from him to prevent a recurrence, but leave him with the calming aid; it's difficult to overdose on that."

Rioletta took the small packages. "Is there anything I need to do to store them properly?"

"Check the paste from time to time and make sure it's not drying out; if it is, boil some water for several minutes and mix that in. Use a tool, not your fingers, to mix it. On the other hand, don't let the tablets get wet at all. They are in a small box within the wrap. It's best if both are kept cool, but you won't have an opportunity to do that while you're traveling, so don't worry about it overmuch."

"Thank you," Rioletta said. "And thank you for your help and your respect for Cardon. I've known Cardon all my life, and I'm still very fond of him."

"I know," Adla clasped Rioletta's hands and smiled. "I'm fond of him too. I have seen some sparks of what he used to be. I hope you'll return having solved this dilemma, and he'll be healthy enough for us to enjoy his personality once again."

"I hope so." Rioletta took the packages to her horse and stowed them carefully in one of her saddlebags, protected from the heat as much as possible. Adla raised a hand in farewell as the group set off down the hillside in the relative cool of the morning, making for the main street of Dobor.

The horses' hooves clopped loudly on the brick of the main street. Few people were up at this hour, only some shopkeepers opening their stores for the day. Nikal greeted several of them as they passed; as both a member of the Kathreftis family and a member of the Council, he was well known in Dobor.

The main street through Dobor continued out of the city to the north, then bent to the northeast towards Tabor, which stood on the eastern side of Hyolon. The group followed it for a couple of hours after leaving Dobor. Hyolon became more visible to their left, and the buildings began to rise as they passed the southern industrial region.

"The buildings look different here," Rioletta noted as she rode alongside Nikal.

"Yes," Nikal said. "We think the eastern side of Hyolon was the side most frequently approached by travelers. It appears to have been constructed to appeal to visitors. The buildings here have facings and facades and friezes, and other decorations like arches and buttresses. Down near Dobor the buildings are rough and undecorated, industrial. But because of the height of the buildings here, collapses are often more catastrophic. The eastern side's considered more dangerous for that reason. Residents of Tabor generally don't enter the Ruined City at all, but we know it provides shelter for the Outcast Council and the other members of the Outcast community; and according to Cardon, the Younger Council used it as well."

The old East Road intersected the Dobor road and ran through the strip of woods between Hyolon and the Tabor vineyards towards the Hyolon Pass to the north. Nikal told them it was seldom used; there were now no facilities or amenities along that route, and it was not maintained. The horse-breeders used it on occasion to loose-herd their horses when they were moving them for sale, but they had been at the Polebray, and it was unlikely any Mahquant or other *quant* would be on it at this time of year. Besides horse-breeders, the road was occasionally used by unsavory characters who had a reason to avoid Tabor.

Several hours north of Dobor the group came upon the intersection with the old East Road in a thick grove. The Dobor road turned east and continued on towards Tabor, well-marked and firm underfoot. The East Road was barely visible through the trees. Nikal paused, and the group brought their horses close together.

"I prefer no one see us start down this road," Nikal said. "There would surely be questions and comments. From here on, we must be more alert; it's possible there could be robbers or other criminals, and I don't know who else might use this route. It's also in poor shape, and we'll have to watch where the horses step. Another two hours should bring us directly west of Tabor and at the closest point to the Ruined City; from there, I don't know where to go."

"I'll be able to figure out how to get to the Younger Council's meeting places from there," Cardon said. "Usually we came in from further north, but I'm sure I'll recognize some of the buildings. There's a greensward there that runs into the city. At one point it must have been a kind of park or recreation ground. There's often water in a raceway and game in the woods, and there are a number of old breweries and wine cellars lining it on this side. The buildings are in fairly good shape and low to the ground, and also a good distance from the high buildings."

"Are they frequented by the Outcasts as well?" Rioletta asked.

Cardon shrugged. "I don't know where the Outcasts live. But certainly the Outcast Council is aware of all the places the Younger Council used. They met frequently, and some of the Outcasts provided guidance to those of the Younger Council who were interested in pursuing further Skills…particularly Rudon. Rudon frequently seemed to know when the Younger Council had arrived, by what means I know not. Whether he or others will note our arrival, I don't know."

"If so, are they likely to be dangerous to us?" Creed asked.

Again Cardon shook his head. "I can't say for sure. I've met a few of them, and they seemed reasonable enough, but I also know what the final draught of the Path of Transformation did to me; and each of them has gone much further along that path than I have. I can only imagine what must be happening in their minds; and for that reason, I would not lay trust in them."

"For that reason no one lays trust in them," Nikal said darkly. "That's why the Forbidden Skills are Forbidden: they cause damage to the self or others. Although I suspect some of it has been exaggerated, tales told over the years. After all, most Skills lie along a continuum; is not part of the diagnosis Healers do a kind of Mind-sharing? And talisman communication perhaps falls in there, too. At the other end of that spectrum is complete Mind-sharing requiring Distraction, but where along the line does it grade from Common to Restricted to Forbidden? For that matter, Andolith Sorcerers specialize in Concealment; I've seen it myself. It seems to me that's along the continuum at the far end of which lies Shape-shifting."

"Many of the Younger Council expressed those same thoughts, Nikal," Cardon said. "Many of the Outcasts go further, and argue that the Forbidden Skills were never meant to be Forbidden except in specific circumstances, in conjunction with specific technologies. Rioletta's studied some of that as a Loremaster."

"I have," Rioletta said, "although I sometimes think my education has been limited. But I don't question that the lines drawn along those continuums you describe are correct, developed over years of trial and error. And the reasoning behind Forbidding certain Skills seems sound to me. It's provided for our successful existence these past hundred years."

"I don't doubt you're right," Nikal said. "I only point out the reasoning of others."

He guided his horse off the hard-packed roadway and onto the narrower path through the trees. It had once been wide enough for two wagons to pass each other, but trees had encroached upon it from either side and vegetation grew in the track. Water had rutted the route in some places and there were occasional branches down upon the road, although it was also apparent that someone cut and removed fallen limbs from time to time. Most likely the horse breeders kept the route at least somewhat clear.

They saw no one for the next two hours. Creed remained on high alert, and once again Rioletta noticed him turning in his saddle, checking behind him as though he thought they might be followed, a hand going to his bow slung across his back as he stood. The woods were close here, and it was difficult to see far ahead or behind or to either side.

The road turned suddenly to the west, and the trees tapered away. Rioletta saw they were now very close to the city. Ruins of stone walls and guardhouses covered in vines loomed around them, and the highest buildings of Hyolon shimmered in the midday heat. Old pavement showed between shocks of grass. A broad brick avenue led straight into the heart of the city from the Old East Road, between two huge buttresses at either terminus of a great wall that seemed to surround a large part of Hyolon. Beyond the open city gate, the avenue seemed oddly bare of encroaching vegetation; perhaps a Protection of some kind still kept it free of grass and vines.

There was something very odd about seeing a city designed to hold thousands of people and hearing no human activity whatsoever. The group stopped and gazed into the city, listening, but there were no sounds but the snorting of the horses and the birds in the trees. The city itself was silent.

Far in the distance, there was a crash as if stone had struck stone.

"Piece of a building falling off," Nikal said. "It happens regularly. This is as good a place as any to stop for lunch. Cardon can take a while to get his bearings."

Rioletta wished they were a little further from the city and its disturbing silence. Perhaps it was the looming buildings, so much larger than any she knew. Perhaps it was the sheer size of the city; it seemed the streets and alleys could hold any number of hidden dangers. Maybe it was the history and the evil she knew must have existed there in the past to make the Dispersal necessary. She wasn't sure. She knew Andor disliked it as well, but it was an irrational feeling, and rather than argue, she dismounted and pulled some of the food out of her saddlebags.

Creed remained on edge as well. "Is it likely the Hyolonal might come out this far?" he asked Nikal.

Nikal glanced at him. "No, they don't frequent this area of the city and they rarely go outside its boundaries anyway. Their strongholds are on the northwest, farthest away from any settlement."

"I don't really understand who the Hyolonal are," Rioletta said. "I know that they are Unskilled, but the Unskilled are usually not dangerous to us. They live together with the Skilled in many settlements and sometimes even intermarry. There were many Unskilled craftsmen at the Polebray."

"Yes, but the Hyolonal are not like other Unskilled," Nikal said. "I don't know how they came to be in Hyolon, but they are a degenerate society. They're dangerous to those who come into the city unprepared, but I actually know very little about their history. Anyway, we're in no danger here."

After lunch, they bypassed the broad brick avenue leading into the heart of Hyolon and continued north along the old road with Cardon leading the way. He pulled up at a point where the city walls curved away from the road.

"From here on, the road gets further and further from the city," he said. "We must strike off towards Hyolon. If we can find the greensward, we can follow that. Once I find the place where Stolen and Justah and I sheltered for those few days last year, I can orient myself and find the grove where the Younger Council lay, with Stolen's help."

"I remember it," Stolen said. "If we climb the wall we used as a lookout, we will be able to set a direction, just as you did when you saw the birds circling."

They struck off through the woods, following winding paths made by animals, drawing ever nearer to Hyolon. At one point, Rioletta realized that they were actually within the very outskirts of the city; the ruins of buildings poked out of the greenery on either side. Eventually they arrived at a broad swath carved out of the forest. Here the vegetation was much lower and the remnants of paved paths could be seen.

"This is the greensward. It runs along most of the north side below the wall," Cardon said. "Many of the buildings along here are outside the wall."

Rioletta examined the buildings as they rode carefully past. They appeared to be a combination of residences and small businesses, perhaps catering to locals and those travelers who ventured off the main routes of the city. Some of the buildings had collapsed completely into their cellars, but others appeared in reasonable shape. Curving away behind them was the tall stone wall, and she could see the tops of buildings on the other side of it.

Nikal pulled up suddenly. "Stop!"

The others pulled up their horses immediately.

"What is it?" Rioletta asked.

"There is a talisman near here," Nikal said, looking around. "I can feel it. Someone has used it frequently. This route is watched, for one reason or another."

"Perhaps the Younger Council Monitored or Viewed it," Andor suggested.

"Likely," Cardon agreed.

But Nikal shook his head. "This has been used more recently than a year ago. But there's nothing to be done about it now; we've already crossed its path, and if anyone was indeed Viewing, they have seen us already."

"It could be Rudon," Cardon said. "If so, he may meet us here, and you'll have your first chance to meet an Outcast Sorcerer. But Rudon is not known for Viewing, as far as I know."

"I've no desire to meet an Outcast," Nikal growled. "He'll find himself at the point of a knife if he appears unexpectedly, or at the tip of one of Creed's arrows, I'll warrant."

The group continued towards a row of low buildings Cardon pointed out, with the wall looming behind.

"Beyond that wall is a huge building with many outbuildings that appears to have been a residence for some important personages, perhaps an embassy," Cardon explained, pointing to the wall. "Here's the wine cellar where we slept last year. It'll be safe enough for tonight. We can set a guard, and the horses will have forage in the greensward this evening. Tomorrow morning we'll climb the wall and I'll try to set the direction."

They dismounted and stowed their belongings in the cellar, which was furnished with scavenged chairs, tables, and beds to make a fairly comfortable apartment. The top part of the building had collapsed in to the first floor, leaving a circle of stone and wood, and within that circle was a fire ring, well-used and full of ash. Chunks of rock and rafters had been dragged around it to form seats, and others thrown against the walls to clear the interior for more space. Stolen picketed the horses not far away in the clearing where there was abundant grass in amongst the encroaching shrubs, and Rioletta made a fire in the pit to heat water and cook dinner.

Creed was more on edge than ever, and paced the area in front of the building until Andor called to him to sit and eat dinner.

"I don't like the fact that there was a talisman there," he said. "And I've been feeling as though we've been followed ever since we left Polebray, except when we were in Dobor."

"Have you seen any sign of anyone?" Nikal asked.

Creed shook his head. "No, it's just a feeling. It's stronger now, like Cardon's voices, I guess. Let's set watches tonight, otherwise I won't sleep."

Despite Creed's misgivings, the night passed uneventfully, and morning dawned bright and sunny with a great cacophony of birds in the greensward. They packed and loaded the horses and left them tied up and ready to go. Rioletta and the others followed Cardon along the row to a section of the old wall, which sloped in one direction and rose to a prominent gateway on the other. The back of the wall was broad and easy to walk on if one watched for loose stones, and they climbed it single-file, up and around as it curved. Rioletta stopped from time to time to look at the huge buildings within the enclosure designated by the wall; certainly the entire village of Andolith could have spent a night in relative comfort inside some of the buildings.

At the very end, where the gateway opened, was a square parapet rising above the level of the wall. Cardon clambered up it using stones as footholds and handholds; the stones appeared to have been laid for just that purpose, almost like a ladder. The rest followed him, and they crowded together on top.

The view was remarkable. To one side were the grounds and buildings of the embassy or convention center; behind that lay the rest of the city, with the tall buildings of the south and east sides easily visible. Below them was the row of houses and shops and the greensward. Beyond that one could look out across the tops of many of the trees to the northeast, out of the city. An even break in the treetops indicated the route of the old East Road.

Cardon pointed to the break.

"I believe the Younger Council was headed for the East Road in that direction, for what purpose I know not," Cardon said. "It eventually leads to the Hyolon Pass, but that's an abandoned route. Stolen, what do you think?"

Stolen stood beside him, gazing out over the trees. "It is that grove there, between us and the mountain with snow still on its side. See, there are scattered ruins; the area was in a place of cisterns and storage buildings, but not heavily built."

"We won't be able to use that mountain as a pointer when we're down in the trees," Cardon said. "But we found it before by simply walking in that direction, so we should be able to do so again."

"I have the direction in my mind," Stolen said. "I remember the form of the trees along the route. I'm good at finding my way in deep woods. We will find it."

The group climbed carefully down the parapet and wall and returned to the horses. Rioletta walked alongside Cardon.

"Are you ready for this?" she asked.

"Yes," answered Cardon, although he looked a little pale. "I want to get it over with. Adla's drugs help, but I still hear the voices, insistent from time to time."

"Well, if we can find them, and Nikal can locate relatives or others to retrieve their remains, it will soon be over," Rioletta said.

"I hope so," Cardon said. He did not sound convinced.

The group mounted and followed Stolen and Cardon through the woods, but soon Stolen pulled up and dismounted.

"The last time I went through here, I was on foot," he said. "Let me lead my horse, and go as I went then. It will be easier."

"I will lead your horse," Rioletta said. "One of us can lead yours if you want to go on foot too, Cardon."

Their progress was slow as Cardon and Stolen examined the woods around them and checked their direction as best they could. Eventually they arrived at a clearing with low vegetation and several obvious stone structures; perhaps it had been a farm or ranch yard.

"This is it," Cardon said quietly. "Here I found all eight of the Younger Council, struck dead. My memory is confused after that."

"There is the stone room where we laid them," Stolen said, pointing to a low-sided square structure. "The roof can be slid aside, and it is not deep within."

"Let's check and make sure all their bodies remain," Nikal said grimly. "Then Andor and I will go to Tabor. We'll mark a route back to this spot; the rest of you should go to some place nearby, and not be seen in case we return with their relatives."

Nikal, Stolen, and Creed approached the stone bin. Rioletta wrapped an arm around Cardon's waist to comfort him as they stood just apart. Behind them, the horses tossed their heads and one whinnied. The three men wrenched the heavy lid back, and threw it off to one side.

Cardon immediately threw his hands up to his ears and collapsed onto his knees. "No! I hear you! I hear you! I'm trying to do what I can!" he screamed.

"Cardon, they are dead!" Creed strode to Cardon and lifted him to his feet by his shirtfront. "Come here! Look at them. They do not live and their voices are not in your head. Look!"

He dragged Cardon to the makeshift crypt, where eight bodies lay stacked, a year dead. Cardon struggled and threw his head to the side, his eyes closed.

"No! They are here! I hear them still! They are not dead!"

"Look at them!" Creed said harshly, shaking Cardon. Cardon reluctantly opened his eyes and rolled his head forward, then stood staring into the crypt.

"I hear them still," he whispered. "I see them here, but their voices still remain."

Suddenly Stolen gave a shout. The rest of the group wheeled about, and Creed dropped Cardon and drew his bow from his back. A man had stepped from the woods on the edge of the clearing.

"Hold!" the man said, raising a hand. "I am unarmed."

Stolen had drawn his machete. He turned sharply to the side as a woman also stepped from behind the trees and moved forward. Both strangers displayed their hands; neither appeared armed. Creed held his bow, arrow nocked, pointed at the man.

The man cautiously stepped closer. "I am Hyphanden, of the Outcast Council of Hyolon," he said with the flash of a smile. "Known to your companion Cardon as Phando. This is my wife, Kwistoctavrina."

The man was tall with dark hair going to gray, and obviously Vrinac, with the narrow face and slight overbite characteristic of the family. The woman bore a striking resemblance to him, although he had introduced her as his wife.

Hyphanden turned slowly, keeping an eye on Creed, and offered a hand to Rioletta, who stood closest to him. Rioletta reached out uncertainly and clasped his hand; he had offered it to her palm up, a gesture of conciliation and respect, and it was customary to accept such a gesture.

Hyphanden released her hand abruptly and strode forward to Cardon, who still sat slumped on the ground. Creed quietly unnocked his arrow, but stepped to the side where he could watch both Hyphanden and Kwistocta. Stolen lowered his machete.

Cardon reached up and grasped Hyphanden's arm. "Phando, I still hear them, although they lie dead here before me. I still hear them!"

"I should certainly hope so," Hyphanden said, "since if you did not hear them, it would mean that they are truly lost for all time; and I personally placed them in the Crypt of Souls to avoid that fate."

Chapter Seven

There was stunned silence for a moment. Rioletta tried to fathom what Hyphanden had just said, but his words made little sense to her.

Nikal stepped forward. "What do you mean? What is the Crypt of Souls?"

Hyphanden squinted up at Nikal from where he had dropped to one knee near Cardon. "It is a story with some length, and although I will gladly tell you, I would prefer a more comfortable location, perhaps with a bottle of good Vrinac wine to share."

"You are the one whose talisman I felt yesterday as we approached," Nikal said.

"Yes," Hyphanden said with a note of disgust, standing up. "And you felt it even though I had done my best to hide its presence from other Viewers. Therefore, you are Nikal of Dobor, unless I miss my guess."

"I am he," Nikal said, clasping hands automatically as Hyphanden proffered his. "I see my reputation precedes me, even to the Ruined City. You are acquainted with Cardon, it appears. That is Stolen, a friend of ours."

"Of course," Hyphanden said with a slight smile. "I know you by rumor, sir. We've never met in person. But I've heard tales, though perhaps not the truth."

"And these are Rioletta and Andor of Andolith's Younger Council, both inducted, and Creed, a hunter of Andolith," Nikal continued formally after Hyphanden and Stolen had clasped hands.

"Sorcerers of Andolith?" Hyphanden said. "You were involved in the rescue of the Elder Council, then? We have heard, although information is often difficult for us to get."

Nikal nodded curtly. "It was they, and I as well. The Elder Council resides in exile in good health, due largely to Andolith's intervention. I expect you'd rather have been rid of them for good."

Hyphanden shrugged. "I'm not particularly fond of the Elder Council, as it was they who Outcast me and set a warrant upon my head. But neither did I wish them any particular harm, nor did I have any purpose for harming them. I made my own decisions long ago, with full knowledge of the possibility of dire consequences."

"Things must be better for you now, with the First Chosen in power. They're not over-fond of the Elder Council, either, and I believe they were contemporaries of yours. Surely they sympathize with you," Nikal continued warily.

"Not so," Hyphanden said. "The First Chosen were indeed peers of mine. In fact, at one time I was Leader of their Council. After my Outcasting, their Council was in disarray. Several other members left and were replaced, but questions remained about their integrity, and they were expelled. The Elders refused to acknowledge their right to succession. However, they were never Stripped of their Skills and remained living free in Tabor. So they were never true Outcasts, and they hold no great love for me. In a roundabout way, my Outcasting eventually led to the dissolution of their Council. They hold our warrants open, and despite their disagreements with the Elders, they can only be seen as a Traditional Council."

"The imprisonment of the Elders was unacceptable," Nikal said. "The actions of the First Chosen and of the Younger Council of Tabor were reprehensible."

"I agree, but I had no part in it," Hyphanden said. "I do not take exception to your rescue of the Elders. In fact, we shelter allies of the Elder Council within Hyolon, including two of the Second Chosen. Come, I'm not here to argue philosophy; there are more pressing things to be discussed."

Hyphanden clasped hands with Andor, but Creed backed away, his hand on the butt of his machete.

Hyphanden spread his hands. "You see I'm unarmed. I present no danger to you or your companions."

"I doubt you need a weapon other than your hands," Creed growled.

"And perhaps my mind," Hyphanden said mildly. "Well, I can't blame you. You're a guard of this group, and you must take your responsibility seriously."

"I knew we were being followed," Creed accused.

"As for that, we have not followed you," Hyphanden said. "We've been Viewing the Row since last year to see who came and went from the Younger Council's meeting spots. When we saw you yesterday and recognized Cardon, we suspected you would come here. This morning we came to this spot ourselves with the intention of meeting you. But others have followed you. We have seen them."

"Them?" Nikal asked. Rioletta and Andor had moved closer as the two spoke, and Rioletta knelt beside Cardon, who was still staring at Hyphanden in a daze.

"There are two of them, yes," Hyphanden said with a slight smile. "As for gender, it's difficult to tell from a distance; but I would make them out to be one male and one female."

"Both traveling together?"

"No, they are not together. One follows you, and the other, as it were, follows the follower. But come, close up the cistern. These people were my acquaintances as well, and the sight of them in this state disturbs me. We'll go elsewhere and talk. I know you have questions, and it may be that I can answer some of those for you. Cardon was also a friend of the Younger Council, and I owe him what I know."

Kwistoctavrina still stood silent some distance away. She had chosen to study the trees of the forest, her head turned away from the open crypt, at which she had not looked. With a glance in her direction, Nikal motioned to Stolen and Creed, and they refitted the top on the stone bier.

"Our intention is to inform their relatives of their location, to provide for proper disposal and closure for their kin," Nikal said.

"It is well," Hyphanden said. He gestured to his wife. "Kwistocta and I have known of their location since their downfall,

71

but without the Younger Council, I have no trustworthy contacts in Tabor and failed to find a way to send a message safely."

Kwistocta seemed to relax with the lid back on the cistern. "Come," she said. "Our horses are off a short distance in the woods. There is an easier route back to the city and to our quarters, which are much more comfortable than the place you stayed last night."

Each of the group clasped hands briefly with her, including Creed. Rioletta found that her clasp was strong and she stood a half-head taller than she or Andor. After her brief introduction, Kwistocta turned quickly and walked into the trees.

"What do you think? Do we trust them?" Andor whispered to Rioletta, Creed, and Nikal.

Nikal fidgeted, fingering the amulet around his neck. "They seem reasonable enough, and I feel no particular deception about them. They risked their lives showing themselves. Creed could easily have shot one or both, and they did not have to come here. Besides, I would like to know what Hyphanden meant when he spoke to Cardon, and how they knew of this grove and the location of the Younger Council."

"Then let's go with them, but remain on guard," Andor said, nodding at Creed. "Now that we know where to find the bodies, Nikal and I can go to Tabor any time."

Rioletta managed to help Cardon to his feet with Creed's assistance, and together they got him upon his horse. The group followed Hyphanden and Kwistocta a short distance through the woods to a path. Their two horses were tied there, and Rioletta realized as they approached that their own horses had given them warning of the Outcasts' approach, though none of them had paid attention.

They followed the Outcasts back towards the city, coming finally to the wall and the small buildings crowded outside it. Rioletta saw the embassy as they passed through a gate in the wall and entered the interior of the city for the first time. They came into a residential area with large, decaying houses behind wrought-iron gates and smaller connecting stone walls. They traveled through winding streets that Rioletta thought must have been laid out to confuse, and finally came to a gate no different in appearance from any other. But Hyphanden raised a hand, and the gate swung open without a sound, as if on well-oiled hinges. The group rode through and up a well-maintained path with a manicured lawn on either side, which from outside had appeared overgrown and disheveled.

"A little Concealment to keep passersby from identifying our residence," Hyphanden smiled as Rioletta stared at the lawns in surprise. Behind them the gates swung closed with a clang.

There were extensive gardens and fruit trees around the back and sides of the stone house, and a snug stable and corrals where they dismounted. They unsaddled the horses and brought their satchels inside. The house was large and well furnished; in fact, it was an estate that had obviously belonged at one time to someone of means. Some of the items were made from materials Rioletta could not identify, and much of it appeared to be antique. She examined a couple of the chairs; they were very well made, upholstered in rich, deeply colored fabrics, and she admired their design. She had somehow not expected members of the Outcast Council to be living in relative luxury; she had imagined them as disheveled and crazy, but Hyphanden and Kwistocta were well-groomed and seemed rational.

Hyphanden helped Cardon to an armchair in the great-room, near a large unlit fireplace surrounded by chairs and settees. The group seated themselves, except for Creed, who remained standing, leaning protectively on the back of Andor's high-backed wing chair.

Kwistocta left the group to bustle about in a kitchen in the back corner of the great-room. She soon brought Cardon a cup of tea. It had a familiar aroma, and Rioletta recognized it as a brew similar to what Adla had supplied. Kwistocta returned to the kitchen and brought out a tray of glasses and a pitcher of cold sparkling wine for the rest of them.

Rioletta accepted a glass with some suspicion, glancing around at the others. The Outcast Sorcerers might prefer unusual drinks…but then again, if they had intended harm, they had had plenty of opportunity already. She sipped the drink curiously; wine was rare in Andolith, and she had never tasted sparkling wine. It was refreshing and light.

Cardon began to look a little better and some color returned to his face. "Phando, we have not seen each other for quite some time," he said, "but I have not been well since the death of the Younger Council."

"In fact, you were not particularly well before," Hyphanden said quietly. "You drank the draught to lead you along the Path of Transformation, against my better judgment; for I've never thought your mind to be strong enough to withstand it, and you did it in the presence of only the Younger Council. Had I been present and consented to your experiment, perhaps I could have controlled the reaction more effectively, but I was not there, I did not consent, and I only heard of the result afterwards."

Cardon looked down. "A serious mistake on my part."

Hyphanden crossed one leg over the other and settled back in his chair. "One of many. You know, when I heard what you had done, I went to the place where the ritual was performed, expecting to find your corpse, but you were not there. I didn't know what had become of you until last year, when you reappeared with your daughter and Stolen. I met with the Younger Council a few days after your arrival, and I was happy to hear that you were alive, but when I heard the story of your illness I realized how close you had been to death or irreversible damage to your mind. And indeed, it appears that some changes have occurred; at the very least, your mind is much more open to intrusion by the thoughts of others."

"That's proved to my advantage in some cases," Cardon said. He glanced at Rioletta. Hyphanden followed his gaze, and Rioletta looked down. Hyphanden's grey eyes were uncomfortably intense.

"When I arrived last year, the Younger Council was preoccupied and secretive," Cardon went on. "Even Marsavrina wouldn't tell me exactly what was going on. We now suspect they had thrown a powerful Forbidden Skill, the one that imprisoned the Elder Council in the tapestries."

"Indeed," Hyphanden said. "Once again, this occurred without my knowledge. Afterwards, they came to us and told us, myself and Kwistocta, what they had done. It was a Skill they had only half-learned, introduced to them by our Council-member Rorudon. I told them they were fools; the Skill they cast has known repercussions, and we could only provide them with such protections as we knew after the fact."

"You had nothing to do with it, then?" Nikal asked. "You identify this Rorudon as a member of your Council, of whom you are the Leader. Yet you did not know he allowed Cardon to take the draught or that he taught the Younger Council these Forbidden Skills."

Hyphanden glanced at Kwistocta. "Rudon, as we usually call him, is a valued member of our Council, but also one who does what he pleases with little concern for what others think. Although our Council is modeled on the Traditional Councils we are familiar with, you must understand that we can hold no one to any standard here. All of us are Outcasts, and the only pressure we can apply is the pressure of our community. If Rudon chooses not to involve us in his activities, there's little I can do other than propose sanctions to be enforced by the community at large."

Nikal sat back. "I suppose that's true. I hadn't thought of it that way."

It was Kwistocta who continued. "We did try to help them. We made them every concoction we knew to counteract the effects of Throwing a Shape-Changing Skill at someone else, and these seemed to be working. As a last precaution, we decided to travel about a day's journey from here to a place in the mountains where we hoped to meet some acquaintances we thought could help us. We traveled towards the Old East Road and the Hyolon Pass. But we had reached only the grove where we met you today when all eight of them were suddenly stricken and dropped to the ground."

"Then you were with them when they died!" Cardon exclaimed.

"We were, both of us," Hyphanden said. "Unfortunately, we did not have time to deal with their bodies; we were forced to leave quickly to protect ourselves. When we returned several days later, we found they had been moved. We found their resting place and decided it was best to leave them there, protected from the ravages of wild animals and birds. But I suspect it was you who found them, Cardon."

"He found them," Rioletta cut in, "and it has disturbed him ever since. All of us have seen what this has done to him."

Hyphanden exchanged a glance with Kwistocta again. "I'm sorry," he said. "I would have stopped it if I could have done so. Remember, they were friends of mine as well."

"Stolen and I found them," Cardon remembered. "My daughter was with us, but I set her in the woods and she did not understand what had happened; she was too young, I hope. This was three days after they left the Row; I saw the birds circling and went to investigate. I saw that all of them were dead; I have known since then that all of them are dead. And yet I've been plagued by their voices, calling out to me in my mind, calling about a crypt of souls, and complaining that they have no key. It has very nearly driven me crazy this last winter, and the closer I got to the Ruined City, the worse it became."

Hyphanden studied Cardon for a minute. "And so you came here intending to provide a proper cremation for them and closure for their families. You assume that once their bodies are properly disposed you will feel less guilt, and the voices will go away."

"Yes, that's what I hope," Cardon said.

"May I ask which voices you hear? Are they specific people?" Kwistocta asked. She sat down near Cardon on a footstool.

"Always I hear Marsavrina and Skadar. This makes some sense to me. Marsavrina was the mother of my child and well known to me, although Skadar was not. And lately…" he paused and glanced at Rioletta, "…lately I seem to hear whispers of others, but I cannot understand what they say. It is only a whisper, although it seems I know the voices."

"Malbec and Chasandahl Vrinal, I suppose," Hyphanden said.

Cardon looked at him sharply. "Yes, but how did you know?"

Hyphanden clasped his hands in his lap and lowered his eyelids slightly, as if in deep thought. "Kwistocta and I are true Outcasts, with warrants upon us for our arrest if we are found outside Hyolon. We fled before the ceremony to Strip us of our knowledge, and it was this act that made us true Outcasts. We joined others living in and around Hyolon, for the Ruined City is large and still has many resources. And here we continue to research and practice the Forbidden Skills. We have discovered much about these Skills, the particulars of which have been mostly lost to Traditional Councils, and we are able to use many of them successfully. We have found and deciphered many hidden records in the city, and learned much about the practices of the Sorcerers of Hyolon before the Dispersal. In particular, many of us have become adept at Mind-sharing techniques, including the Distractions necessary to keep one from forever becoming entrapped in the other person's mind."

He paused, and Nikal spoke up. "It is said amongst those of the Dobor Council that Mind-sharing techniques can be used to rescue the minds of those killed through the casting or mis-casting of Skills."

Hyphanden nodded. "And thus you anticipate my next words," he said. "Indeed it is possible to rescue the consciousness of a person recently dead, provided that person has been killed strictly by Skill. The mind of a person dead of injury, or illness, or old age, is not available. Remember that Kwistocta and I were with the Younger Council when they were stricken. We knew immediately what had happened. We each went to the Council-member who had fallen closest to us: I to Marsavrina and Kwistocta to Skadar. In such a way we were able to bring the consciousness, or the template of it, of each of them wholly into our own minds, and store them in a part of our minds we kept willfully separate. It was risky for us, as we had never done such a thing before; but we are both Skilled at Mind-Sharing. Then we moved to Malbec and Chasan; but they had been down for a while before we were able to go to them, and we were not able to take all of their consciousness. Only a part was available to us, and none of the others were available at all. They are truly dead and gone, for all time."

"But does that mean that the consciousness of these members of the Younger Council still reside in your minds?" Rioletta asked, astonished.

"No!" Hyphanden replied. "It was difficult for us to keep that part walled off from the rest of our minds. We were unprepared and did not have the potions we needed to create a successful separation. We knew we would not be able to maintain that temporary separation for long. We fled immediately to the rest of the Outcast Council, leaving the bodies lie. Neither of us dared sleep, and we were awake for three days, until such time as we had successfully transferred their templates into storage."

"What kind of storage?" Nikal asked. Rioletta shuddered involuntarily. There was something unnerving about talking of storing peoples' minds absent their bodies.

Once again Hyphanden hesitated, as if trying to formulate his words. "One of the things we have discovered in the city is a storage place for minds that have been removed through Mind-sharing. We call it the Crypt of Souls. It exists below the main

Council-house of Hyolon. We have known of it for years, although we had never used it until last year. We discovered the method for transferring the templates, or patterns of consciousness, into storage; it is not too difficult to do, although it takes some preparation. I can only describe the Crypt of Souls as looking something like a giant honeycomb…and there are more minds in there than the four we stored, although who put them there and who they are…we do not know."

"You mean these minds still exist, in storage, conscious and alive?" Cardon asked, sitting up very straight.

"Well, alive, at least, if you want to call a mind without a body alive," Hyphanden said. "A mind must have a matrix upon which to build itself; without that matrix, it is nothing, it does not exist. In the body, it has the physical form of the brain. During the removal via Mind-sharing, it is sustained for only a few seconds upon a tenuous matrix of mist, which cannot last, and then takes up residence in the structures of the host mind. But the Crypt provides a sort of matrix of its own. As for conscious, that is something we have not known until now. But you told me you heard their voices, and that confirms for me that they must be conscious in some form."

"Then that is an awful thing," Stolen said in his quiet voice. "I was imprisoned in a similar way for thirteen years, able to sense the world around me but at its mercy, unable to move or control my own destiny."

"Yes," Hyphanden agreed, with a curious glance at Stolen. "It is meant to be a temporary thing, and we thought it was better than death, although if we do not remove them and replace them in some body, perhaps that will not be the case."

"And if you do remove them, they will stop bothering me," Cardon said. "Although I am already most relieved to know I'm not totally insane."

"No, although why they've been contacting you, I don't know," Hyphanden said. "I would have thought they'd come into the minds of those who rescued them. But Marsavrina had a close bond with you, and your mind is very open, as I have said. Perhaps Skadar and the other two are following her lead."

"But how can we replace them in a physical body?" Rioletta asked. "Obviously their own bodies are not suitable for such a purpose."

Hyphanden glanced at her. "Well, that's an issue. We do not know how to open the Crypt of Souls, only how to store minds in it. We know some information about opening it: we know that it requires a physical key, for example, and the concoction of a draught, and of course there must be a body to receive the mind on a permanent basis. A recently, very recently, dead person would probably suffice; or perhaps temporarily an animal or animated non-sentient object, but we are not sure."

Cardon groaned. "So you can put these minds in the Crypt, but you cannot get them out. They are stuck there, repeating their half-conscious desires to me."

"I'm afraid that's true," Hyphanden said. "But I've been seeking information about opening the Crypt of Souls. I am a Loremaster, experienced in research. There are some other things I have found out, which I will relate to you later. But I suggest we eat dinner and relax for the evening. In the morning, Nikal and Andor can ride to Tabor and locate the relatives of the Younger Council and bring them back to the grove if you still want to do so. The rest of you can stay here in hiding. Then we can discuss what we will need to do to relieve Cardon's distress and rescue Marsavrina and Skadar from the Crypt."

Rioletta went to the kitchen with Kwistocta to help prepare dinner. There were fresh vegetables and fruits from the garden and an impressive variety of breads, pastas, and sauces to choose from, as well as a well-stocked wine-cellar just off the kitchen.

"Some of this comes as trade from others," Kwistocta said. "All of the Outcasts trade among ourselves, like any other village. We have a large greenhouse to provide us with fresh vegetables over the winter. But some things are difficult to come by, for they require trade with others outside the community, such as many of the spices. I miss the Younger Council's help in those matters."

"How many of you are there?" Rioletta wondered.

"On the Outcast Council? It is structured like a normal Sorcerers' Council, and in Tabor the traditional number is eight, so we have followed the model we know."

"And all of you are Vrinac?" Rioletta asked hesitantly.

Kwistocta glanced at her and smiled. "Yes, we are all Vrinac, but Vrinac is a group of families, not a single one. The most populous families are Vrinal, Buradoc, and Surinac. And yes,

79

Hyphanden and I are both Vrinal and thus closely related, but that is not unusual in Tabor. We are first cousins; we are married because we are Outcasts and don't have to obey the rules of the Tabor Council or the Charter, although we have no children."

Rioletta nodded. "How many other Outcasts in total are there?"

Kwistocta paused. "I'm not sure. Probably some hundred-fifty, including the Council and those that drift in and out of Hyolon. Some are from Tabor; others are from other cities and Councils. Not all were inducted Sorcerers, but all are of the Skilled people. Most are our age or younger. In the beginning, when Hyolon was first used as an Outcast refuge, fifty years ago now, many died while they were rediscovering the Forbidden Skills. Others died from violent encounters with the Hyolonal, for which they were unprepared. Now we know more and are safer, and more of us survive."

"You're not exactly what I expected," Rioletta admitted.

Kwistocta laughed shortly. "You expected us to be insane, running around with our hair uncombed, raving and throwing Forbidden Skills left and right?"

Rioletta shrugged apologetically. "That's something like what I've always been taught."

"Of course," Kwistocta said somewhat bitterly. "The Traditional Councils wouldn't want their acolytes knowing that you can practice the Forbidden Skills extensively and remain sane, particularly if you're careful with the draughts and potions. I was taught the same thing myself, and I was quite nervous when Hyphanden and I first tried extending ourselves along the continuum of Mind-sharing. But in fact most of those who live in our community are quite rational and we live normal lives. There are a few rogue Sorcerers around, those who have truly damaged their own minds through uncontrolled experimentation, and also through clumsy Stripping during their Outcasting, but they're not part of our community."

"I wasn't aware there was any difference between rogue Sorcerers and Outcasts, to tell the truth," Rioletta said. "I suppose I imagined that all who lived in Hyolon were the same; I certainly didn't imagine a community with people living in estates with large gardens and trade relations."

"Come, let's take this food out," Kwistocta said. "Later we can tell you more about our community and the city of Hyolon if you wish."

The dinner was good and served with more wine, similar to that of Tabor but homemade by the Outcasts, who had carried their Vrinac winemaking knowledge with them to Hyolon. Even Creed appeared to be relaxing; he sat in a large chair near the fireplace with a plate balanced upon his knee and a glass of wine near him on the floor.

Rioletta resumed her spot on the other side of the fireplace. It was topped by a heavy wood mantle, upon which sat a number of objects. They appeared to be antiques, probably gathered from Hyolon by the Outcasts as décor. Rioletta squinted at a small metallic obelisk; it had an odd blue sheen, and she struggled to remember where she'd seen that glow before.

"Tell us more of what you know about opening the Crypt of Souls," Nikal urged Hyphanden as he finished his dinner. "You said you had found further information."

"Certainly. I propose a trade," Hyphanden said, looking directly at Rioletta with a slight smile. "Information for information. You tell us how you came to make the acquaintance of our friend Stolen, here, and I'll tell you everything I know about opening the Crypt of Souls."

"No deal!" Nikal said immediately, but Stolen had started to speak at the same time.

"Obviously you realize that the stories passed around about my origins are not true," Stolen said.

Hyphanden interlaced his fingers and leaned back in his chair. "Of course. I'm familiar with the Forbidden Skills. No one I know has come far enough along the Path of Transformation to produce offspring that carried on their traits, although I've wondered about the possibility of inheritable changes. And I imagine I'd know about anyone who was *that* Skilled in Shape-changing. He or she would be an Outcast, and the main refuge for Outcasts in this region is Hyolon."

Rioletta exchanged glances with Nikal; she had not thought about how the story that Stolen was born of Outcasts would sound to an actual Outcast.

"You're a Changeling," Hyphanden continued, addressing Stolen. "That is, you were born one of the Skilled people and you were changed afterwards, by someone or something more powerful in such Skills than anyone I've ever met."

"You're right," Stolen began, but Rioletta interrupted him. "Stolen, remember your bargain," she warned. "Don't jeopardize your safety."

Stolen shrugged. "I feel little loyalty to the Lefollah at this point," he said. "I'm more concerned with getting the information we need to help Cardon. The bargain's fair, and I'll tell what I know of my origins. After all, these Outcasts are no longer part of your society, and not bound by your agreements, is that not right?"

Hyphanden smiled again and turned his gaze back to Rioletta. "I know, or suspect, more," he said. "There is a bond between the two of you. What Skills have you practiced, against the recommendations of your Council?"

"Me?" Rioletta exclaimed. "I am a Traditional and an Inducted member of the Younger Council! I've done nothing against the Charter of Dispersal or the Andolith Charter!"

"No? But you have had contact with Shape-changers, and practiced some of their Skills yourself, to at least a small degree. I can feel it."

"I have not!" Rioletta exclaimed, feeling a flush rising to her cheeks. She looked around at the faces of her companions, all of whom were regarding her with interest.

"But you found the Lefollah and learned to speak their language," Stolen said gently to her. "You are a Loremaster, and you know that language carries power. In a small way, you have formed a bond with the Lefollah, and they are, as Hyphanden says, powerful Shape-changers."

Stolen turned back to Hyphanden and leaned forward with his elbows on his knees. As the rest of them listened, he told Hyphanden and Kwistocta all he knew of his origins, his childhood in the grove of the Lefollah, the kidnapping of Rioletta, and his imprisonment among the Twisted Trees.

When he had finished, there was silence for a long moment. Hyphanden seemed lost in thought. "There are stories, of course. I've read accounts in some of the books I've found here in the city. And Mynador, the oldest member of our Council, has some knowledge of those who broker children. But we have never encountered a true Changeling. It sheds some light on certain information I've found."

"A bargain's a bargain," Nikal said impatiently. "Now you know about Stolen and the Lefollah, so you tell us what more you know about the Crypt."

Hyphanden nodded. "Well, opening the Crypt to remove minds is much more complex than entering minds into it. The Sorcerers of Hyolon intended that those minds not be taken out except by consensus, perhaps to avoid their purposeful destruction as revenge or punishment. Thus, opening the Crypt requires certain equipment and certain people who must work together in agreement."

"That makes sense," Nikal said. "The old Sorcerers were good at creating checks and balances upon their own powers."

"Perhaps. At any rate, I have found some references to a Key to the Crypt. It's apparently some object that contains not only physical items but the specific instructions for how to perform the Skills and other actions necessary to open it. There are several people who must be gathered together including a Loremaster and one Skilled in Monitoring and Viewing. Second, a non-Sorcerer, Skilled or Unskilled, must work with these two, for the physical lock can only be opened by one who is not inducted. It seems that the physical lock is complex, and must be opened in a specific series, using a variety of special tools. Third, there must be a body for the souls to be transferred into. And lastly, there must be a person who must be a Healer or Mind-sharer and preferably experienced in the Path of Transformation, who must take a special draught brewed to specific instructions, and who's then available to actually receive the minds when they are removed from the matrix of the Crypt. This person holds the minds temporarily until they are transferred into the new body. He's called the Receiver. We know also that there is in existence somewhere an Index or Translator with which to identify the minds in the matrix of the Crypt. But, we still do not know where to find the Key or the instructions regarding how to proceed."

Rioletta sat quite still. She ventured a quick glance at Nikal and found him staring fixedly at her. She looked away hurriedly, and the satchel at her side seemed suddenly bulky and obvious. For she knew, without a doubt, that the book she carried in it was the Key to the Crypt of Souls.

Chapter Eight

As soon as they retired to their room that evening, Nikal closed the door and stood with his back to it.

"Give me the book," he demanded.

"What are you going to do?" Rioletta reluctantly pulled the book from her satchel. She had never seen him in this mood since the first time she met him, when he defended himself against the Councils of the Sydian at Andolith.

"It's obvious, isn't it?" he replied, taking the book. "I have to View it to confirm whether or not it's the Key to the Crypt of Souls."

He strode across the room to a chair and threw himself into it, then opened the book on his lap as he had when he Monitored it before. He looked up at Rioletta, who had not moved.

"Well, come and stand by me in case I need your help," he said impatiently. "It's not normal to View a book, and I don't know what will happen."

Rioletta went to him and stood by the chair with a hand on his shoulder, although she didn't know what she would be able to do should he need help. Nikal relaxed, one hand lying on the book to keep it open. His eyes closed, but Rioletta could see a flicker beneath his eyelids.

In a moment he took a breath and let it out with an audible sigh. "Yes, it's working. It's difficult, though. It's not set up for modern Viewers; the format's a little different."

Rioletta looked over his shoulder. Nikal turned the pages slowly, as if searching for the right place. He went back and forth between several pages a few times before settling on a particular one. Rioletta could see that the page had an illustration of a plant growing in front of a stacked stone wall.

"I can see a room with an odd-looking wall. It must be the Crypt of Souls, because it looks as Hyphanden described, like a huge honeycomb. To the left of it is a panel. Now I'm seeing how to use the tools of the card. It goes quickly through the card sides. You fit them into a slot one at a time in a specific order. The order is not specified; you'll have to figure that from the plant plates. Now the procedure is done, and a change comes over the honeycomb; the cells become more open."

He paused. "That is all, except for a credit at the end. It's a cryptoglyph, and I can't decipher it right now, but I can draw it if you bring me a paper."

Rioletta quickly opened her satchel again and removed a pen and small pad of paper, which she carried with her to write recipes and the like. Nikal took it and quickly wrote a series of shapes. Then he closed the book.

"I have no doubt this is the Key," he told Rioletta. "I wonder why it came to me?"

"Perhaps only coincidence," Rioletta said. "Or perhaps it was looking for someone who was a strong Viewer. But now that we know what it is, what shall we do?"

Nikal considered. "I'm not sure. All my life I've been told that the Outcast Council are crazy and untrustworthy. Hyphanden and Kwistocta seem to belie that, but I can't bring myself to simply throw away all my years of training. Maybe I'm wrong, but I don't like the idea of simply turning this thing over to Hyphanden. On the other hand, it seems we can't free Marsavrina and Skadar without them; we don't know where the Council-house is or how to access it, or even how to move safely through the city. And if we don't free them, they'll remain imprisoned, and Cardon will certainly eventually lose his own mind."

"On the other hand, now that I know Marsavrina and the others still survive, in some form anyway, I'm not sure how I feel about freeing them," Rioletta said. "From what we know, they purposefully imprisoned the Elder Council, and we don't know why. It may be they are dangerous people."

"True," Nikal said, "but you faced the same decision with Stolen. If we don't do it, Cardon will continue to suffer."

"How do you feel about going to Tabor tomorrow with Andor?" Rioletta asked, sitting down on the bed. Nikal handed her the book, and she replaced it in her satchel.

"It's somewhat risky for us to go. It may be that the Younger Council's relatives will want to question or accuse us, especially Andor. But I think in the end we will come out all right; we hold the trump card in that we alone know where the bodies are located. I feel less comfortable with leaving you here. Cardon is useless; I know you are fond of him, but you can't disagree with that. Stolen will do his best to protect you, but his judgment is to be questioned simply because he has limited exposure to human beings and the way they act. Creed is certainly an asset, but he can't protect all of you at once. You yourself have little skill with a bow or machete, and none of you can Throw Skills. Perhaps your greatest threat is from the Outcasts, anyway, and I assure you, they are powerful Sorcerers in command of many, many Skills we can only begin to imagine."

"Perhaps we should wait until morning to make our decision," Rioletta said. "If all seems well, you can go; if not, we will all go together somewhere else."

"Very well," Nikal said. "Let's put a locking Skill on the door. Not that I think Hyphanden couldn't break it if he wanted, especially in his own house. But I will sleep better knowing it is there."

Nikal placed the Skill on the door, and Rioletta checked it. She had some limited Skill at Locking, a Skill typical among those of Andolith, and had learned some from Pateret, who was an expert. It seemed secure enough to her, but the book now seemed to prickle at the edge of her mind, as if she had suddenly become more aware of it.

The door was heavy dark wood and the walls of stone, so no sounds intruded upon them from elsewhere in the house. The bed was deep and comfortable, especially after having camped for so many days, and Rioletta slept soundly.

In the morning, Nikal had made up his mind about going to Tabor.

"I'm not going. I don't like the idea of leaving you here, and besides, there's the matter of us being followed by more than one person, according to Hyphanden."

"We were being followed before," Rioletta pointed out.

"Yes, but it would be much easier for two of us to be set upon than six of us. And after all, we're in no great hurry now; we know proper disposal won't cure Cardon's problem. But I would like to get a message to Adla and to Ladon telling them what we're doing."

"I'm not sure how we're going to do that from within Hyolon."

"Me either," Nikal mused "I'd like to meet with the rest of our group somewhere away from Hyphanden and Kwistocta to discuss what's to be done about the book. Maybe someone will have an idea about how to pass a message."

Rioletta and Nikal joined the others for breakfast. They were later than the rest; their room was on the west side of the building, shaded by large trees, and thus the heat and summer sun had not awakened them as early. Hyphanden already sat in the great-room with Stolen. Rioletta took her plate to the chair she had been in the evening before, by the heavy mantled fireplace.

"You have learned to speak the human language well," Hyphanden said to Stolen. "Your appearance is somewhat different than I'd heard from the Younger Council."

"Yes, I have fewer leaves by design," Stolen admitted. "I have learned something about making them drop when I want to, and if I leave them alone and abandon them, they then shrivel and die. I've cleared them from my face and only continue to grow them where most human men grow hair anyway. But look, I've discovered something else recently."

He held out an arm. "While we traveled from Polebray to Tabor, my friends questioned whether I could grow new leaves if I desired. I told them I had never tried; I am not interested in producing more leaves, but in losing them to make myself appear more human, and I don't remember ever thinking about the leaves I grew with the Lefollah. But my curiosity was aroused, so I made an attempt. See here: this leaf is a new one, as is this one here."

He pointed out a new leaf on the back of each arm. "I have grown them to maturity in a week. But watch what else I can do."

Stolen grabbed hold of the leaf and gave it a firm tug. He grimaced, and the leaf popped off his skin, leaving a small mark that oozed a drop of blood. He dropped the leaf on the ground, and immediately it stood up on its points and scuttered around the room.

Hyphanden laughed out loud. Rioletta shuddered and pulled her feet away; she could only think of the thousands of Leaves that had invaded Andolith, searching for Justah after they fled with her from the Grove of Lefollah.

In a minute, Stolen brought the leaf back to him, and it crawled up the chair and onto his arm and reattached itself.

"Now I know something about how the Lefollah drop their branches to form a twig body," Stolen said. "It is a thing I don't remember being taught. But it seemed to come to me readily."

"It's quite interesting, and I would like to spend some time with you, to learn more of what you know," Hyphanden said. "Certainly your Skills are akin to Shape-shifting Skills. But as far as we know, no one, no human, has ever successfully accomplished true Shape-shifting. Misdirection and Concealment are as close as most can come, and only a few develop the ability, after much hardship, to Throw a Skill such as the Younger Council Threw at the Elder Council. And that proved deadly, and our best potions could not prevent those deaths. A careful analysis of your knowledge could perhaps show us where we have gone wrong, and what could be done differently to improve our success."

"Stolen is of Andolith now," Rioletta said abruptly. "I don't mean to impugn your hospitality, but Ladon would never approve of such a discussion. The Forbidden Skills are still Forbidden, at least for us. Despite the fact that we, all of us, have crossed back and forth over that line that appears to separate Forbidden from Restricted, we should not be actively supporting these practices."

Hyphanden glanced at Kwistocta, as though for support. "Of course," he said. "I apologize. It's not my intention to turn you into Outcasts, although the life is more acceptable than you might have been told, as you can observe for yourselves. And I note that you cannot precisely define that line, as you put it, which separates

Forbidden from Restricted; neither can anyone else. It is precisely this problem that causes some, such as the Younger Council, to find themselves on what is obviously the wrong side of that line through incremental advances. Isn't that right, Cardon?"

Cardon shrugged uncomfortably. "It wasn't so much incremental as physical," he said. "I fell across the line, rather than anything else, through lust and curiosity, and perhaps a childish belief that I was invincible, or better than others. The results of that have been disastrous; I've destroyed my own health, and I have a five-year-old daughter who grows leaves out of her head."

He glanced quickly at Stolen, who only raised his eyebrows. Nikal cleared his throat in the silence that followed, and sat forward in his chair, placing his plate on the floor beside him.

"Hyphanden, we would like to meet in private, the six of us, to discuss what we have learned here and decide upon our next move. I hope you'll forgive us the desire to find a place where we can be sure we are not overheard."

"I understand," Hyphanden said. "You do not want me or Kwistocta to hear what you say. I give you my word that if you want to meet in any room of this house, I will leave you alone and not strive to overhear you, no matter how curious I may be. But if you prefer, I can point you to some places outside the walls of our compound where you will be relatively safe, at least if you follow our directions and do not stray into the heart of Hyolon."

"I think that would be preferable," Nikal said.

Kwistocta stepped forward. "There are a series of parapets and walls that at one time formed a kind of barrier around this area of the city. You can access one of those walls from the back of our property, and if you follow it you will see it connects like a raised pathway to many other houses. You can make your way for several miles through the neighborhood in relative safety due to your height above the streets. Besides, the Hyolonal don't usually come into this area, although some of our friends have told us they have been seen near here more frequently recently."

"Why is that?" Andor asked. "I'd think this would be a prime area to loot."

"Perhaps it was at one time," Kwistocta said. "Of course, the Hyolonal would have known about this area and suspected that a great deal of useful belongings could be found here. Many of the

90

properties were looted a hundred years ago, but others have Protections of one type or another and can't be accessed by the Unskilled."

"I know about the Hyolonal," Nikal said. "My people go into the city to salvage glass, and we're always on the alert for them. They're lightly armed and unorganized. We've never had any real issue with them the few times we've seen them."

Kwistocta shrugged. "They wouldn't attack a large group with an obvious guard. But they can be dangerous to small groups, whom they might seek to rob."

"We will be careful," Nikal said. "Show us how to get to this wall."

The group filed out the back of the house and between the fruit trees and gardens to the back wall. There was a set of stairs rising up to the top.

"Once you step beyond our wall, you are out of our Protection," Kwistocta said. "You will need to contact us to allow you back in. But we will be watching for you."

Creed led the way up the stairs, and after a brief look around, he turned to the left. The rest of them trooped after with Stolen at the back, his machete at his waist. The wall was about two feet wide with a low lip of stone and occasional parapets. On their right it plunged into a ravine, heavily overgrown so they could not see what might have been there at one point. On their left it connected with a series of other walls, as Kwistocta had told them it would. These walls surrounded other estates, some ruined, some intact but overgrown. Rioletta suspected the intact ones remained protected by some Lock Skill or other Protection now unknown.

Eventually Creed led them to a point where a broad parapet looked down onto a square; there was a set of steps on either side that would bring a traveler on the wall down to the plaza. At the bottom of each stair was a kiosk which had apparently once housed a gate; but the gateways stood open and unprotected now. Despite that, it was a relatively safe place: they could see in all directions, and were they to be attacked, they would have only to defend the two staircases and the route behind them from their superior position.

They settled themselves in a ring on the flat top of the parapet. Without further ado, Rioletta pulled the book out of her satchel and handed it to Nikal. He held it aloft.

"This book I purchased from a salvager at the Polebray," Nikal said. "I searched all along their stalls, because I felt drawn to their wares. I imagined that it was the antiquity that drew me, and because I searched for a gift for a Loremaster, I was naturally drawn to books. This is the one I eventually purchased, and I made a gift of it to Rioletta. Soon after we discovered that the book contained several secrets. I now believe that those secrets were what drew me to it, although I do not yet completely understand why. But let me tell you what we discovered about the book."

Nikal reviewed Rioletta's discovery of the card in the back and the unusual tools hidden in it. He related how they had discovered that the six edges of the card fitted the pattern drawn under six of the plants. He told them how Rioletta had caused the book to Read itself to her and animated the drawings trying to find the purpose for the card, and how the numbers of the plants had been revealed. Finally, he told them how he had Monitored the book and discovered the recipe, and then Viewed it and discovered the use for the card's tools.

"From this information, we know now what this book is," Nikal said, holding it up again. "It is indeed the Key to the Crypt of Souls."

Cardon looked up sharply, and the others glanced at one another. "Are you sure?" he said.

"Yes, we are after last night's Viewing," Nikal said. "The book confirms what Hyphanden told us."

"Have you told Hyphanden?" Andor asked.

Nikal shook his head. "No. I wanted to talk to all of you beforehand. We cannot continue without Hyphanden or Kwistocta, as we don't know where the Crypt is located other than in the Council-house, and we don't know how to proceed safely. But if we tell him about this Key, we play our hand. I do not wholly trust him yet; we have heard stories all our lives, all of us, of the Outcast Sorcerers and the damage they have done to their minds. We know that the Outcast Rudon led the Younger Council to their deaths through instructing them in a dangerous Forbidden Skill. So I ask you: what shall we do, and how shall we do it?"

92

There was silence. No one seemed to have a good suggestion as to how to proceed. Rioletta herself was undecided.

Finally Andor spoke up. "What if we tell Hyphanden we believe we have the Key, but don't tell him what it is or show it to him? Then we won't play our entire hand, and he will only be able to take it from us by force."

"Of which he is probably entirely capable," Nikal said grimly. "Don't forget that both of them, and their cohorts, are undoubtedly much more powerful than any of us, or all of us combined, due to their practice of the Forbidden Skills."

"All of this may be for naught, anyway," Rioletta said. "Even though Hyphanden knows the location and we have the Key, we have not fulfilled all of the requirements. Obviously we have a Loremaster and thus that part is fulfilled. Hyphanden himself is a Loremaster, as am I. Nikal has played the role of Monitor and Viewer. Creed is a non-sorcerer; I doubt his Skill in Stealth would count against him. But we have not got the ingredients to make the potion, and even if we can obtain them, who will take it and become the Receiver? I know the plants, and many of them are deadly by themselves. It must be a dangerous brew. And we don't have the Index the book refers to; although it's possible we would be able to identify Marsavrina and the others known to Cardon and Hyphanden anyway through some other means."

"As for that, I suppose it would fall to me to become the Receiver," Cardon said. "It makes sense. Marsavrina and Skadar are already thoroughly familiar with my mind, and I have already taken, and survived, potions that are likely similar. I am willing to take that risk."

Nikal shook his head. "Cardon, you are weak. I mean no offense, but this thing has ravaged your mind and body. If there were another, I would reject your offer immediately. But there may be no other."

"Of course, there's still the problem of a body to put each of the minds into," Rioletta said.

"Hyphanden said we might be able to use an animal temporarily," Cardon said. "Perhaps a horse."

"That hardly solves the problem," Nikal said. "I can't imagine it would be successful to permanently put each of the minds in a horse! Eventually each mind will still have to go into its own human body, and for that we must have either a corpse that has died within a very short time, or some other thing that I cannot imagine. I will not commit murder to restore Marsavrina and Skadar."

There was silence once again.

"Perhaps I could grow one."

Everyone looked at Stolen.

He shrugged uncomfortably. "It seems that perhaps, if I can grow leaves, I might be able to grow branches. In that case, I might be able to grow enough to form a body, perhaps a small and unsturdy one, and I might be able to maintain it with my own mind until it received one of its own."

No one spoke. They all continued to stare at Stolen, and Rioletta considered the implications. Surely it would violate the accord they had made with the Lefollah, although Stolen seemed unconcerned. Yet a twig body might be preferable to the body of a horse, with its unfamiliar configuration and size.

Then Creed hissed, "Look!" and pointed down below into the square.

The group reacted to his tone and quickly lowered themselves on the parapet; Rioletta, Andor, and Cardon faded to stone, utilizing Concealment. Below them they could see a group of some eight individuals, scruffy and ill-clothed, armed with rudimentary weapons such as slings and poles. The eight walked carefully and slowly, a step at a time, towards the base of the parapet, as if stalking something.

Suddenly the Hyolonal sprang forward as one. There was a cry from below, and a person darted out into the open, away from the wall. The Hyolonal threatened him, each one advancing and swinging a pole or sling, then retreating. The person reciprocated with a knife drawn from his belt; and his skill was such that he managed to keep them at bay, though he was vastly outnumbered and surrounded.

"Not fair," Creed said, standing up on the parapet. He snatched his bow from his back, nocked an arrow, and sent it flying down off the wall. It was not aimed at any one person; but it sizzled through the air between several of them, and the Hyolonal stopped cold and stared upwards at the parapet. The Andolith group piled down the stairs towards them, Creed in the lead, yelling.

94

The Hyolonal stood their ground, although uncertainly, holding their poles before them. As they reached the bottom steps, Nikal Threw a Blocking Skill at them and bowled several of them over. Stolen and Cardon brandished their machetes, and a few swipes broke two of the poles. The knife-wielding stranger pressed his attack as well, and sliced through the hanging sleeves of two of the Hyolonal. At this, the eight attackers turned and fled, pursued by a streak of fire from Nikal.

Creed held another arrow to his bow and sighted on the back of one of the Hyolonal, but he did not fire. As the group reached a corner of the square, he brought it down and put the arrow away.

Then he turned to where the stranger stood, hands on knees, catching his breath. The rest of the group stood silent and uncomfortable as Creed turned.

The man was Durigon Cautes.

Chapter Nine

Creed stood in shocked silence for a moment; then the muscles in his jaw began to tense.

"Creed!" Andor said in a loud voice. "We need to get out of here! We're still in danger."

Rioletta looked around quickly. Indeed, there was no way to tell if they had vanquished the Hyolonal or if the group would return with more support.

"All right," Creed growled. "Up the stairs to the parapet, quick."

"Duri, are you injured?" Andor asked brusquely.

"I can walk," Duri said. "I got a pole across the ribs. Probably broke one, maybe more." He looked pale, and there was a thin line of sweat on his brow.

Andor supported Duri and escorted him to the gate at the bottom of the stairs. They climbed as quickly as Duri could manage it, followed by Rioletta supporting Cardon, who was out of breath, the exertion and adrenalin of the encounter taking its toll on him in his weakened state. Creed stayed in the rear, looking over his shoulder and holding his bow.

Once on the wall, though, Creed was forced to take the lead. None of the rest of them was sure of the route he had taken to get there. Stolen fell back, machete in hand, with Nikal near him.

Rioletta wished she had paid better attention on the way there. With her poor defensive Skills, she was forced to stay in the middle of the group. But they saw no other Hyolonal as they made their way back to the residence of Hyphanden and Kwistocta.

At the top of the wall behind the estate they paused. Within a minute Kwistocta came out and frowned at them.

"You bring another."

"Yes, and he is injured," Andor said. "He is known to us. Will you let us all in? We had an encounter with the Hyolonal."

"Please wait," Kwistocta said, and disappeared back inside.

"She's not pleased," Rioletta said. "But we'll just have to wait and see what happens."

Creed turned to Duri, who stood sweating and pale with an arm wrapped over his ribcage.

"You followed us," he said accusingly.

"Yes, well," Duri gasped, "that was not necessarily by design, but I'm not an idiot, either."

"What do you mean?" Andor demanded, standing in a position that blocked Creed's access to Duri. Creed looked threateningly over her shoulder.

"It was known all over the Polebray that you harbored two individuals said to have been born of those who practiced the Forbidden Skills. Obviously that means you have contact with those who practice those Skills. I assumed they must be Outcasts."

"But how did you know we were coming here?" Rioletta put in.

Duri shrugged. "Once I was kicked out of the Polebray, I set up my camp around to the south, hoping to catch some of the vendors as they came out. I stayed enough out of the way so I wasn't eating dust from the roadway. Your little group came out the east gate, but then you turned and skirted the Polebray on the south side. Obviously you weren't going back to Andolith, and I saw you had two of Dobor with you, plus one of the Forbidden offspring. So I assumed you were going to Dobor, and from there, it's not a long way to Hyolon and the Outcasts, is it?"

"And you actually wanted contact with the Outcasts?" Andor asked incredulously.

Duri grinned, although it turned more to a grimace as a spasm of pain caused him to clutch his ribs again. "I've learned a lot during the time I've been away from Andolith. One thing I've learned is that if someone is trying to keep you from knowing something, it's probably because that knowledge is valuable. I'm of no village; no Council controls my actions. Therefore, nothing is Forbidden to me any more than it is to the Hyolonal."

"You're no Sorcerer," Creed said. "You couldn't make use of what the Outcasts know if you had it."

"I may not have been formally trained as a Sorcerer, but I can learn, and I don't mind taking risks," Duri told him.

"Obviously," Andor said, as Hyphanden and Kwistocta returned to the wall.

Hyphanden looked up at Duri with an intense stare, from which Duri did not turn away.

"This man is an acquaintance of yours?" he asked the group.

"Yes, and he was attacked by the Hyolonal," Rioletta said.

"And he is one of those who followed you," noted Hyphanden. He laid a hand on the stair rail and motioned them to come down. "We will contact Rorudon, who is more Skilled in Healing than we are."

"I know Rudon," Cardon said as they descended the steps. "I met him several times; it was he who had the most contact with the Younger Council and instructed them. What he taught them caused their deaths; I cannot forgive him that, Healer or not. I can do healing work myself, and I specialize in injury. All I need is access to some of the healing herbs and other ingredients. Do you grow such here?"

"I'll show you what we have," Kwistocta said, "but you're weak and affected by the potions I've given you. You may not have the strength to do much good."

Cardon and Kwistocta hurried off towards the west side of the house. Rioletta slid the glass back door aside for Duri and the rest of the group went inside. Duri settled gingerly into a chair in the great room.

"Have you no horse?" Hyphanden asked. "You had when I saw you from afar."

"Of course," Duri said. "I left him corralled east of here with most of my gear and came into the city on foot, following the track left by these people."

"We can bring the horse here," Hyphanden said. "I'll arrange it, providing the Hyolonal haven't found him yet."

"I set some Concealment around him," Duri said. "It's likely they won't mess with him if they find him."

"And yet you have no mark of a Sorcerer about you," Hyphanden mused. "Yet you set Concealments, you have avoided my talismans, and you also have Skills in tracking."

"And a few other things," Duri said. "But remember all the Skilled of Andolith have Huntsman Skills."

Rioletta studied Duri with interest. With less history with him than Creed or Andor, she had developed less of an opinion, and harbored no particular bad feelings towards him. She had not known that a non-Sorcerer could learn Sorcerer-level Skills by himself.

Cardon and Kwistocta came back into the room. Rioletta helped Duri strip off his supple leather vest and shirt and the tight thin garment he wore beneath; he was wiry but well-muscled, with an ugly dark red mark across his ribcage. Cardon pulled a stool up next to Duri's chair and leaned forward to examine the injury. Duri turned his head away but endured the examination with little change of expression.

Kwistocta, who had been preparing a poultice in the kitchen, brought a bowl out to Cardon. "I have sent a message to Rudon anyway. He may have cures you're not familiar with, Cardon."

"Or couldn't use if I was familiar with them," Cardon agreed. "It's your choice; I have no say in the matter. But I can certainly give you painkillers, Duri."

"Maybe later, but I don't want them now," Duri said. "Go ahead with your treatment; I'll talk with the others, if they'll accommodate distracting me."

Rioletta sat down near Duri. "I'll distract you if I can," she said. "I don't remember you that well; I was about thirteen when you left. Tell us about where you went and what you've been doing."

"I remember you," Duri grimaced. "You're the girl who was kidnapped and showed up a few days later. I had nothing to do with that, although there were some who accused me."

"No, I'm well aware you weren't involved," Rioletta said, purposefully avoiding Stolen's eyes. She took Duri's elbow to help support his arm while Cardon poked at his ribcage. As she moved his arm across his chest, she noticed a small object attached to Duri's belt. Duri quickly put his other hand over the object, unclipped it, and stuffed it into the pocket of his vest, which lay beside him on a footstool. Rioletta glanced around, but no one except perhaps Hyphanden had noticed.

She turned back to Duri and prompted him, "You left Andolith after your fight with Creed. I know that much."

"Yes, at the suggestion of old Mosse of the Council." Duri related how his parents had sent him to West Ford to live with friends who ran a shop. He had been apprenticed to those friends, who specialized in vests and tunics and overshirts with hidden interior pockets and slots to hide and store things. He described satchels and wallets, belts and boots, all intended to help travelers come through a robbery with at least some of their money intact.

Rioletta kept his attention, encouraging him to speak and look directly at her. Out of the corner of her eye, she noticed Hyphanden take Duri's vest and shirt to hang on the pegs on the wall behind his back, and she saw him remove the small item from the vest pocket and examine it quickly before putting it away.

"Also they traded in knives," Duri continued. "I saw right away the knives they carried weren't carving knives, but for the purpose of defense. And all manner of people came through there, from all manner of places. I met traders and merchants, to be sure, and idle visitors; but also mercenaries and guards and others with an interest in self-protection. Many of them stayed with my foster-family, and I heard many stories."

Duri paused and looked down at Cardon, who was prodding his ribcage again. Rioletta put a hand on his cheek and turned his face towards hers. "Keep talking."

"Two years after I arrived in West Ford, I signed on with a trade party. We crossed the Rhamphor and traveled many days to the west, past the Polebray, out through the plains, past the ridge of rock where you crossed north. There are many other cities to the west of us, some ruined and some intact but uninhabited. And there are many other settlements, some more violent, some more different from Andolith than you could possibly imagine."

"That is true," Hyphanden said. "Of course, the Dispersal was not limited to the area around Hyolon. All of the cities throughout the world known to us were abandoned at that time. We

101

have the distinction of living in the city that was the capital of this region and one of the main players in the Dispersal, but there were many other large and important cities."

Rioletta looked at him, forgetting Duri for a moment. "Why would some of the cities remain intact, while others crumble like Hyolon?" It had never occurred to her to wonder what the other cities of the Dispersal were actually like; if she had thought about it, she would have assumed they were much like Hyolon, doomed to fall slowly to pieces.

"Many Councils set Protections around their cities as they left to keep them from being looted; but these Skills trapped any left behind inside the city with no way to leave it. Trophandra, the Leader of the Hyolon Council, did not allow such a Skill to be set; in so doing, she allowed the survival of the Hyolonal. They were originally the Unskilled who inhabited the city but refused to leave during the Dispersal. They can come and go as they please and supplement their diet with hunting and fishing and get fresh water as necessary. The Hyolonal have become a degenerate society…but in other places, those trapped within the cities died horrible deaths of starvation and thirst."

Rioletta squinted at Hyphanden, not sure whether he spoke the truth. This was another part of the Dispersal she had never been taught about. Certainly she had been taught that Trophandra was one of the main forces behind the Dispersal, but she had never heard that anyone was left behind or trapped within abandoned cities.

Duri grunted in pain and Rioletta turned back to him with a start. "Where did you learn the knife-fighting techniques?" she asked him hurriedly.

"All over," Duri replied. "I needed some way to protect myself. As Hyphanden noted, I'm not a Sorcerer, although I know more Skills than many. I learned whenever and whatever I could. Now I travel with the confidence that I can protect myself."

"Oh?" Creed put in. "You weren't doing such a great job there at the bottom of the wall in the plaza."

Duri grinned. "No, but I was distracted. I was concentrating on a Listening Skill so I could overhear what you were saying up there above me. You don't believe I have this Skill? Shall I repeat what I heard? Your host might be interested in what you've been concealing from him."

102

Nikal glanced at Hyphanden, then around at the rest of the group. "There's no need," he said slowly. "I'll tell him myself. Hyphanden, we hold the Key to the Crypt of Souls."

There was a long silence, during which Hyphanden stared fixedly at Nikal. The rest of the group glanced around among themselves; the decision to reveal the Key had not been made. But Rioletta could see that revealing it on their own terms was better than allowing Duri to tell whatever he had heard from below the wall.

"I suspected as much," Hyphanden finally said, with a note of satisfaction. "I've known of you for quite some time, Nikal, and it seemed to me that if anyone had inherited the Key, it would be you."

"Why would you suspect that?" Nikal asked.

"Because I believe you to be the direct descendent of Likendahl, the founder of Dobor, and, as far as we have been able to discover, he was entrusted with the task of preparing the Key, whatever form it takes. I would expect he left his mark on it."

Nikal looked at Rioletta. "I never looked to see who, eh, prepared it," Nikal said discreetly. "I am indeed a direct descendent of Likendahl. But I did not inherit it; I found it at the Polebray and bought it without realizing what I had. But the mere fact that it was prepared by Likendahl wouldn't draw me to it."

"But there's the cryptoglyph upon it that you Viewed. It could be Likendahl's graph," Rioletta reminded him, carefully avoiding suggesting that the object was a book, as Nikal had done.

"Yes. A cryptoglyph could be constructed to call to relatives, even distant ones," Nikal agreed. "You seem to know quite a bit that you reveal only in bits and pieces, Hyphanden."

Hyphanden raised his eyebrows. "I have been open with you, for the most part. I have very little to hide. I told you what I know about the Crypt. I must reserve something for myself, because I want to be involved in freeing the minds I implanted there, if it comes to pass. I still hold a few cards: the location of the Council-house; the Skills necessary to enter it and find and access the Crypt of Souls; and how to move through the city with the optimum of safety. Also, Kwistocta and I are the only ones who know where in the Crypt we placed the particular minds you seek; remember I told you there are many others there.

"You hold this card: I do not know what form the Key takes, and thus do not know what to look for, except if I Mind-share with one of you, and that you would surely know and resist. I know what I described to you earlier. I know what kind of people must be brought together to open it. I see that at least some of those requirements are fulfilled, and you have the actual Key, with its included directions, I assume. You only need a body into which to place the freed minds."

"We may have solved that problem too," Nikal said. "We will hold the secret of the Key to ourselves for the time being, but you have guessed much of our plan."

Nikal described Stolen's idea to Hyphanden. Having seen Stolen's mobile leaf before, Hyphanden did not seem particularly surprised, but Duri gaped.

"How many of these bodies can you grow, and how quickly?" Hyphanden asked.

"I don't know," Stolen said. "I suspect it will be slow and difficult. I'll need a lot of food and a place to root myself and gather sunlight."

Hyphanden mused. "If you were only able to create one, we might be able to transfer both Marsavrina and Skadar into it, at least temporarily. It would be difficult for two to share the same mind, but possible if they maintained compartmentalization. Even if they didn't, a shared mind with a mobile body would be better than none at all."

"What about the other two?" Rioletta asked. "Certainly we couldn't put four minds into one body!"

"No, I think that would be far too confusing," Hyphanden said. "And we can't put them in their own bodies; I doubt they are complete enough to manage a body by themselves. It is only parts and bits of their consciousness that remains. I think they will have to be left in the Crypt, or else transferred into some living person, someone who is willing to allow his own structure to fill in the missing parts of the templates of Malbec and Chasan's minds."

"It will be hard to find someone who would accept bits and parts of two dead Sorcerers' minds into their own," Kwistocta said. "It would have to be someone from the Outcast community. No one controlled by a Traditional Council would be allowed to do such a thing."

Hyphanden nodded, but his eyes narrowed. "There are other possibilities," he said, but did not elaborate. He turned to Duri instead. Rioletta, distracted by Stolen, Hyphanden, and Kwistocta, had forgotten once again about Duri, but Cardon had stopped prodding at him for the moment anyway.

"Your story is an interesting one," Hyphanden said. "There are indeed many strange cities and settlements far to the west of here. I see you carry not only the Skills and physical arts you've learned, and the knives and clothing you've adopted, but also other items, such as the device in your vest. It is quite unusual."

Duri glanced down at his belt, then looked around for his vest. "I'll thank you not to go poking through my personal belongings," he growled.

"I picked up your vest upside-down and it fell out of the pocket," Hyphanden lied easily. "I apologize."

Duri's eyes registered suspicion. "It is only a compass," he said.

"More than a compass," Hyphanden said. "It appears to be a device for marking routes and mapping, is it not?"

"Well, yes," Duri admitted. "But it requires other units similar to it and in communication with it to function properly. In most places it doesn't work at all, but it seems to be working well around here. I can triangulate with it, which means there are at least two other similar devices in operation somewhere around."

"Hmm." Hyphanden said. "Devices that communicate with each other continuously are Forbidden. And so I surmise that you have been in an area where the inhabitants practice the Forbidden Technologies."

Duri smiled. "You surmise correctly. I usually don't admit that; but after all, you practice the Forbidden Skills, so what does it matter?"

"Do the inhabitants of the places you've traveled to practice both?" Hyphanden asked.

Duri shook his head. "No. No Skills at all in the places where the Technologies exist. And as far as continuous communication, this device can be turned off, and it has no interface with the mind that I can tell."

"I'm interested in the fact that this device functions at all in this area. I'm not aware of any others. But perhaps you'd best leave it concealed for now; we can discuss it more later." Hyphanden placed his hands on the arms of his chair and began to rise.

"Well, I suspect we could all use some lunch. And Rudon will be here soon, and he will expect it."

As Kwistocta and Hyphanden went to the kitchen, Rioletta moved closer to Cardon. "Were you able to see what plants grow in their medicinal garden?" she asked in a low voice.

Cardon nodded. "Their garden includes most of the plants I've seen used to create potions, brews, teas, salves, and everything else you can think of. It's quite complete. A few of the plants usually grow wild and aren't easy to cultivate. I suspect you'll find most of what you need for the Key there."

"Of course, we can ask Kwistocta for them if we don't care if she knows the ingredients," Rioletta said, glancing at Nikal.

"No, I think it's best to keep a few secrets for now," Nikal said. "Let's not give them the recipe or let them know what form the Key takes."

They heard an unfamiliar voice near the back of the house and Hyphanden strode down the flagstone hallway. There was a hushed conversation by the front door, and it was some minutes before Rioletta heard them coming back towards the great-room.

"Rudon," Cardon said bitterly. "It was he who guided the Younger Council when they requested help, and he who supplied them with the recipe for the potion I took, although he was not there at the time I took it. Hyphanden will tell you that the Outcasts don't recruit people into their society, that people come to them on their own, but if Rudon wasn't recruiting the Younger Council, I don't know what you'd call it."

A man walked swiftly into the room, looked around, and settled his gaze on Duri. The man was shorter and more muscular in appearance than Hyphanden. His face was round and his skin tanned as if he spent time outside; he rubbed his hands together and bounced on his feet as he walked and grinned a wide grin. The he spied Cardon, and stopped short.

"Ah, Cardon," he said, with just a note of discomfort. "I'm glad to see you alive and well. I didn't get a chance to meet personally with you last year when you were here, but I heard of your visit, and was happy to know you survived your little encounter."

Cardon did not reply. Rioletta thought Rudon looked happy and friendly. Unlike many of the Vrinal, his eyes were dark blue, and they sparkled with apparent amusement. She wondered how much Cardon's bad experience with the Transformative potion had colored his perception.

Rudon turned to Duri. "So, you've encountered the Hyolonal," he said, taking up the stool Cardon vacated for him. "I'm told you put up a good fight. But a pole across the ribs is uncomfortable. We'll see what we can do. I see someone has already made a beginning: quite good, quite good." He glanced at Cardon and smiled. "But I have other means at my disposal."

Rudon wore a complicated vest with many pockets, clips, and straps on it. Various objects stuck out of the pockets. Rioletta supposed he carried medical supplies in it, but she wasn't sure. In addition he carried a satchel, which he swung around to pull out a few packets of cloth, folded or sewn closed over whatever the ingredients were. Then he leaned forward and felt Duri's ribs. Once again, Duri remained impassive.

"Hmm," Rudon said. "Of course, you can help with the healing yourself. It is only a matter of directing internal energy, like when you Throw a Skill."

"I don't know how to Throw Skills," Duri said.

"No?" Rudon raised his eyebrows. "But you can direct your energy outwards, can you not? And if you can do that, you can Throw. Cardon here can Throw Skills; you don't need to be an extremely accomplished Sorcerer."

"As for that, I'm not a Sorcerer at all," Duri said.

"You can Throw Skills?" Rioletta asked Cardon at the same time.

"Not as far as I know," Cardon said.

"Sure you can," Rudon repeated. "You can make fire in your hand, can't you? Well, that's an example of directing energy out of yourself. Throwing is the same thing. But we're not here to discuss Throwing Skills; we need to get our friend here, who claims not to be a Sorcerer, healed up."

Suddenly he seemed to notice Rioletta. She felt an odd prickle at the back of her mind and drew a sharp breath. A moment later, the feeling was gone, but it reminded her of the feeling she used to have when Leaves were around.

Rudon quickly stuck out a hand. "We've not been introduced," he said with a smile. "A Loremaster, or I miss my guess. A rare specialty these days. And Inducted?"

Rioletta took his hand. "Your guess is correct, and I'm a member of the Younger Council of Andolith."

Rudon grinned again and turned back to Duri, handing him a packet. "We'll wrap that onto you and I'll use it like a talisman, as you yourself can, to focus on the injured spot. A broken rib is no fun, but by tomorrow you'll be able to move around fairly well; and in a few days it will have knitted itself quite nicely. We'll spend a few sessions now and again working on it."

When Duri was bandaged and helped back into a shirt, Kwistocta, who had been standing behind the group, beckoned them all into the room near the kitchen where food had been laid out on a long serving table near the back.

"Well, Phando," Rudon said, grinning as he piled cheese and bread on a plate. "I think your idea is a sound one. He's suitable, and I think all other conditions are also met."

Rioletta continued to pick and choose from the foods spread across the table, trying not to look in Rudon's direction. What did he mean by that?

"Very well," Hyphanden said. "Then we will advance with the idea. But there's no need for us to discuss it now; have your lunch."

Rudon retired to the fireplace with his heaping plate; Rioletta caught Nikal's eye. She didn't know what Rudon had found out, but it was apparent he was talking about Duri.

Chapter Ten

During their meal, Rudon talked animatedly to each of them in turn. He asked rapid-fire questions about Andolith, its location, the make-up of its Council, its crafts and history. Although he had been raised near Tabor, he revealed, he had never been to Andolith, only to West Ford and Matbor. He questioned Stolen and listened to his story with rapt attention. He asked Rioletta about her experiences as a Loremaster in an isolated Traditional village, and seemed interested that she had learned to Monitor and View with Nikal. Rudon helped himself to the wine, and Rioletta remembered Cardon describing him as one who enjoyed his leisure, who had befriended Malbec of the Younger Council by introducing him to party tricks.

Hyphanden looked up suddenly from his plate. "Someone's arriving."

"Yes," Kwistocta said. "It looks like the two you sent to the Row."

Hyphanden nodded at Duri as he rose. "Your horse has arrived, if all has gone well."

In a few minutes, Hyphanden returned from outside with two young men. One of them wore the formal high collar common among the Skilled of Tabor.

"These are Kerdahl and Stetsor, new Outcasts of a slightly different kind," he said, introducing them. "These two fought openly

109

against the First Chosen last year. Stetsor is in fact a grandson and namesake of one of the Elders. When the Second Chosen fled, their supporters were given the choice of swearing allegiance to the First Chosen or leaving Tabor. Some of those who chose to leave went to West Ford, some elsewhere. Ironically, some of them wound up here living the lives of Outcasts, although they are perhaps further away from us philosophically than they are from the First Chosen. We have a number of them here, now; in fact, we've had to open a new estate to house them."

"I prefer to think of myself as temporarily dislocated, rather than as an Outcast," Kerdahl said somewhat stiffly. "I maintain my Traditional orientation. But we are indebted to the Outcast Council for accepting us here."

"I assume you found the horse without problem," Kwistocta said. "No Hyolonal were there?"

"The horse was there as described, with a minor Concealment around it. We had little problem breaking it. We saw no Hyolonal in the area." Kerdahl grinned suddenly, and Rioletta saw the Vrinal in his wolfish grin, which transformed him from a serious young man to one with a mischievous air. "But I'm afraid we found ourselves on the wrong end of a nocked arrow when we went to leave."

Hyphanden raised his eyebrows and looked from Kerdahl to Stetsor.

Stetsor grinned as well. "True enough! Nocked by a woman!"

"A woman?" Hyphanden asked. "I didn't see her arrive, but I've been busy and not Viewing the talisman at the Row regularly."

Kerdahl nodded. "After we convinced her we were not there to steal the horse but to care for it, she consented to come down off the wall and talk to us. She was not a Sorcerer, but certainly one of the Skilled. She had the appearance of a guard or hunter. She told us she was Rath of Luth. I don't know where Luth is, but she said she was Andian."

"Luth is a satellite of Andolith," Rioletta said. "It's one of the Sydian settlements beholden to our Council for guidance. Most of them refer to themselves as Andian. Rath of Luth is known to us, but I have no idea what she might be doing here or why she would have followed us."

110

"As for that, she told us outright," Kerdahl said. "She asked about the owner of the horse, and we told her he was under the care of the Outcast Council. She said she had followed him after noticing that he followed a group of her friends, suspecting he meant them harm. We told her the rest of the group was also under the care of Hyphanden, and that no harm would come to them. She said she'd go to Tabor, where she knows some people, but that she would check back in a few days in case anyone wanted her to carry a message."

"Good," Nikal said. "She'll probably send a message to Ladon telling him what she knows; and I can hope she'll think to send one to Adla as well."

"I wonder if Ladon sent her, or if she came of her own accord," Rioletta said.

"Either way, I feel more at ease knowing she knows our whereabouts. Perhaps she'll be able to carry the message about the Younger Council. We'll have to find out who she knows in Tabor and what her relationship is with them when she returns," Nikal said.

"Now, Duri, do you think you can ride a bit?" Hyphanden asked.

Duri shrugged. "I can. Whether it'll be pleasant or not is another matter. Where is it you want me to go, or are you having me escorted out of the city?"

"Quite the contrary," Hyphanden said with a smile. "If you are able, I'd like you to accompany Kerdahl and Stetsor to the bachelor estate, where you'll have a room for yourself and stable for your horse. Thus you may begin to become part of the Outcast society."

Duri looked at him without comment, his dark eyes inscrutable. He collected his shirt and vest. Rioletta held his shirt for him as he painfully worked his arms into the sleeves. When they were gone, Nikal turned to Hyphanden.

"What is it you intend to do? Why offer to make Duri a part of this society?"

Hyphanden smiled. "I think Duri would make a fine repository for the partial minds of Malbec and Chasan, don't you? Rudon agrees; he confirmed my evaluation while treating him."

111

"But why him?" Andor demanded. "And what makes you think he'll accept?"

"Has he not already told you he was interested in contacting the Outcasts? Your conversation outside on the wall as you waited was open to me; I wanted some advance knowledge of the stranger you returned with."

Nikal spread his hands in a gesture of incredulity, but Hyphanden shook his head. "Don't worry, I Monitored only that part; the rest of what you said has not been compromised, except that which you chose to tell me yourself. So Duri has an interest in us, he is free from the influence of any Council, and he has no particular family. He has traveled and is likely known or accepted in many circles; he might be useful to us as a conduit between Hyolon and others. His mind is supple enough to have been a Sorcerer..."

Creed snorted, and Hyphanden raised his eyebrows, but then went on, "...like it or not, and he obviously has learned some Skills on his own, as well as the physical arts. But there is a more important point: he has already partitioned his mind. Whoever accepts the minds of Malbec and Chasandahl will have to be able to keep them separate from his own, at least in the short term. Duri has already built at least one partition; there is a part of his own mind he chooses not to access. Perhaps it's a repository of objectionable impulses, or perhaps memories he wishes to suppress. Whichever, he has already done it. I have no confirmation he'll accept my offer, of course. I suspect it will seem interesting to him, though. In exchange for the use of his mind, he receives the partial minds of two Sorcerers, complete with whatever Skills and knowledge survive. If he does accept, he will certainly have to stay here, at least in the short term; we'll have to see how he reacts, and many would find him untrustworthy if they knew."

"I find him untrustworthy as it is," Creed growled.

"Well, if all goes well, you'll be free of him for a long time," Hyphanden said.

"And I perceive you have another motive," Nikal said. "He openly told us he has associated with those who practice the Forbidden Technologies. Your interpretation of the Charter and the Technologies and Skills is a rationalization to excuse your own malfeasance, I suspect. But what better way to test your theories:

find one who is versed in one, and see what happens when you add the other!"

Hyphanden scowled at Nikal for a moment, then smiled, although his hands remained tight on the arms of his chair.

"Your reputation doesn't do you justice, Nikal of Dobor," he said. "I have heard your Viewing Skills extend beyond that which is normally part of such a Skill."

Nikal snorted. "It took no special Skill to see that, only attention to your own words. Will you tell Duri he's to be part of your experiment? If not, I'll make sure I do."

"He will know everything and make his decision freely," Hyphanden said. "Decisions made in the absence of complete information are not true decisions, but manipulated choices. My life's goal is to obtain the most complete information I can, and I would not do him, or any other, the disservice of withholding any of it."

Nikal fell silent at that; perhaps he felt it unwise to antagonize Hyphanden, especially in his own home. In the uncomfortable break, Rudon rose to gain their attention. "Now let's have a bit of fun," he said. "I'll show you a few tricks; you see who can guess how I do them and what Skills are at work."

The group watched as Rudon performed a series of minor tricks, although Hyphanden brooded in his chair and did not participate. Rudon was very skillful and deft, but more surprising to Rioletta was the fact that many of his tricks required only the combining of Restricted Skills and did not cross the line to the Forbidden. He also challenged them to place Protections on small items, and then rapidly broke their Skills. He was certainly entertaining, but Rioletta tried to remind herself to be cautious; this was undoubtedly how Rudon had first introduced himself to Malbec and the Younger Council.

That evening Hyphanden called a meeting of the entire Outcast Council. Besides Hyphanden, Kwistocta, and Rudon, the Inner Circle of the Council included Mynador, a woman some years older than the others, upright and severe in appearance. She had been in Hyolon longer than anyone else in the Outcast community, and she was an Outcast of Matbor, reputedly the only one ever.

The rest of the Council consisted of Gomphos and Tarbos, Outcasts from Ankara, and Dacent, a young Skilled man who had been Expelled from his community for practicing Sorcerer-level Skills. The eighth spot was vacant, and temporarily occupied by Caladoc of the Second Chosen of Tabor, to Rioletta's surprise. Like Kerdahl and Stetsor, he had fled the city after the coup, along with Cayondahl, another member of the Second Chosen.

After introductions, Hyphanden covered the arrival of the Andolith group, Stolen's story, and the possibility of opening the Crypt to retrieve the Younger Council. Most of the Council agreed quickly with the proposal, but Mynador expressed some reservations.

"We have no idea what minds are stored within the Crypt," she told the Council in a rasping voice. "We do not have this Index, which you believe would allow us to identify who they are and what their background is. These are most likely not minds we want to allow back into the world; they were placed there for a reason."

"Kwistocta and I remember which cells we placed the four minds of the Younger Council into," Hyphanden argued. "All the information I have suggests it's possible to pick and choose which minds we want to remove. We'll take those, then close the Crypt up again. We won't bother the other minds."

"At least until such time as we can identify them," Rudon said eagerly. "Once we know who's there, we'll have the ability to open it as we choose now that we have the Key, and perhaps use the minds. Think of the knowledge we could gain, and how quickly we could gain it!"

"I think that's a bad idea," Kwistocta said. "We do not have the Skills to take out and put back minds from our own repeatedly, and we don't know what besides their Skills we might get. It sounds dangerous to me; I'm with Mynador on this."

"Besides, the Key does not belong to us," Hyphanden said. "I would count on using it only this one time, to rescue the Younger Council."

Rioletta and the rest of her group listened quietly while the Council argued; there was little they could add to the conversation. In fact, it was a conversation Rioletta could hardly believe she was hearing; only a week before, she would never have imagined discussing the removal and re-internment of bodiless minds.

"All the more reason to remove at least a few of the other minds at the same time we rescue the Younger Council." Rudon leaned forward, his dark blue eyes intense. "We have information suggesting how the Crypt was constructed. We could create temporary storage for them."

"I agree with you to some degree," Hyphanden said. "We could probably create some kind of temporary storage. But I think we would need to spend time in advance creating partitions within the minds of whoever would accept them, and we don't have the time to do that. And we should have the Index to enable us to choose wisely."

"I don't think we should attempt to access hundred-year-old minds even with the Index," Kwistocta said. "The knowledge we might gain is not worth the risk."

"All right," Hyphanden said with a sigh. "Let's go through it all again. Somebody write down the pros and cons of each of our courses of action, and we'll try to look at it objectively. Let's remember that our main purpose is to rescue what's left of the Younger Council, and try to keep our personal desires out of it."

He looked pointedly at Rudon, but Rudon smiled and raised his eyebrows. "I will if you will."

"I'll take notes if you want," Rioletta volunteered. "I have nothing to contribute, so I can listen and write without interruption."

Kwistocta provided her with a pen and paper, and the Council continued their discussion, with Rioletta occasionally reading back the notes. Eventually they elected to access the Crypt only for long enough to retrieve the Younger Council. Hyphanden voted with the majority with the understanding that they could revisit the issue later; Rudon reluctantly agreed, and the Council finally adjourned for the night.

Rioletta, Stolen, and Andor stood near the front door to bid a formal goodnight to the members of the Council as they left for the evening. Suddenly Rioletta felt a presence; she turned around quickly to see Mynador lurking behind them, staring fixedly at Stolen.

Mynador took a few steps closer and reached out towards Stolen. "Many children's stories are based on that which we fear, and that which we fear is often based in reality," she said in a hoarse voice scarcely above a whisper. Stolen and Rioletta exchanged glances; was she talking about Stolen as the source of childhood fears? "Something I know about the trade in children, and those who broker it," she continued. "There are things I know, and more I can guess. Remember the children's tales."

Mynador straightened and brushed past them out the door. Rioletta, Andor, and Stolen looked after her.

"Creepy," Andor said. "I wonder what she meant?"

"Not sure, and not sure I care to know," Stolen said with a shrug. "I'll be locking the bedroom door tonight, though."

The next morning Rioletta arose with an odd feeling of emptiness. For the first time in a long time she had nothing in particular to do, and she knew it would be that way for the foreseeable future, until all the preparations had been made to go to the Crypt.

It was early and the house was quiet. She walked out through the great-room into the garden and saw Stolen standing in the sun. His back was to her, and she stopped so as not to attract his attention. He quickly removed his clothing, then dug his feet into the soil and threw his head back and arms wide. As he did so, the leaves on his back, arms, and in his hair unfurled and stood out from his skin. Rioletta realized he was taking energy directly from the sun. Tiny thin struts emerged from his thighs and shins and along his arms: the beginnings of branches.

Rioletta turned away into the house without disturbing Stolen. Within a few minutes she was joined by Nikal and the rest of the household. Rudon arrived and helped himself to breakfast, then engaged Cardon, Nikal, and Hyphanden in a discussion about where to draw the line between Restricted and Forbidden. Rioletta listened but stayed out of it; she was a little concerned the discussion might rise to an argument between Nikal and Hyphanden, but Rudon seemed to be able to turn the conversation at the right time, and things remained civil.

Cardon told Rudon about the Andolith Council's journey to Tabor and the stealing of the tapestries containing the Elder Council. Cardon had animated drawings of horses to three dimensions to distract attention from them as they broke into the Council-house, but he lamented their brief life and how they dissipated within a few minutes.

"This is the kind of thing I was talking about," Rudon said. "Is such a thing truly Forbidden, or does it not rise to that level?"

"Ladon seemed to think it was Forbidden," Cardon said. "His reasoning was that I was creating a semblance of life that I could not sustain."

"I can show you how to keep them alive for much longer," Rudon told him. "Also, I can teach you how to call them back to you or to where they came from, and how to draw them in advance and then Throw a Skill at them from a distance to animate them."

"That would be useful," Cardon said. "I wouldn't feel so bad about using the Skill if I could return the drawings to their original state."

"Let's go out in the garden," Rudon said. "We'll work on it where your Throwing won't go awry! Can you draw something more fearsome than horses?"

"Not really," Cardon admitted. "Horses are what I've practiced and I'm best at."

"Well, horses aren't particularly scary or vicious. Maybe you can draw some teeth and claws, or something. Let's start with something smaller, though. Perhaps bunnies…"

Rudon and Cardon went to the garden, leaving Nikal and Hyphanden to carry on the conversation. To Rioletta's surprise, Nikal seemed interested in the discussion, and he seemed to be holding his temper. He leaned forward, his elbows on his knees, ticking off points on his fingers, while Hyphanden slouched in his chair with a slight smile, deftly countering Nikal's arguments. Rioletta was pretty sure Hyphanden would come out on top, not necessarily because his arguments were more sound, but because he was a Loremaster and Nikal was not. She was not interested in engaging Hyphanden in such a discussion herself; some part of her mind preferred not to hear his arguments and challenges to the Traditional interpretation of the Charter.

Rioletta was left to seek the company of Andor and Creed. She found them outside on top of the wall behind the estate. Creed was bored; he was hunting small animals from the spine of the wall, and risked going down into the greensward to get them. Andor and Rioletta sat on the wall and watched.

They had not been there long when Rudon joined them. "Well, Cardon will be occupied for a while practicing Throwing his Skills at his drawings," he said. "Kwistocta's setting Protections to keep those voices out of Cardon's head, and Nikal and Phando are arguing philosophy. Stolen's growing like a weed, literally. But I'm afraid Hyolon's not a good place for recreation for the rest of you."

"We're likely to be rattling around this place for a while, too," Creed said. "It'll take a while for Stolen to grow twigs."

"Well, there's no need for you to be stuck at Phando's. You can visit the rest of us, and parts of the city are safe enough." Rudon grinned and feinted teasingly at Creed. "You're a warrior, Creed! You can protect these young women, can't you?"

Creed responded by knocking Rudon's hands to the side, raising his own defensively, but he didn't return the grin. "I'm a Hunter, not a warrior."

"Besides, we know nothing about the city," Rioletta said. "It wouldn't be so interesting to go walking around looking at buildings with chunks falling off on our heads."

"True, some areas are safer and more interesting than others," Rudon said, readjusting his shirt. "If you want, I'll take you on a tour."

Andor jumped up. "Let me get my satchel!" She hurried back towards the estate.

Rioletta adjusted her shoes for walking while they waited, and Creed slung his bow over his back. Rioletta had her own satchel with her, with the book in it. For now she kept it with her at all times. She wasn't sure what Hyphanden would do if he had the information from the book; if he could free Marsavrina and Skadar without their involvement, it would be fine with her. But Nikal insisted they keep the book secret and guard it at all times.

When Andor returned, they set off along the top of the wall following Rudon. He set a quick pace and led them south through the neighborhood, first along walls and then along connected balconies. The second and third-story balconies were like raised streets and they passed many small storefronts and apartments.

Although the height of the buildings and the size of the city still seemed strange, Rioletta was beginning to feel a little more comfortable there. Certainly the city was not sterile; besides the Hyolonal and the Outcasts, many animals lived in and around it. Animals as large as deer and coyotes walked the streets before fading back into the trees that encroached on all sides; birds flew in and nested high on the buildings. Of course, there were rats and mice, but also squirrels living in the rock piles where buildings had crumbled and fallen down. She heard their chirps and warnings as they passed by. Sometimes they did hear rockfall from far away, when some construction or another lost a wall or roof tiles. But a hundred years had not been long enough to destroy the foundations of the best-built estates, and much of the city seemed quite solid.

"We're heading for the Museum District," Rudon said. "We won't access the main museum today; it's dangerous, full of old Protections we don't fully understand. It must have been very important to the residents of Hyolon, given the way they left it. But there are smaller ones in the same area, showcases for collections and tourist shops and such, and not all of them have been looted."

"Maybe I could pick up a souvenir or two," Creed mused.

Rudon glanced back at him. "I wouldn't slip anything in your satchel if I were you. You never know what the old Sorcerers might have left. If there's something that truly interests you, we'll take it back and maybe have Mynador look it over. She's good at detecting those old Skills. I can detect Protections, but there are others."

"Sure," Creed agreed. "I wasn't advocating theft. But no one I know has ever been to Hyolon, and it'd be great to have something from here I got myself."

"Have you got something to trade?" Rudon grinned. "Some of the old things won't let you take them unless you leave something of equal value in their place!"

Creed shook his head. "Maybe I'd better drop the idea altogether!"

Rudon stopped at a rail on one of the balconies. From there Rioletta could see a broad, paved boulevard, opening into squares at regular intervals. She recognized it as the one they had seen during their journey to Hyolon, when they'd stopped for lunch after leaving Dobor.

"The main avenue into Hyolon," Rudon said. "The big gates are about a mile east. We'll cross here. Use your Concealment while we're on the ground."

They hurried across the open ground. On the other side Rudon led them through a complex maze of buildings, and they dropped their Concealment. Just as they did, Creed stopped and frowned.

"I caught motion on top of that building," he said, nodding at a rectangular construction.

"Probably just a bird or a squirrel," Rudon said lightly.

Creed followed as the rest of them moved on, but Rioletta noticed that he kept looking up at the building's roof, on high alert. She doubted a Hunter of Andolith had mistaken a squirrel for something to be concerned about, and her own senses heighten in response to his vigilance.

Eventually they came to a walled section, and on one corner of the wall was a high spire. Rudon paused to break some Protections, and they entered the spire and made their way up a spiral staircase to the top. Narrow doorways led to an outside balcony far above the streets. The four of them stepped out. Rioletta cautiously tested the balcony for integrity, but it appeared strong.

"What a view!" Andor exclaimed.

Rudon smiled smugly. "From here you can see west all the way up the main boulevard to the main square. The spires in the far distance, beyond the central plaza, are the Council-house. To the south is the Museum District, and to the north you can see the Embassy near our estates."

Rioletta walked slowly around the balcony. She squinted out to the east towards Tabor and in the direction of Andolith, but the view that way was blocked by trees and a low fog rising off the vineyards and mustard fields.

Creed came around behind her and paused as well. "Nice view," Rioletta confirmed.

But Creed scowled. "Don't like it. We're exposed up here. Anybody could see us and see how many of us there are."

They went back around to the other side and trailed single-file down the stair. Back down on the street, Rudon led them along a row of small storefronts. A few had been looted, but most still bore enough Protections to remain impervious to the Hyolonal and others who sought to trade in antiques. Rudon took them into a few Protected buildings, easily dropping the Skills. Some exhibited paintings and other fine art, but one seemed to specialize in small amulets, talismans, and the like.

Rudon stopped outside that one and squinted up at the carved letters in the lintel over the door. "I'm not sure where these things came from," he said, glancing at Rioletta. "Can you read the words, young Loremaster?"

Rioletta stepped back and focused on the letters. The language was unfamiliar to her. She tried a translate Skill, but although the letters took on a more familiar shape, the words made no sense.

"I can't," she admitted. "I've never encountered this language before. I don't know the Skills."

"No?" Rudon looked at her. "You are only of your Younger Council, though. You won't be inducted into the Special Skills until you are in the Elder Council, and perhaps the Inner Circle."

"Special Skills?" Rioletta frowned. "As far as I know, there are no secret Special Skills held only by the Elders in Andolith."

"Ah," Rudon said. "Nor in most Councils, anymore. I thought Andolith might be different, in its isolation. There used to be such Skills in all Councils, but the Dispersal was more violent and disruptive than anyone imagined at the time, and many of those were lost."

Rioletta did not know how to reply; Special Skills were mentioned in the Charter, but as far as she knew, Andolith had none. Then again, even if they did, she probably would not know about them as a member of the Younger Council. For a moment she felt a tiny bit of doubt about her Council. Was it possible Ladon was in possession of some concealed knowledge? Her thoughts returned to Mosse Amwiska, her mentor and the one who had sent her to find the Lefollah. Mosse had died before Rioletta completed her task, and anything she'd wished to pass on upon Rioletta's induction had been lost.

"Well, I'm pretty sure the things in here aren't originally from Hyolon," Rudon said. "So taking a few of them wouldn't amount to theft or looting, in my opinion." He stood in front of the door for a few moments, until it produced a loud click. Then he opened it and stood aside.

Rioletta browsed through the showcases. Most of the cases were closed and Protected, but a few objects sat exposed on shelves and stands. As usual in a Protected building, there was no dust.

Creed eyed a small pocketknife with the skyline of an unidentified city etched in its handle on one side and archaic script on the other. It opened smoothly with a small click that became a buzz, and a tiny blue spark sat upon the blade's tip.

"Self-sharpening," Creed said. "Okay if I take this?"

Rudon took a brief look at it and handed it back with a nod of assent. Andor chose a smooth chain with the same blue color as the spark on Creed's knife, but Rioletta wasn't taken by any particular piece besides the ones locked away in the showcases.

"Here, how about this, Rio?" Andor handed her a small silver-blue disk with a hole in the middle and etchings around the edge. "You could slip it on the chain you already wear, next to your talisman."

"Hmm," Rudon said, examining the disk. "Looks like an amplifier. No harm in that; it will amplify your talisman."

Rioletta slipped the chain holding Nikal's talisman off and opened it to add the tiny disk. It clinked against the talisman once, then seemed to cushion itself with a faint ring of blue light.

They began making their way back through the district, with Rudon making small talk and pointing out features of the city. Eventually they came to the wall with the spire and stepped out through the gate.

They stepped into the midst of a group of Hyolonal.

Creed snatched his bow off his back, but there were fifty or sixty Hyolonal in a horseshoe-shaped ring, all dangling slings or gripping spears. There was no way for Creed to even choose a target.

The Hyolonal stood silent and still. Not one of them moved to counter Creed's bow. Creed, Andor, and Rioletta stood as still as the Hyolonal. Rioletta had no idea what to do; she found herself wondering, for a fleet second, what the Hyolonal would do to an Inducted Sorcerer if they were able to capture one.

Rudon stepped forward then, his hands out in a placating manner. He said not a word, but walked slowly towards the Hyolonal. When he reached a certain distance from them, they began to step backwards as though an invisible wall was pressing against them, maintaining the structure of the horseshoe shape as they backed. Rudon pressed forward slowly, and suddenly the Hyolonal turned as if one, and all of them disappeared quickly and quietly into the streets and alleyways.

Creed let out an audible breath. Rioletta felt her heart rate beginning to decrease and she looked at Andor, who had drawn the only weapon she wore--a small belt knife.

Only Rudon seemed unconcerned; he sauntered back to them with a grin. "Guess they didn't want to deal with an Outcast Sorcerer," he bragged. "I can go anywhere in this city. None of them will mess with me."

They made their way back through the city carefully and on high alert, their jovial mood vanished. It was mid-afternoon when they returned to the estate. Rudon left them at the gate to go to his own residence.

Nikal had been looking for Rioletta. "I was beginning to get worried. Where did you go?"

"I'm sorry I didn't tell you. We didn't expect to be gone quite so long. Rudon gave us a tour," Rioletta said. "We went to the Museum District."

"You were out roaming around with Rudon? You know his reputation! He's the one who recruited the Younger Council!"

Rioletta flushed. "Nikal, I'm not in danger of being recruited to the Forbidden Skills by Rudon. Besides, he protected us from a group of Hyolonal on our way back. There must have been fifty or sixty!"

"Fifty or sixty?" Hyphanden frowned. "I've rarely seen more than ten or fifteen in a group. I can't imagine why they didn't attack you."

"The way they just faded away was even weirder," Creed said, shaking his head. "There wasn't much I could've done, maybe take out one or two. We were lucky they were so afraid of Rudon."

Hyphanden shook his head again. "Rudon doesn't have any special relationship with the Hyolonal as far as I know, or any special power over them. I'm not sure what was going on."

They were forced to stop speculating for the moment as Kerdahl and Stetsor arrived. This time they brought Rath with them; Hyphanden had set them to watching the Row, waiting for her return. She entered the estate on obvious alert, aware of all her surroundings; but when she saw Rioletta and Andor, Creed, and Nikal, she relaxed.

"Rath! Glad to see you," Andor said, clasping her hand. "Welcome to the Ruined City!"

"A little less ruined than I'd been led to believe," Rath said, looking around the great room. "It appears you're all safe. I hope my decision to trust these people was well-founded."

Rath told them that she had intended to return to Luth via Andolith, as they had planned. But after Duri was expelled from the Polebray, she had followed him to see where he set up his camp. "It was only for my own peace of mind. Later, when you left, I realized your route around the Polebray would take you close to Duri's camp. I told Ladon I would follow, just in case. Sure enough, Duri packed up and pursued you, although he never came too close."

"So you followed him," Creed said. "I wonder which one of you I was sensing while we were travelling."

"I followed him all the way to Dobor, then again as he followed you here," Rath said. "When he entered the city itself, I kept track of his whereabouts but remained near his horse, since I figured he would have to come back for it eventually. I met Kerdahl and Stetsor when they collected his belongings. They gave me word of you; I returned to Tabor, where I have friends among the Security Force. From there I sent a message to Ladon and another to Adla, Nikal; I hope that is as you would have wished. I'll take back whatever message you want, if I'm to be allowed to leave here."

"You're not a captive, and can leave any time you want," Hyphanden said somewhat stiffly. "We ask only that you not reveal any particulars of the Protections we use that you might see while here."

"Agreed," Rath said. "I didn't intend offense."

"You have strong tracking Skills, apparently," Hyphanden said more amiably, "if you continued to keep track of Duri after he entered the city, when he was out of your view."

Rath smiled and lifted the hem of her vest, revealing a small device on her belt. It strongly resembled the one Duri had displayed.

"In the presence of other such devices, these can track each other, although it's best if there are at least three. A talisman or familiar object can serve as a third in a pinch, though. I was aware Duri had one; I saw it among his belongings at the Polebray. So I employed my own…little Skill required."

"Isn't that Forbidden Technology, though?" Rioletta asked, as Rath handed her the small object to examine.

Rath shrugged. "It does remain in communication with another device when it's activated, which can be interpreted as Forbidden. But it is possible to turn it off and it doesn't rely on an interface with the mind. I use it rarely, and in this case I used it protectively. Let Ladon dispute it if he will; he is my Council-leader now, after all. But I don't think he will."

"Where did you get it?" Hyphanden asked as Rioletta passed it to him.

Rath shrugged. "During my travels. I'm afraid I have no similar devices to interest you, nor do I trade in them. But besides Duri's, this device has communicated with others in this immediate area, so I know others exist here."

Hyphanden nodded and passed it to Nikal, who immediately handed it back to Rath, as though he disliked touching it.

"Let us tell you what we intend, and why we've been staying here," Nikal said. "You can take that information to Ladon, or send it if you think it safe."

"I'd prefer to stay in the area until you're headed home," Rath said. "I suspect you might need help at that point...or perhaps *you* will not, Nikal, but Sorcerers of Andolith traveling in Tabor very well might. I have contacts here, and know the roads."

"That's true, we're not very welcome in Tabor. But how will we be able to contact you?" Rioletta asked.

"I'll keep an eye on that row of buildings where Duri's horse was, if that's a good spot for you," Rath said. "When you're ready to go, show up there, or leave me messages in the building."

"Be careful," Creed said. "There are Hyolonal, and they might show up in that area."

Rath smiled. "I've dealt with the Hyolonal before, and others of their ilk. They are not particularly bold when confronted with deadly force. They want only to take what they can get and leave safely. But I thank you for your concern, and I'll be wary."

Rath spent the night and departed the next morning.

"Choose the messenger to Andolith carefully," Rioletta said as she clasped Rath's hand in farewell. "I'm sure Ladon won't be pleased, and the messenger had best be prepared for his reaction!"

Rath smiled. "I'm sure I can find someone to take on the job, but it may require a few extra coins. If I don't hear from you within a reasonable amount of time, I'll start making plans to come in here and rescue you. There are some who'd be bold enough to enter the Ruined City for such a mission."

"I hope it won't be necessary, but I'm glad you're watching out for us." Rioletta watched as Rath mounted her horse and started down the sloping drive. Rath turned to wave at the bottom, but just then she passed out of Hyphanden's Concealment and faded from view as though hidden by a fog.

Chapter Eleven

One morning Rioletta walked into the living room to a strange scene. Stolen was sprawled in a large easy chair, unclothed except for short trousers. Rudon sat nearby on a stool, blotting blood from Stolen's arms and legs. Hyphanden stood wordlessly looking on. And beside Stolen stood a being Rioletta had not seen for more than a year: a Twig Person, the mobile body of a Lefollah.

The Twig Person was less complete than those she had seen before. It was shorter than Stolen, very slender, with a limited number of branches comprising its arms, legs, and torso. Its body was filled in with leaves. There was a horizontal bar across its face about a third of the way down its head, and there Rioletta could see two small sparkling black eyes.

"How in control of it are you?" Hyphanden asked, as other members of the party quietly gathered around.

For answer, the Twig Being suddenly walked across the room to the table at the back wall, picked up a piece of fruit in spindly fingers, appeared to examine it, and returned it to Stolen. The Twig Person walked with the quick steps Rioletta remembered from the Lefollah, bouncing slightly on springy twig feet.

"It is me, and I am it," Stolen replied, turning the fruit in his hand. "I control it as completely as I control my own hand. It has no thought separate from me. Should it get too far from me, it would

127

cease to have connection to my mind and would stop, unable to make its own decision to go on. Eventually it would fall apart, unless I could go to it and collect it. But you propose to give it its own mind. I do not know what will happen then. It's like giving a part of my body its own mind."

"Is there in fact any matrix, any brain, for Marsavrina and Skadar to be transferred into, then?" Rioletta asked.

Stolen shrugged. "I cannot tell. The Lefollah are able to give their Twig Bodies specific instructions and maintain only minimal contact with them while they complete the tasks on their own."

"That suggests to me that the Lefollah Twigs have at least some repository for thought," Hyphanden said.

"But I am not Lefollah, and this Twig Body is not one of theirs, nor is it made by an experienced creator," Stolen said. "I can't guarantee how like one of theirs this is."

"I suppose we can only try," Hyphanden said. "We have come up with no other solution, and we can't wait forever. It's time to go to the Crypt of Souls."

"First we'll have to prepare the potion for Cardon," Kwistocta said. She turned to Rioletta. "I assume you have the recipe?"

"Yes," Rioletta said. "I've written it down. We'll need six plants, different parts of each one, and some other ingredients. Most of them are available in your garden, but one I'm not sure of."

"Rudon will be able to help us with that, I'm sure," Kwistocta said. "He knows where to get all the wild-growing ingredients and keeps some stores of them. Let me see the recipe, and I'll decide whether it needs to be made directly before we go, or can be made and kept for a period of time."

Rioletta brought the recipe, which she had written down, rather than the book itself, of which she made no mention. Kwistocta took it and frowned.

"I'm sure you realize that several of these are deadly poisons," Kwistocta said. "Two of them are not bad, but the other four are very dangerous, even in small amounts. Nevertheless, it's a typical recipe for a Mind-sharing Distraction. But this won't make a potion at all, not something that could be drunk."

"What will it make?" Rioletta asked, looking at the recipe from beside Kwistocta.

"Perhaps a salve, or cream," Kwistocta said. "It may be meant to be rubbed on the hands, face, or elsewhere on the body where the blood vessels are numerous and close to the surface. Were there not other instructions?"

"There are other instructions, but none about how to apply this," Rioletta said. "At least, if we've discovered all the secrets of the Key."

She glanced at Nikal. He looked at the floor for a minute, then caught Hyphanden's eye.

"Perhaps it's time we showed them the Key," he said grudgingly. "We may not be able to ferret out everything it's got to say. There are other Skills that could be applied to it, and those are Skills we don't practice or perhaps even understand. We need to make sure we've got all the information it holds before we proceed, I'm sure you'll agree."

Rioletta looked around. There were resolute nods of agreement, so she removed the book from her satchel, and handed it wordlessly to Hyphanden.

He took it carefully and turned it over, but did not open it.

"Show me what secrets you've found already, and I'll see what else I can do," he said. "I caution you to continue to keep it concealed from others. Certainly there are other Outcasts, rogues, not within the Council's community. I expect there are some who would go to some lengths to get their hands on this."

"To what lengths would they go?" Andor asked. "Surely they wouldn't confront a group of Sorcerers such as the Outcast Council to get something like this book. It only opens the Crypt, where unknown minds are stored, isn't that correct?"

Hyphanden nodded. "Of course. Unknown minds, but we can be fairly sure they were minds put there before the Dispersal. They were minds for which someone was willing to risk his or her safety. They are stored in the Council-house. What do you think of them?"

Nikal nodded. "Most likely they're the minds of Sorcerers of Hyolon, perhaps the Outcasts of their time. The knowledge they hold must be vastly more expansive than ours."

"Indeed," Hyphanden said. "We have had to recreate the Forbidden Skills slowly and with limited information and much risk.

129

Think of what it would be like to have all those Skills suddenly at one's disposal, with little effort."

"Is it not tempting to you?" Nikal asked.

Hyphanden stared at Nikal from under his brows, and weighed the book in his hand. "Yes, tempting," he answered slowly. "At one time in my life I was susceptible to temptation, the downfall of the Skilled, and I followed the Path of Transformation and became an Outcast. Since then I have developed Skills beyond the imagination of most Sorcerers today. Do not think I couldn't take this from you, all of you, quite easily. Do not think I couldn't discover what you have discovered. But I am older and more experienced now. I have a life I enjoy, and temptation is no longer such a failing of mine. Recall also that the opening of the Crypt requires a team of people, not just one or even two. I will go no further than to rescue the minds we've planned on. You have my word."

No one said anything.

Rioletta felt a prickle at the back of her neck as she wondered just what Skills Hyphanden did in fact possess. But there was little they could do now but forge ahead and hope he would keep his word.

The next morning, just as the sun was coming up, the group set out for the Council-house. Hyphanden and Kwistocta led the way, followed by Nikal, Rioletta, Andor, Creed, Cardon, and Stolen with his Twig Being trailing along behind him. Rudon also accompanied them, having been an acquaintance of the Younger Council and by now well versed in their plans.

They went on foot, as horses would draw too much attention and would have to be left behind when they entered the Council-house anyway. They began by leaving the estate via the rear wall and followed it past many other estates, through the large neighborhood that had once housed the wealthy of Hyolon.

Rioletta walked just behind Hyphanden and Kwistocta, while Creed and Rudon brought up the rear. Hyphanden glanced over his shoulder and spoke in a low voice to Kwistocta.

"We shouldn't have brought Rudon along. I know he was a friend of the Younger Council, but he also led them to their demise. I don't think he deserves to be there when we rescue them. Who knows how they'll react?"

"He's a Skilled Healer and a Protection-breaker," Kwistocta answered. "We may have need of either or both of those Skills. Besides, he's part of the Inner Council; we have no right to refuse him."

Hyphanden snorted, but he made no further complaint. He and Kwistocta pointed out the estates of other Council-members and Outcasts in good standing with the community as they travelled. Eventually they arrived at a well-kept home with high, narrow walls; this was the Bachelor residence, where Kerdahl, Stetsor, and now Duri lived. Duri was waiting for them on top of the wall, with his characteristic cocky grin.

"Are you prepared, Duri?" Hyphanden asked. "There is still time to refuse."

"Are you kidding? I'm looking forward to it," Duri replied, without a hint of anxiety. He fell in behind Creed at the back. Rioletta noticed that Creed purposefully drew aside and motioned Duri to pass him on the wall. Duri shrugged and moved forward, allowing Creed the vital rear-guard position.

They passed the spur of wall that led to the parapet and plaza where Duri had been cornered and injured by the Hyolonal. Rioletta turned to Duri, her memory piqued. "How are your ribs?"

"Very well, little pain anymore," Duri replied. "I've been introduced to some potions that allowed me to heal faster than normal, and learned to concentrate my attention on the talisman bandage of Rudon, although I can't say everything is perfect yet. I wouldn't want to take a hard fall. But it doesn't bother me to walk."

The wall continued, leading on to the west at a rising angle, and finally connected with an upper story of a tall building, with many windows devoid of glass. Rioletta tried not to look off the side of the wall; the height was dizzying, and the wall seemed to have become thinner.

"Salvage teams have been here," Nikal noted. "If the glass had all broken, there would be shards, but see how clean it is? Our salvage teams take everything away with them, we can use it all."

"You and I will have to have a discussion about where to draw the line between looting and *salvage*," Hyphanden said with a grin.

Nikal stopped and glared at Hyphanden, but he didn't reply.

131

"Of course, it also makes it less attractive to the Hyolonal, since the weather can come in through the openings," Hyphanden continued. "Although they aren't apt to live in the tall buildings anyway; too dangerous. This one is not in good condition, but we will have to enter it. The wall ends here for a distance, and we'll have to descend to the ground and cross open space to find another spur."

Kwistocta motioned at the door at which they'd arrived, and then pushed it open cautiously. She entered the building first, stepping carefully, and led the way through the interior. There were many desks and the frames of chairs scattered about; anything wood had been removed, as well as hinges and forged metal objects, but heavy items of metal had been left behind. Interior wallboard lay slumped and broken across the floor. In some places wall struts had been removed, probably for firewood. As they passed open doorways, it was obvious that the building was slowly collapsing; piles of rubble could be seen here and there.

"Let's go quickly," Hyphanden said. "If there are any Hyolonal, it's best to take them by surprise anyway. And I don't like this building; no Healer I know can repair people who've been crushed by tons of falling material."

They reached a staircase and descended, turned, and continued down floor after floor to the ground level. Rioletta lost track of the number of floors they passed; the office building must have housed more workers than the entire population of Andolith. The staircase ended in a large lobby with scraps of carpet and a huge double doorway with no door ahead of them. Kwistocta led them out the opening, and they turned to the right in the courtyard.

As they emerged from the sheltered yard onto the street, they saw a small group of Hyolonal ahead of them, standing by the corner of a building across the plaza. They were dressed in browns and tans, holding sticks and slings, but it appeared this was a group of young teens, rather than an adult crew. One of the teens pointed, the rest squinted, and then they silently faded away.

"At least they didn't attack us," Creed said.

"No, but that doesn't mean much," Hyphanden replied. "There were only a few of them, and young. Perhaps they went to get others, or perhaps they'll only spy on us to see what we do. A group of Sorcerers doesn't often make its way through the streets of

Hyolon; they'll know we're up to something, and it might be interesting for them to find out where we go and what we do."

"We'll be on alert, then," Creed said. He held his bow in his left hand as they walked, and readjusted the machete he had slung awkwardly on his belt.

They went quickly along the street, almost at a run. Then Kwistocta ducked into another courtyard, this one more overgrown than the last, and led the way to another doorway. This one still had doors, although they had been ripped open and flung to either side. They were ornate and heavy, and leaned at precarious angles, hinges having been removed long ago.

This building appeared to be less an office and more a lodge of some type, with small private rooms and the remains of more comfortable furniture. They climbed the stairs, rising to a height similar to the one they'd been at previously. Rioletta's legs began to ache, and she was glad when Kwistocta turned off onto a floor and then wound through a series of small rooms and closets to an exterior doorway. Once again, they were back on the wall. The city center loomed to their left, many tall buildings punctuated with large piles of rubble where a few had completely collapsed. The area below and around them began to appear more residential, with lower buildings and large spreading open tracts that might have been communal gardens. Here and there in those tracts Rioletta glimpsed riotous flowers, once domestic, now feral and overgrown.

The wall began to dip downwards, with missing chunks and no side walls or parapets. The group followed it down to the ground, where it turned sharply and ended at a low fence surrounding one of the tracts.

"From here on there is no wall," Kwistocta said. "We'll be traveling along the ground, although we'll take a roundabout route through many buildings in order to avoid any eyes that might be upon us. We are deep in Hyolonal territory now; this is the area of the city they prefer, because there are houses in decent shape which require little upkeep and no settlements around the outside of the city, only wild woods in which they can hunt and fish. Unfortunately, the Council-house is in this area. In a city this size, the Sorcerers undoubtedly didn't care to be in the busy center. We believe some of them lived in this area, though the older and more powerful probably lived where we live now."

The group turned out onto a narrow street between low houses and stone fences surrounding the communal gardens. After winding along similar streets for some time, Kwistocta motioned them to a halt.

She leaned towards them and lowered her voice. "This is the closest we'll come to known Hyolonal residences," she said. "Just two blocks away are houses we know to be occupied. It's likely there are people roaming these streets, and we must go quickly and as quietly and unobtrusively as possible."

"Shall we use Concealment?" Rioletta asked.

Kwistocta shook her head. "I don't think that's necessary, and it uses up energy we might need in the Crypt."

As they moved along behind a row of what appeared to have been shops, Rioletta saw glimpses of houses where the vegetation had been cut back and the dirt yards trampled. In the yards were stacks of wood, metal, and scrap. The houses could hardly have been said to be well kept, but they had a lived-in look, and in the distance she could hear the yells of children, perhaps playing among the heaps.

A few blocks later, the occupied residences dwindled.

"There'll be no more houses," Kwistocta said, "but we're not out of danger from them. In fact, it appears we're being followed."

Creed and Duri both glanced around. No one could be seen, but Kwistocta's comment put them all on edge.

"How dangerous are they, really?" Rioletta asked. "Rath seemed to think they're easily dissuaded, and their weapons seem primitive."

"Most of them are easily dissuaded, it's true," Kwistocta said. "Here, though, is their home turf. They are more motivated to defend this territory, and they'll have more people and perhaps better weapons. We can surely flee from them successfully, using Throwing Skills and the like; nevertheless, it's always possible one could get in a strike with a spear or rock, and we wouldn't have time to stop and treat an injury. It's best not to risk such a thing, especially with a small group such as ours."

As they continued through the city, Rioletta soon became aware that they were, indeed, being followed. Occasionally she heard nearby calls similar to those of birds and other animals. Eventually, the Hyolonal began to appear in the open behind and to the sides of them. There were a great many of them, wordlessly watching and following, all carrying sticks, spears, and slings.

"We have passed into another Hyolonal territory, but the Hyolonal from the first territory have not dropped away," Hyphanden said. "Generally they defend only a particular area in clans or family groups, and they will drop away and be replaced by others as we pass through those regions. But today they seem only to be growing in numbers, almost as if they've developed some sort of pact or treaty with one another, although that's unlikely."

"Why unlikely?" asked Rioletta. "Has anyone ever tried to negotiate with them for safe passage or some such?"

Hyphanden glanced at her. "Of course, many have tried in the past to negotiate with them, and another attempt is made every few years. But each clan makes agreements only for itself. Therefore, any pact made with a single family is worthless; the other families will take advantage as they can, and soon the pact will be broken. They do not form alliances with each other, at least not for long periods of time, as far as we can tell."

"It's time to hurry," Kwistocta said. "Now that they have pinpointed our location, they can certainly figure where we go, despite our defenses. We cannot become invisible, even if we use Concealment, nor are we invincible, and there are few of us and many of them. Let's get to the Council-house as fast as we can, for they won't enter there."

The group picked up speed, Creed and Duri with bows at the ready and Stolen and Cardon with machetes drawn. Andor grabbed Stolen's Twig Being by a spindly arm and supported it as she went, allowing Stolen a bit more mental freedom; the thing trotted along next to her without protest. Kwistocta set up a Protection around them, ceding the lead to Hyphanden; the Skill appeared as a translucent wave that traveled out ahead and to the sides of them, and Rudon kept it up to the rear of them as well. Once again, Rioletta felt at a loss, for she had no such Skills to contribute.

"It is only a Shock-wave, easy enough to maintain," Kwistocta said. "It will throw them back if it strikes them, but won't cause more serious damage."

The group rounded another corner at a trot, and Rioletta began to feel an odd rhythmic pulsing in her ears. In another block, it resolved into a sound: a steady, deep thrumming click. In a few more blocks, they entered an open plaza, and directly across from them was their destination and the source of the sound.

The Council-house, easily identifiable because of its typical multi-storied long-house style, faced them from across the plaza. It was as ornate as the Tabor Council-house, but of slightly different form, a large and solid building with flying buttresses and spires on each corner, and friezes and bas relieves decorating the upper walls.

A single narrow doorway was visible at ground level, and in front of it swung a giant pendulum, the timekeeper of a huge multi-dialed clock mounted upon the face of the building. The pendulum clicked at each upstroke, then swung with startling speed, as if propelled, down to its zenith just a foot from the ground. The circumference of the pendulum was carved into scimitar-like blades, and they appeared to be honed to a sharp edge. Between each stroke, the door was visible for only a few seconds.

They ran across the plaza with a horseshoe of Hyolonal behind them, many hundreds now, although they kept a set distance and did not press an attack. As they ran, Kwistocta dropped the Protection, and threw another Skill forward. The Council-house door popped open, swinging inward.

"Time your entry well!" Hyphanden yelled. "Rioletta, you first. Stolen, Cardon, Andor, can you get the Twig Being in?"

Rioletta ran full speed at the door. As the pendulum clicked to one side, she ran through and staggered into an antechamber on the other side. She barely stopped herself before she ran headlong into a wall. Stolen followed, and then his Twig Being, propelled by Andor as well as pulled mentally by Stolen. Cardon and Andor followed together, running into each other at the door, so the pendulum swung down close behind them. Kwistocta was next, then Nikal, Duri, Creed, Hyphanden, and finally, after several swings more, Rudon. The door shut with a snap. All of them stood in the antechamber, catching their breath.

"Not hard to get by, if you pay attention, but the Hyolonal can't open the door remotely, and won't risk squeezing up against the building to give it a try while that pendulum rushes by behind them," Hyphanden said with a grin.

"What keeps it going? Is it a Skill?" Rioletta wondered, looking up at the ceiling of the antechamber, from which the clicking of the pendulum and clock machinery could be heard.

"It's an ancient Skill of some type plus a Technology, plates that gather the energy of the sun and cause the expansion of fluid in enclosed pipes," Hyphanden said. "I've examined the machinery myself, but that's all I know about it. The plates haven't been salvaged because of the Protections of the building."

Kwistocta was staring at the door. "I don't like it," she said bluntly. "I've never seen that many Hyolonal all gathered in one place. There were several hundred around us by the time we arrived. It will be hard to get back out again, if they're still there. We'll have to be prepared to fight, and several of us may end up incapacitated or weak after the Crypt. I'd like to know what's going on."

Hyphanden shook his head. "We'll cross that bridge when we get to it. We can probably escape, although I'd prefer not to cause too much carnage amongst the Hyolonal. If we have to, we'll hole up here for a while and try to send a message for help. Rudon is adept at Protections as well, and should be able to keep us secure, right, Rudon?"

Rudon smiled. "I'm sure I can think of something. But now we have a task at hand."

Hyphanden nodded. "Yes. Let's start by setting a few extra Protections here, just in case. Cardon, draw a few horses, or whatever you've been practicing, and leave them to guard the entry."

"I'll put up a Bell Skill," Rudon said. "That way we'll know if anyone comes through the doorway, and Cardon or I can wake the horses remotely."

Cardon pulled several charcoal pencils from the pocket of his Mahquant vest and began drawing horses upon the walls of the antechamber. They were not like the horses he had previously drawn, though; these ones had long, sinuous necks, sharp teeth, and claws rather than hooves. Last he added eyes, with slit pupils like a snake's. Even without animation, they were frightening enough in appearance that some might be dissuaded from passing them.

The building was lit by sconces arranged along the walls at regular intervals. They glowed with enough light to make navigating the hallways reasonable. Hyphanden led the way out of the antechamber and down a staircase to a broad basement; it was furnished as a lounge, with none of the décor disturbed. The

Council-members might have left the day before; Rioletta did not notice even a layer of dust on the tabletops or bookshelves.

At the far end of the lounge were several similar-looking doors. Hyphanden chose one and opened it. It led to a small chamber that appeared to be a bedroom or sleep-in study, although there were no personal items visible within it.

Hyphanden paused in the doorway. "Stay back," he commanded. "Rudon, come here. You've never been further than this; I'll show you how to break this Protection."

Rudon stepped forward with a grin and stood beside Hyphanden. To their right, within the doorjamb, was a tiny opening with a sphere that appeared to be floating on its own. Hyphanden touched it lightly with a finger, and it sparked momentarily. Then he flicked it upwards and an entire section of the doorjamb scrolled into the ceiling. Revealed behind it was a plate with a series of indentations; Hyphanden touched several of these in some sort of order, then waited while the jamb snapped down into place again. In a few seconds the entire bedroom began to re-arrange itself; all of the furniture folded itself up, stood itself on end, or moved to one side or another.

"I imagine this was a guard room," Hyphanden said. "Someone would have been assigned to remain here at all hours of the day."

He strode into the room and waved his hand in the approximate shape of a square, with Rudon right behind him looking on intently. A line appeared on the floor, outlining a door. In a moment the door sagged inwards and became a set of stairs. As soon as it appeared solid, Hyphanden stepped down upon it and the rest followed him. Rioletta glanced back as she descended and noticed that the hatch above them was barely visible, shimmering as though they were underwater. The entry to the stairs had readjusted itself to become a Concealment behind them.

As they went down, it became darker and darker, until Andor announced she would find a light.

"Don't bother," Kwistocta said. "No light penetrates this dark. It is a Dark Skill of some type, which we don't have the knowledge to break. We have to go on by feel. Reach above your head and you'll find a rail on the ceiling. Run a hand along it; the walls fall away into hallways and chambers on either side. If you can't reach the rail, hold onto someone in front of you," she added, as Andor snorted. Andor and Stolen were the shortest in the group, besides the Twig Being.

Rioletta reached up and found the rail. It was thin and cool beneath her fingers. It seemed to hover just below the low ceiling. She ran her hand lightly along it as they went, her other hand out in front to protect her in case the person in front of her stopped short.

They continued on for a while in this manner. From time to time a breath of cold air seemed to indicate an opening into another passageway or room. Occasionally the air gusted out with a strange hollow sound like the exhalation of some giant beast. Several times they passed glowing colored shapes that Kwistocta told them were Protected doorways into other chambers and halls. Rioletta heard small sounds, too; she tried to tell herself it was only rats and mice.

It was hard to judge distance in the dark, and their speed had slowed, but eventually Creed announced he was sure they had come much farther than the length of the building above them.

"I'm sure we have," Hyphanden said. "This warren of rooms and halls is completely underground; I have little idea what is in most of them. We've managed to break the Protections on a few of them and discovered everything from rooms of unintelligible files to strange devices and objects. There's years of discovery in this place; enough to last me the rest of my life. It's one of my favorite places to explore. I discovered the directions to get to the Crypt in amongst the books of the turret at our estate. Kwistocta has been here too, although Rudon has not."

"Despite my being part of the Inner Circle," Rudon grumbled. "That will change, though, now."

"We turn here," Hyphanden warned. They turned to the right, and Hyphanden opened a plain-looking stone door lit with a dull overhead light with a simple Unlocking Skill. It opened soundlessly and slowly, and a curious odor emanated from within. The group stepped into the chamber, and the door silently closed behind them. Lights rose slowly until the chamber was reasonably well illuminated.

It was a fairly small room. There were a few stools along the right-hand wall, and disconcertingly, what appeared to be a pile of bones in one corner. There was also an odd-looking wall to their left, with the appearance of an off-white wax with large hexagonal scores etched into it. The wall of wax stopped just short of the corner of the room, and within the small space between it and the corner was a square of metal about a foot long with a single circular indentation in it.

Both Rioletta and Nikal were aware of what they were looking at; Nikal had Viewed it and described it to Rioletta. The wall was the Crypt itself; the square was the lock into which the parts of the key had to be inserted.

"What else did you discover from the book?" Nikal asked Hyphanden as they stood looking.

"Nothing," Hyphanden said grimly. He removed the book from his satchel and handed it to Nikal. "I know only what you know, now, other than the fact that I could read Likendahl's glyph at the end and thus confirmed that the book belonged to him personally at one time. We will have to guess how to apply the potion. And I did not discover what the Index to which the book refers is; there is only a Table of Contents in the book. However, it shouldn't be necessary in order to retrieve the Younger Council. I know where I put them, and Cardon will be able to feel them."

"Let's prepare, then, if you're all ready," Kwistocta said, looking at Cardon.

Cardon swallowed visibly and stepped forward to Kwistocta. She pointed to one of the stools, and he sat down upon it, face pallid in the half-light. Nikal sat on another stool, opened the book on his lap, and removed the key, which he handed to Rioletta. In turn, she opened it to reveal the small tools and six sides and handed the parts to Creed.

Kwistocta removed a packet of the salve from her satchel. She pulled on a pair of snug leather gloves and unwrapped the packet slowly and carefully. Once it was open, she extended it to Cardon.

"Take some and rub it into the palms of your hands," she instructed. Cardon did so without hesitation.

"Duri, you must take a very small amount as well, and remember all we have taught you in the past two weeks."

Duri rubbed his fingers in the paste, and then rubbed it into his palms vigorously. Kwistocta carefully re-wrapped the remainder of the salve and stowed it in her satchel.

"What next?" Andor asked nervously.

"Now we wait," Kwistocta said. "It will take a half-hour or so for the potion to enter Cardon's system, and I think we should not open the Crypt until that time. We'll want to do what we need to do quickly and get it closed again."

She sat down upon a third stool, close to Cardon, and rubbed his back in a comforting manner. Cardon sat silent, occasionally glancing at the palms of his hands or rubbing them together as though he still felt the potion upon them. Duri sat upon another stool, his dark eyes darting from one to another of the party. Rudon stood in a corner, watching them both, bouncing restlessly on his toes. Rioletta, unable to relax, watched each of them in turn. The thought crossed her mind that it could be the last time she would see Cardon alive; she was unconvinced that he was strong enough to withstand this ordeal. She pushed the thought away as quickly as she could.

Chapter Twelve

As time wore on, Cardon became restless. His eyelids began to droop and his breathing became audible. Finally Kwistocta looked up at Hyphanden.

"It's time. He is fully under the influence of the drug now."

Kwistocta helped Cardon up. Duri stood up himself; he seemed slightly unstable, but fully in control.

"Now we have to use the Key in the correct sequence," Nikal said. "Creed, are you ready?"

Creed nodded. He examined all the little parts again.

Nikal took a deep breath and concentrated on the pages of the book. In a moment he began to speak mechanically. Slowly, he described what he saw.

"There should be a disk with a circle cut out of the middle. Silver, with a bluish sheen and inscriptions upon it. Place that in the indentation on the plate."

Creed quickly inserted the disk, and a tiny square hole appeared below it. Nikal directed him to place the end of one of the tools in the hole and pump it up and down. There was click, and a door on the plate swung open, revealing other indentations and holes. Nikal explained which tool to use in what order. Where he encountered directions that referenced one of the six plants, Rioletta referred to her notes and chose the correct notched side of the card for Creed. The sides were slid through or pressed into slots in the lock.

Finally Nikal looked up. "Those are all of the directions," he announced. All of them stared at the wall, but for a moment nothing happened.

The hexagonal shapes etched into the surface seemed to rotate, the surface began to clear and then slowly disappeared altogether, revealing open cells underneath. Creed stepped back quickly. Some of these cells appeared to be filled with a golden, viscous material.

Kwistocta turned Cardon to the wall and moved him to one side, holding him by the shoulders.

"Cardon," Kwistocta whispered, "concentrate on the calls you hear from Marsavrina. Invite her into your mind. Find her here in the matrix before you."

Cardon staggered slightly, and reached out for the wall, but Kwistocta quickly knocked his hand down. A moment later, one of the cells seemed to shimmer, and the golden ooze within it began to run out. As it did it vaporized, becoming a golden haze. The haze floated towards Cardon, then slowly disappeared as it reached him. Rioletta saw him shudder, and he continued to shake violently as though he was cold.

"Good!" Kwistocta said. "Now call Skadar. I will help you; I am still strong. We will not abandon you. Find him and take him into your mind."

Cardon opened his eyes slightly, and began to scan the wall slowly. For a few minutes, nothing happened. Then another cell began to ooze forward and vaporize. Cardon turned towards it, and accepted the golden mist as it floated towards him. His knees began to buckle, but Kwistocta held him firmly.

"Malbec and Chasandahl!" she commanded. "They are only part-minds, they will not be so much. Find them!"

This time there was a long pause; then almost as one, two cells deteriorated into mist. A moment later, Kwistocta turned Cardon around sharply by the shoulders to face the group.

"Duri!" she cried. Hyphanden, who had been standing next to Duri, yanked him forward to Cardon. Duri wore a blank look now; the drug was obviously affecting him.

Kwistocta and Hyphanden grouped closely together with Duri and Cardon, all of them touching one another. Duri struggled briefly, and a golden mist seemed to hover around them. Then it was gone and Duri staggered back, his eyes wide.

In a moment he regained his balance and focus. Andor grabbed his arm and led him to one of the vacant stools and ordered him to sit. He sat down obediently, and Andor crouched beside him. Rioletta glanced only briefly at them; she concentrated on Cardon, hoping to help him with her own mind.

Stolen brought the Twig Person forward. "This will be more difficult," Hyphanden muttered to Kwistocta. Cardon stood still, head back, shaking, Kwistocta supporting his shoulders. Hyphanden took Cardon's hands and placed them in the area of the Twig Person's shoulders.

"You have to explain this, Cardon," he said. "You have to let Marsavrina and Skadar know they cannot stay in your mind. They must go into this being in order to gain independence. They must share for now, but it's better than where they have been."

Cardon seemed to be struggling. His jaw clenched and he alternately opened and closed his eyes. But the golden mist appeared again, hovered, then disappeared into the Twig Being as though sucked in.

The Twig Being leaped backwards and ran into a corner of the room. Stolen staggered away with a cry and clutched his head. Hyphanden darted after the Twig Being and restrained it in the corner, crying out to Marsavrina and Skadardahl. Creed jumped to help him, and Nikal grabbed Stolen, who fell to his knees.

Rioletta leaped to catch Cardon as he crumpled to the ground. Kwistocta supported him, but he slumped over, unconscious. Rioletta rolled him onto his back, and she and Kwistocta knelt beside him.

"Cardon!" Rioletta cried, shaking his shoulders. Even in the dim light, she could see he was deathly pale. She bent closer to him; she could feel no breath. She tilted his head back; it was well known that unconscious people sometimes failed to breathe due to the position of head and neck. But he still did not draw breath.

Kwistocta took his wrist and then felt his neck. "His heart beats yet, but it is slow and it will not continue if he does not breathe. I'm afraid the dose of poison coupled with his weakened state may have been too much for him. The only antidote I have is in liquid form; if we pour it into his mouth now, he will not be able to swallow it; it may run into his lungs."

Rioletta opened her satchel and rummaged in it until she found a small packet. It was Adla's antidote for the sleeping potion she'd given to Cardon in Dobor.

Rioletta opened the packet. It was dry, and beginning to crumble.

"Quick, Kwistocta! Use some of your liquid antidote and your glove to mix this paste," she demanded. Kwistocta brought out a small vial and moistened the paste, then mixed it with her gloved hand. Without direction, she pulled Cardon's mouth open and rubbed some of the paste along his gums and under his tongue.

At first there was no response, but then Cardon took a long, gasping breath. He began to breathe slowly on his own as Rioletta held his head. A small amount of color began to return to his cheeks.

"Perhaps a little more," Kwistocta said, rubbing some more of the paste into his mouth. Cardon breathed more regularly. His eyes opened, although they remained unfocused, and he turned his head away when Kwistocta tried to open his mouth again. Rioletta brought out the tablets Adla had given her, and spoke to him sharply.

"Cardon! Open your mouth and swallow this tablet! Do as I say."

Kwistocta pulled Cardon to a sitting position. Rioletta held Kwistocta's liquid to his lips and Cardon reluctantly swallowed a small amount with a shudder. Then she forced a tablet into his mouth and he swallowed it down, choking a little. He remained sitting on his own; the antidote appeared to be working.

Rioletta relaxed a bit and glanced around the room. Everyone had been watching as Cardon struggled for breath; now they began to turn their attention to each other.

"Are you all right, Stolen?" Andor asked.

Stolen nodded. "It was quite painful," he admitted. "It was as if something was ripped away from my brain, as if someone I cared about suddenly disappeared. But I am feeling better now; there is only an emptiness. The Twig Being is quite gone from me."

The group turned to where Creed and Hyphanden stood in the corner with the thing that was now Marsavrina/Skadar. It looked around at them with small sparkling black and amber eyes, and it seemed there was knowledge within them.

"Marsavrina, are you there?" Hyphanden asked.

The being turned quickly to him and looked him in the face. Then it nodded once.

"And Skadar?"

Once again, the being nodded. Then it fastened its eyes on Duri, who had risen unsteadily and approached it. Duri stared back at the unblinking black eyes.

"The minds of Malbec and Chasandahl are within me," Duri said hoarsely. "They are more complete than perhaps you knew, Hyphanden. I hold them separate for now; but eventually I will be able to speak their messages."

"Then we are in better shape than I thought we might be," Hyphanden said. "We have only to see if we can bring Cardon to full consciousness, and then we can at least retire to an upstairs room to rest. But we can take our time now."

"I don't think so," Creed said. "How do you close this thing?"

Hyphanden spun around, and Kwistocta jumped to her feet. The Crypt of Souls stood fully open, many cells filled with gold. The minds were restless; they pulsed and oozed, some of them now hanging over the lips of their cells. And in front of them stood Rudon, arms raised, eyes blazing, a cloud of golden mist hovering around his head and entire body.

"Rudon! No!" Hyphanden shouted. He lunged for Rudon, but pulled himself up short before touching the cloud.

"Creed! Run the key in reverse!" he shouted. Creed took a single long step to the lock, but as he did so, the cloud began to move in his direction.

Hyphanden stepped between Rudon and Creed. "Nikal! Can you View the directions?"

Nikal had already grabbed the book, but his concentration was broken. He fell to his knees on the floor and opened the book with shaking hands.

But he did not need to View it. Creed, ignoring the battle of wills that erupted between Hyphanden, Rudon, and the golden mist beside him, efficiently and quickly ran the entire sequence in reverse, without a mistake. A moment later, the cells began to cloud over; the restless ooze pulled back inside, and the wall regained its solid form, only the etched hexagons revealing the matrix within it.

The remainder of the minds were trapped, but the ones that had turned to mist were outside the matrix, and hovered between Rudon and Hyphanden as though frozen. Kwistocta jumped to her husband's side, but as she did, Rudon suddenly threw his arms forward. The mist rushed towards Hyphanden and Kwistocta as though released, and in a moment it had disappeared into them. Both of them staggered, and Hyphanden fell to the floor.

Rudon leaped past them towards the door, which swung open at his command. Creed ran for him and drew his machete, but Rudon darted out the door, turned quickly, and threw his arms forward. Creed tumbled back into the room in a back somersault, and regained his feet just as the door slammed.

"Leave him!" Hyphanden ordered. He had regained his feet and was standing with one hand on his knee, the other on the wall. "Do you have the book?"

"Yes," Nikal replied. "He did not try to take it."

"He thinks he will have access to it later; why risk himself, the coward?" Hyphanden said with a grimace. "Creed, are you all right?"

"I'm fine," Creed replied.

"I'm not sure why," Hyphanden said. "That was more than just a Blocking Skill Rudon Threw at you; it could have killed you and all of us in here, but you seemed to absorb it. Do you have some Protection on you?"

Creed shook his head, but Rioletta's hand went to her talisman, where the strange amplifier from the museum district hung.

"Hyphanden, Kwistocta, what happened?" Nikal demanded. "Are you both all right?"

"I have had several minds enter into my own; whose, I know not, but I have set up a temporary block," Hyphanden replied. "It was already prepared; remember, I held the mind of Marsavrina and the partial mind of Malbec within my own for several days."

"And I have similarly partitioned my mind," Kwistocta winced as she gained control of herself. "Perhaps we will be able to return here and replace these minds in the matrix, but right now I think we should move from this room. I suspect Rudon's strange control over the Hyolonal has been explained; he's managed to create some alliance with them. It's likely he'll soon let them in to loot the Council-house, and we must be in a position of defense by then." Creed and Nikal went to Cardon and hauled him to his feet, where he stood shaking. Rioletta got him to swallow another of the tablets, followed by the rest of Kwistocta's remedy.

"How shall we go?" Nikal asked. "Are you well enough to lead us?"

"Yes," Hyphanden said. "Unfortunately, I'm not familiar enough with this underground network to suggest we try and escape or hide along here. We'll have to go back to the ground floor; from there we can access the upper levels of the Council-house and the roof, where I think we'll be safer and have the upper hand. The Council-house is attached by an arched bridge to another building; it's probably unstable, but might prove a means of escape."

Kwistocta opened the door and let Hyphanden through first. Creed and Nikal took turns supporting Cardon. Rioletta grasped Duri by the hand and led him along, and Andor took the Twig Being by the arm. Stolen was able to follow along on his own.

Once the door closed behind them, they were left in the dark to traverse the long hall, which slanted slightly uphill. Rioletta staggered along uncertainly with one hand on the rail and the other still leading Duri. Occasionally she bumped into Cardon or Nikal. They listened for sounds of the Hyolonal or Rudon, but heard nothing. Finally they climbed the steps to the guardroom, and cautiously entered it. Hyphanden took the time to return the room to normal, to at least temporarily protect the lower chambers from the Hyolonal. From there they crossed the long open library and rose to the antechamber where the exterior door was located.

Just as they entered the antechamber, a silence descended on the room. The clock with its pendulum had stopped. A moment later, the door burst open.

At first, no one came through the door. Hyphanden pointed to a staircase leading up from the opposite side of the chamber. Kwistocta ran to it, and Rioletta pushed Duri ahead of her. But as they gained the staircase, Hyolonal flooded into the room, yelling and brandishing spears and sticks. They saw the group on the steps and surged forward.

Nikal, Hyphanden, and Cardon all turned at the same moment, and all three of them Threw the animation Skill at Cardon's horses. Cardon's Skill leaped out ahead, then gained energy from the other two and slammed into the wall and the drawings. It rolled back over itself in a visible crest like a translucent wave and flowed back into the room.

The horses leapt off the wall and shook themselves into three dimensions. With a roar, each horse snaked its sinuous neck around, peered down at the Hyolonal cowering beneath it, and began to slash back and forth with teeth and claws, slit-pupiled eyes glowing.

The Hyolonal scattered with screams. More of them, piling in through the door, blocked the egress of the first ones, and it quickly became a scene of chaos and carnage.

The group had paused on the stairs, hoping the Hyolonal would be quickly vanquished. But now Nikal began to urge them onward.

"We'd better go fast! Leave the horses!"

"What's the matter?" Rioletta asked.

"The animation Skill was too powerful! It splashed all over the room. Look!"

A chair joined the fray, bashing itself to splinters against the onslaught of Hyolonal. Several paperweights threw themselves through the air, books flew off the shelves, and pens and pencil streaked around like darts. One of them barely missed Creed, who ducked just in time. The group turned and fled up the stairs, but it seemed the effect was following them: in the next room, a paperweight rocked restlessly on a desk, and an illustrated book of plants, open on a desk, began to spew vicious thistles.

"Rudon's fault," Hyphanden gasped as he took two steps at a time. "He probably put a Protective Skill over Cardon's drawings to keep them from responding to the Animation. But he didn't expect three of us to Throw at them at the same time. We overpowered his Skill, but it caused splashback. So other objects are becoming animated in ripples. We can hope it will become too weak at the edges to continue."

The group wound up and up, past the main audience hall, through several stories of bedrooms, living spaces, and offices, until at last Hyphanden threw open a door and they came out onto a flat roof. The roof was half-covered with what had at one time been a garden; the other half included the sun-plates and machinery to run the giant clock, which was affixed to the side of the building and towered above the roofline. The pendulum hovered at a strange angle, as though frozen in mid-swing. It seemed to strain restlessly to move again, the gleaming upper balance twitching as though alive.

On the opposite side of the roof, a graceful bridge built in a high narrow arch lifted dizzyingly into the air, spanned several hundred yards, and finally ended halfway up a tall, narrow structure that shone like polished brass in the sun.

"Make for the bridge!" Hyphanden ordered. He turned aside and ran to the machinery behind the clock. Kwistocta led the others to the span, but the arch did not appear stable. It was obvious that parts of it had given way and dropped to the pavement a hundred feet below. There were gaping holes in the pathway and in the walls enclosing the bridge.

Kwistocta threw open the gate before the bridge, and the group paused there, turning to meet any Hyolonal who might come up the stairs behind them. Rioletta stood behind Creed, wishing she had some weapon or Skill she could use to help. Kwistocta began rapidly working a Supportive Skill, casting it up the bridge, where it rolled forward further with each gesture like an unfurling carpet.

Hyphanden worked at the machinery. With a loud clunk, the exposed gears began to turn again. There were screams from below as the down-rushing blade of the pendulum caught a few of the Hyolonal, and on the upswing drops of blood were flung into the air and splattered on the rooftop. But many Hyolonal were already inside; a number of them appeared at the top of the staircase and piled through the door. Hyphanden threw a Blocking Skill at them and ran to join the others.

"That should deter any others from entering, at least in the short term," he panted. "No doubt Rudon promised them they could salvage the Council-house if they helped him, and if they kill us, they can have our estate as well. But I'm loathe to give it up easily; there are many books stored here we haven't deciphered yet."

Rioletta saw more Hyolonal appear on the roof. At least some had managed to avoid the horses and the pendulum. They approached cautiously, spears leveled, hiding behind machinery and retaining walls.

She felt a slap on her arm, and turned to Duri. "Here," he said. "If worse comes to worse, do what you can to defend yourself. Do not worry about me."

He handed her a knife, sharp and curved and with a hilt that fit Rioletta's hand easily. He held another himself. She was unfamiliar with using knives for anything but cutting vegetables, but she gripped it firmly and it gave her some sense of security.

"Cardon! Call your horses!" Nikal cried. Cardon had not yet spoken a word; but at Nikal's direction, he turned and raised a hand. In a few moments, shouting could be heard from the stairwell; no further Hyolonal appeared, but the toothed horses leapt out onto the roof. They bore down upon the Hyolonal, who scattered in chaos, some fleeing back down the stairs, others throwing spears and slinging rocks, and still others racing towards the group huddled at the doorway to the unstable arch.

Hyphanden and Nikal both Threw Blocking Skills, and the Hyolonal tumbled about, spears, rocks, and slings flying here and there. Some fell completely over the edge of the roof and disappeared. The horses, however, appeared to see the Sorcerers for the first time, and as if developing a new target, they lunged across the roof in their direction.

"Cardon! Call them off!" Nikal shouted. Cardon raised his hands again, but the horses did not respond.

"It's not working!" Hyphanden yelled. "Rudon's influence! We will have to take the bridge after all! Quick, and cross it as fast as you can! There's no telling how long we'll be able to keep it stable!"

Kwistocta turned and fled up the narrow roofed bridge, which was wide enough to accommodate only a single file. Rioletta followed, with the Twig Being close behind. But the horses were already upon them; one of them reached the edge of the roof, whipped its sinuous neck around, and grabbed Andor by the elbow. Its teeth sank to bone, and it lifted her bodily. Andor screamed and flailed for the knife at her belt with her other hand, but the creature shook her back and forth like a terrier with a rat.

Creed leapt forward with his machete raised, and brought it down on the creature's neck with a force that should have severed its head. A great rent appeared on its neck, but no blood showed. The horse snapped its head around, and seeing Creed, dropped

Stolen: Crypt of Souls

Andor on the very edge of the roof. She rolled quickly to her feet and scrambled away from the edge; but within a few paces she staggered and fell in a faint, blood streaming from her arm.

Creed hacked again at the beast's neck, and Stolen and Cardon joined him with their own machetes. Several other horses joined the attack, and the three could only swing wildly at them with the heavy blades. Rioletta ran back down the bridge, but Hyphanden blocked her way.

Creed ducked under the neck of the first horse and reached Andor. He gathered her up easily in his arms, and made for the arch.

When Creed was inside, stumbling sideways along the span with Andor in his arms, Cardon and Stolen broke off their defense and raced for the gate. As soon as they were safe within, Hyphanden slammed the gate, and they fled along the passageway, the sound and vibration of bodies slamming into the bridge abutment following them.

The noise and swaying were terrifying, but the bridge held for all of them to cross. At the far end, they gathered in a small room in the metallic building to which the span was attached. Rioletta fought to get her breath; she still held Duri's knife clutched in her hand.

A moment later, the wall of the building ripped away as the span fell behind them. Sharp shards of metal rained down among them, and they were forced to run again as the floor crumbled and the ceiling followed.

They reached an interior room where they could pause at least briefly. Creed laid Andor down on the floor, and Cardon and Rioletta knelt down beside her immediately.

"Now we have need of Rudon," Hyphanden said bitterly.

Andor's left arm was obviously broken in at least two places, the upper and the lower, and great fang marks marred it. She was pale and unresponsive. Rioletta examined the arm as best she could.

"What is our plan now?" she asked. "Are we safe here? Can we summon help and wait?"

"No!" Hyphanden said. "Undoubtedly Rudon, wherever he is, will induce the Hyolonal to enter this building from the bottom and search for us in here. This is not a building under any kind of Protection, as far as I know; from here we must go down to the street and go from building to building into the center of town, and from there work our way back to the estates. I know of no other passage."

"I do," Kwistocta said quietly.

Hyphanden turned quickly to her, with a look of alarm on his face.

"Kwistocta! No! Don't try and access information from those you hold in your mind! You don't know who they may be; it's far too dangerous."

Kwistocta knelt by Andor. "Bind her arm up as best you can for now. We will carry her until we arrive at a safe place where we can treat her more effectively. Do it quickly and follow me."

Chapter Thirteen

Rioletta and Cardon quickly bandaged Andor's arm, using strips of cloth hurriedly torn from Cardon's and Duri's undershirts. Then they helped position her so Creed could carry her more easily, partially over his shoulder, with one of his arms supporting her under the legs. Andor had become more responsive, but she still was very pale, and did not speak. She laid her head on Creed's shoulder, but her eyes remained open, and she was able to hold on to Creed with her good arm.

Rioletta took Andor's satchel and Stolen took Creed's bows and arrows. Kwistocta led them silently and swiftly through the deteriorating building, following the information she accessed from the minds she had absorbed at the Crypt.

"Hyphanden, how many minds do you hold?" Nikal asked as they ran. Hyphanden was beginning to look worn, and stumbled repeatedly on blocks on the floor.

"Four, but two of them are less than complete," Hyphanden gasped. "Kwistocta holds three, and they are whole."

"Cannot you simply expel them, without putting them into anything?" Nikal asked.

"We could, but that would be the end of them forever. Remember, these are minds that have been stored for more than a hundred years, and we know not who they are. I dislike the thought

155

of simply killing them. I've been seeking for years the kind of information these minds undoubtedly contain; but it's true that if we can't return to the Crypt, or find some suitable receptor for these minds, we may have to simply let them go or force them out. And we have limited time; neither of us dared sleep when we stored Marsavrina and the Younger Council, for fear that the partitions in our minds would break down. We have greater experience than we did then; still, it would be very difficult."

Kwistocta stopped suddenly at a wall. They had descended several floors. Through the windows, Rioletta could see Hyolonal beginning to gather near the entry to the building. The wall did not appear any different from any other wall in the building, but Rioletta guessed it was a Concealment, and when she concentrated upon it she could break through the Skill. Kwistocta passed a hand in front of it; there was in fact a narrow door. She stepped through it, and the rest followed.

They had entered the interior of a wide wall and followed along inside, surrounded by struts and joists. Rioletta pulled a light out of her satchel and found another in Andor's, which she handed to Duri. There was no Dark Skill here, and the lights were sufficient to show their way. Kwistocta took the bends and turns unerringly, choosing one offshoot and then another, until eventually they arrived at a dead end. She opened another door and they stepped out into a room different in appearance from the ones in the previous building.

"We are now in the next building over," she said. "The walls are connected between the buildings at certain points, although it is difficult to see from the ground due to the perspective. They were built that way on purpose, to conceal the connection. The purpose was to provide an escape route for the Council-members from the Council-house to the Security House near the center of the city."

Hyphanden took her by the arm. "Kwistocta! Confine yourself to accessing vital information only. Do not let any of the rest of it leak into your mind!"

But Kwistocta pulled her arm away and hurried through the room into a hallway. The others struggled to keep up; she was nearly running, and Creed readjusted Andor in his arms, the sweat streaming down his face. There was no breath of air in this building, which seemed sealed very tight, and the July heat was stifling.

156

Ahead of them, a rug slid back onto itself in a series of wrinkles, and a hatch outlined itself in the floor. Through this they descended along a narrow staircase, from there into another wall space, and so they traveled, following Kwistocta through seven buildings, descending a floor or two in each. Doors and passageways were concealed through Skills and tricks of perspective; in one case, Kwistocta stepped confidently out onto what appeared to be thin air. The span over which she walked had been Concealed so it appeared the same as the environment around it. Rioletta gritted her teeth and forced herself to follow in Kwistocta's footsteps, not looking from side to side.

Finally they entered a huge ground-floor cart-house where their footsteps echoed unnervingly on the smooth stone floor. They crammed themselves into a tiny room on one side, and at Kwistocta's command it moved down several floors. When the door opened, they followed an underground passageway for a distance Rioletta estimated to be nearly a mile, stopping once to allow Creed to rest.

Along this passageway rooms and halls shot off at various angles. Kwistocta passed them all, until she chose a particular hall and a door that led them up a flight of stairs. At the top of the flight was a series of doors, which she opened easily. The final door opened into a large chamber set with desks and cabinets.

"The Security House, from which Guards were dispatched," Kwistocta said curtly. "We are now in the central part of the city. From here we should be able to send a message. But whom can we trust?"

"Anyone," Hyphanden replied. "I will try the rest of the Council. I don't believe any of them are involved in this; certainly not all. We can hope that if some are, the ones who support us will overpower those who do not."

"No!" Kwistocta warned him. "Send a specific message to a chosen person. If you send a message to all the Council, Rudon will receive it as well."

"Of course," Hyphanden said, looking shaken. He pulled out a talisman on a cord around his neck, similar to the one Rioletta wore to contact Nikal, with a small metal disk strung next to it. He stood silent for a moment, holding it enclosed within one hand. His eyes closed, and he nodded a few times.

157

Then he opened his eyes. "I have received a return message from Cayondahl of the Second Chosen, and Lastravrina, who is with him. They will gather horses and come to our aid. They will also contact Kerdahl and the others at the bachelor's estate. Cayon is a Healer; that will be well."

"Should we wait here?" Rioletta asked, "Or should we continue in their direction?"

"Wait," Hyphanden said. "I suspect that is safer. Unless Kwistocta knows otherwise."

Kwistocta sat down heavily on an upholstered chair. Her eyes looked blank. Hyphanden stared at her in obvious concern, his hands knotted, but he did not go to her or touch her, and when Rioletta made a move to comfort her, he waved her away.

"Do not touch her. It is too dangerous. Do not touch me, either."

Kwistocta closed her eyes, and appeared to be deep in concentration.

Cardon and Rioletta made Andor as comfortable as they could on the floor, supported by Creed's legs. Then Cardon and Duri found armchairs to rest in. After a quick look around, Nikal approached a series of glass-fronted cabinets along one wall and motioned Rioletta to come over. Inside were firearms, both long guns and handguns, arranged in sets of three, as though stored by a particular guard, or intended to be handed to one upon check-out.

"I wonder why they didn't take these when they left?" he said. "They would be valuable and useful. There appears to be a strong Protection on them, or I would take them myself to use now."

"There are many things we don't understand about the Dispersal," Hyphanden said, glancing briefly at Nikal before returning his gaze to Kwistocta. "We can't break those Protections, or I would give you access to the firearms."

Rioletta jumped at a small noise from the corner, and Cardon and Duri started up, but it was only the creaking of an old building. Every small noise made them nervous as they waited in the silence.

Finally, Hyphanden leapt up. "They are here," he announced. "Cayon signals me."

Creed gathered Andor up, and they followed Hyphanden and Kwistocta through the hall to the front door, a great heavy affair of hammered metal. The door swung outward to reveal a large courtyard.

Directly before the door were a number of mounted Sorcerers. Several of them held bows, arrows nocked, pointed directly at the stunned group in the doorway. Others wielded knives or raised short, knobby sticks, which Rioletta had occasionally seen used as an aid to Throwing a Skill.

"What are you doing?" Hyphanden shouted angrily. "We are wounded and exhausted and need your help!"

Cayondahl, in the front, slowly lowered his bow, and the others followed suit, although they looked around suspiciously.

"I'm sorry, Hyphanden, but we weren't sure what was going on. We gathered as many Sorcerers as we could and rode to your estate to gather your mounts and those of your guests, as you requested. But as we traveled here, I received a private message from Rorudon via my talisman. Rudon told me you had been set upon by Hyolonal during your mission, and that several of your group had been killed. He said any message I might receive from you was undoubtedly a trick and I should disregard it. I couldn't conceive who could manage such a trick; your voice is distinctive. So we ignored his warnings and rode here, but I couldn't in good conscience allow these people to meet you without some self-protection."

"Of course, Cayon," Hyphanden said more evenly. "Indeed we were set upon by Hyolonal and nearly killed, but they were under Rudon's guidance. He has betrayed us, and you were right to be suspicious. But now we need your help. I will tell you more along the way."

The riders dismounted and Kerdahl brought the Andolith horses closer. Andor was handed up to Creed after he mounted; his big horse could carry them both easily. Stolen took Marsavrina/Skadar behind him; the Twig Being mounted easily and lightly, as if it had been riding for years. Rioletta took her own horse, still carrying Andor's satchel and Duri's knife. She held the knife more loosely now. Duri had put his into its sheath concealed somewhere on his person, but she had nowhere to store hers safely. They followed Cayon through the courtyard and out into the central city. Hyphanden quickly filled Cayon in on the details of what had occurred.

"We saw no Hyolonal at all during our ride here," Cayon said. "If it is as you say, doubtless they are all gathered near the Council-house. But when they cannot find you there, they may come here in anger. How many did you leave dead?"

"I have no idea," Hyphanden said. "Cardon's horses slew some and our Blocking Skills threw some off the roof and others against the walls hard enough to have killed them. The pendulum may have sliced a few. But as far as numbers, I have no concept. Anyway, it would be stupid of them to attack the estates; we have powerful Protections in place there, unless Rudon has managed to disable them while we were detained. It was he who was with me when we first entered Trophandra's home, my estate, many years ago, and we broke the Protections and set up our own, so he is familiar with them and Skilled at breaking them as well. But we will have the advantage from inside, and we have many Skills we can Throw at them."

"Perhaps," Cayon said, "but it will make our forays into the city more dangerous in the short term at the very least. Hopefully Rudon will take himself somewhere else in disgrace and we won't have to engage him. We will set up a guard around your estate to make sure he can't enter, no matter what he may have done to your Protections in our absence. But there's no law we can bring to bear against him."

"I'll present what I know to the Council at large," Hyphanden said. "We will have him banned from the Council and community; he can take up his position amongst the rogue Outcasts if he wants."

"I wonder what turned him, and how long he's planned this?" Cayon asked.

"I should have been more suspicious of him before," Hyphanden said. "I was aware that he actively recruited the Younger Council to learn the Forbidden Skills. He has always held a grudge against the Elder Council who Outcast him, unlike many of us who have taken the responsibility for our punishment upon ourselves. I now suspect he may have primed the Younger Council to betray the Elders. But I suspect more than that; I believe he used a Forbidden Technology to manipulate them. Perhaps when he learned we intended to free Marsavrina and Skadar, he realized they would tell of his involvement, and the Outcast Council would disapprove and banish him from Hyolon. So he took the opportunity to seize the minds in the Crypt."

"What Technology are you talking about?" Cardon asked. "I saw, as I have told before, that Malbec carried a talisman or other object on his belt the last time I saw him, and that he referred to it constantly. Now that I've seen Duri's mapping device, I know that they resemble one another."

"Yes. I suspect Rudon provided each of the Younger Council with such a device, although geared more to communication than mapping. He used that Technology, coupled with Skills, to manipulate their minds. He may now have retrieved the devices from where the Younger Council lay, and he may be using them with the Hyolonal." Hyphanden shook his head. "I should have confronted him before."

The group rode warily up to the front gate of the estate, and Hyphanden raised his hand. The Concealment faded away as they rode up towards the house. They dismounted at the front; there was no obvious intrusion, and the Protections on the house seemed intact.

One of the Outcasts took Rioletta's reins as she dismounted. "We'll take the horses and set up a guard around the house," Cayon said. "I'll come in with you, though; your friend needs immediate treatment."

As they went through into the great-room, Kwistocta, who was in the lead, stopped suddenly. She turned to face Hyphanden; her eyes rolled up into her head, and she fell to the floor. A moment later her back arched and her breath caught in her throat as she seized.

"Kwistocta!" Hyphanden shouted. He threw himself to the floor, almost on top of her, and grabbed her head in his hands, turning her face to him. She did not respond, but he shouted her name again and commanded her to open her eyes. Rioletta and Cardon rushed to her side and bent over her, unsure what to do.

Her eyes did open, but they were unfocused. Gradually she relaxed somewhat, as Cayon knelt by her side. Hyphanden continued to stare into her eyes.

"Her partitions against the intruding minds have broken down; she accessed them too freely when she led us out of the

Council-house," Hyphanden said. "She hasn't the strength to control them now, and her mind is becoming disordered."

"Hyphanden…" Cayon began, but Hyphanden hushed him harshly.

"There is only one remedy: those minds must be removed from hers," he said. He shook Kwistocta slightly, and her eyes rolled down and met his. Hyphanden let his head drop forward until his forehead touched hers; no one else in the room dared move or speak.

Hyphanden shuddered, but Kwistocta seemed to relax. Then her eyes sprang wide open, fully focused. She leapt to her feet, then crouched next to Hyphanden, who pushed himself slowly to his knees.

"Hyphanden! What have you done?" she demanded. Hyphanden looked up at her with a grim smile.

"I'm doing quite well, better than you would think, with seven extra minds in mine," he said weakly. He planted one foot and rose, adjusted his shirt, and looked around. "Cayon, Andor needs your help immediately. Kwistocta, if you are feeling better, Duri will need help strengthening his partitions. We must also deal with the Twig Being, but that can wait."

Cayon moved to where Creed had laid Andor on a couch, but Kwistocta remained with Hyphanden. She clutched his arm firmly, forcing him to turn to her.

"Hyphanden, you cannot sustain seven minds in your own, especially when they were thrust there with you unprepared. You must cast them out!"

"I surely cannot sustain them," Hyphanden agreed. "I am exhausted and will have to sleep, for one thing. But I am loathe to cast them out. I do not know who they are, only that they have lain imprisoned in the Crypt for at least one hundred years. And one of them gave us access to information that saved our lives; how ungrateful it would be to then expel him into the void forever!"

"But you cannot return them to the Crypt, at least not any time soon," Kwistocta argued. "And there is no one here either strong enough, or properly prepared, to accept them. If your mind collapses under the strain, all of the minds will be wasted, including your own."

"Yes, but recall that Duri also carries the partial minds of Malbec and Chasan. Would you expel them into the void if he cannot keep them? Do we not need a way to keep them safe?"

Hyphanden turned on his heel and strode into the kitchen. He opened a lower cupboard and removed a large wooden box. It was weathered by years of use, waxed and oiled, with tight seams and a hinged lid. He tossed it on a table and then turned to search the cupboards again, pulling out a metal canister of wax.

"What are you going to do?" Nikal asked. He and Rioletta had followed Hyphanden into the kitchen.

"I'm making a Crypt," Hyphanden said shortly.

Nikal stared at him. "Of course! But have you the knowledge?"

"Perhaps," Hyphanden said. "It will not be like the one in the Council-house. But I have read quite a bit about the Crypt in books I've taken from the Council-house and elsewhere. I have some idea of how it was constructed. And I have thought about this before; I almost prepared it before we left, just in case. I should have done so, but at least I have the idea set in my mind. Where is Rioletta?"

Rioletta stepped closer to him. "What do you need?"

"Go to my chambers," Hyphanden ordered. "There you will find many cases of books. There is a set near the window, to the right. You are skilled at reading texts with hidden meanings–bring me the ones marked with the clock with the pendulum. You will have to use your Loremaster Skills upon it, for it cannot be seen on the covers. Those are from the Council-house. I will have you read the passages I need out loud to me. Nikal, I will need you to bring me tools and supplies as I ask for them. Can Cardon help, or is he too weak?"

"I'm here, and getting better every minute," Cardon replied. In fact, he was the only one of them who appeared stronger than he had when they had begun their journey that morning.

"I will need certain plants from the garden," Hyphanden said. "I'll count on you to fetch and prepare them. Here is what we must do: we will use this box as a frame, and build a physical matrix within it. Then we must prepare a substrate for the minds; the minds themselves have no form, but must order themselves by being inserted into a substrate with a definite structure. The golden ooze and mist you saw at the Council-house was that form. We will build something similar; I hope it will be sufficient. And this must be large enough to accommodate the seven minds I hold, Duri's two if necessary, and the two of Marsavrina and Skadar, if necessary. A matrix of three cells by four would work."

Rioletta, Nikal, and Cardon were soon engaged in helping Hyphanden work as quickly as possible. Rioletta brought an armload of books and spread them out on one of the settees in the great-room, where she could leave them open to specific passages and bring them in to Hyphanden as necessary. Nearby, Cayon and Creed bent over Andor. Cayon unwrapped the arm to get a better view. Andor was awake, but very pale and quiet.

As Cayon worked on Andor, Kwistocta sat in a large armchair next to Rioletta's settee and beckoned Duri to her. He was also pale, and seemed quieter than usual, without his characteristic grin.

"Come, sit in front of me, and I will help you create better partitions for the minds you accepted," Kwistocta said. "If it is too much for you, we will remove one or both when Hyphanden is through."

Duri sat on the edge of the chair, and Kwistocta pulled him back until he leaned against her. She was taller than he, and she had little trouble looking over his shoulder and reaching around him as though hugging him from behind. She opened one hand, and revealed a cube within it. Rioletta watched in curiosity, glancing up occasionally from the books she scanned.

"This is a Distraction device," Kwistocta said. "They are Forbidden, but the Mind-sharing we are about to do requires at least some Distraction for you. Consume it; it contains potions to relax your mind as well as drugs to make you physically ill if you do not respond with an antidote. You will have to come completely back into your own mind to take that remedy, or the potion will bring you back unpleasantly."

"Great," Duri said as he gingerly removed it from her hand and examined it. "I can see why these devices are Forbidden. I know submersion in icy water and pain devices are some of the other Distractions used by Mind-sharers. But it seems that Hyphanden was able to share your mind enough to remove those others from it without any Distraction!"

164

Kwistocta smiled. "Hyphanden and I have shared minds many times, for more than thirty years," she said. "Neither of us requires a Distraction from the other, or wants one. Besides, although it is carefully covered up, there is at least one other Distraction that is not nearly as heinous as the other techniques. In fact, it's this very Distraction that lures some young people into studying Mind-sharing, and from there into the Path of Transformation and other Forbidden Skills."

"What's that?" Duri asked, as Kwistocta settled herself and pulled his head back onto her shoulder.

"Intercourse," Kwistocta said with a wry grin. "But I'm afraid your only choice today is this potion. Now be quiet and open your mind to me."

Chapter Fourteen

When Hyphanden was satisfied with what he had created, he sat in a chair at the table in the kitchen with the box in front of him. Rioletta and Nikal stood nearby, but not too near: neither of them wanted any contact with the minds Hyphanden disgorged into the box. It was difficult to tell how successful he might have been, although Rioletta saw the golden mist leave Hyphanden and enter the box. Hyphanden rose wordlessly and went to the great-room, where he slumped in an armchair. Nikal, with a glance at Rioletta, carefully closed and latched the top of the box and slid it gently to the back of the table, against the wall.

Kwistocta brought Hyphanden tea that included a calming aid and a sleep inducer, as well as a drug he had requested. Within a few minutes, he fell deeply asleep.

"I'd like to move him to our bedroom," Kwistocta said, gazing down at him. "He'll wake up cramped if he sleeps here all night."

"We can get him there," Creed said. "Come on, Cardon."

Creed slipped an arm under Hyphanden's shoulder and caught one of his hands. Cardon took up the other side, and with Hyphanden between them, they brought him to the back chambers and laid him on his bed. Rioletta followed with the stack of books she'd retrieved earlier; he would have to shelve them himself, as she didn't remember where she'd taken them from. Cardon brought Kwistocta a cup of tea, and then followed Rioletta out the door.

By early evening, Duri was also sleeping in a drug-induced collapse on a settee, Stolen had fallen asleep in a chair, and Creed had removed Andor to their room, where she also slept with the help of medication. Rioletta could see Cayon and Kerdahl and the rest of those assigned to sit guard over the estate outside, aligned along the walls.

Nikal and Rioletta went to their own room, where Rioletta fell asleep almost immediately. She did not stir until the next morning, when she awoke somewhat stiff from not moving for many hours. She washed her face and dressed, and then went out to the sitting room and kitchen, leaving Nikal still drowsing.

Cardon and Stolen were already up, as was Kwistocta. Cardon looked much improved, despite his collapse of the day before. He smiled quickly when Rioletta walked in, a smile she had not seen for a long time. She couldn't help but return it.

She walked into the kitchen to greet Kwistocta and perhaps help with whatever chores needed doing. Kwistocta smiled as well; she seemed relaxed and recovered.

"How is Hyphanden?" Rioletta asked.

"He's up and about, looking fairly rested," Kwistocta said. "The sleep did him good. He was even up before me. I hope for his sake his Crypt-substitute worked, for he fretted about whether or not the minds had been destroyed. I suppose I should check and see if it looks stable this morning, if the substrate appears to be holding together."

The box sat on the back of the kitchen table. She pulled it towards her and flipped open the lid.

"The matrix and substrate appear stable," she said, but then frowned. "Rioletta, tell me, can you see which of the cells are occupied?"

Rioletta bent over the box and stared at the wax block within it. She could clearly see etched hexagons with cells behind them. Several of them appeared to be filled or partially filled with a silvery substance, blurred behind the front cover of the matrix.

"It looks like these six cells are occupied, or partially occupied," Rioletta answered, pointing to the cells.

"Six," Kwistocta stated. "Hyphanden took on four minds, two complete and two partial, and I took three complete, which he later took from me."

"That makes seven," Rioletta said, and looked again at the matrix. But she saw only six filled cells.

Kwistocta slammed the box shut with an expression of frustration.

"What has happened to the seventh mind?" Rioletta asked. "Was it destroyed, or did it somehow escape or leak out? Or perhaps Hyphanden combined the two partial minds into one space."

"No, oh, no, I don't think so," Kwistocta said. "Hyphanden never put it in here, or he took it out again this morning. It's still in his mind."

She turned on her heel, and strode into the great-room, where Hyphanden had just arrived from the backyard gardens and thrown himself into his customary large chair near the fireplace.

"Hyphanden!" Kwistocta demanded. "Where is the seventh mind?"

Hyphanden looked up at her and smiled guiltily. "Right here, quite safe, Tocta. I have no trouble maintaining the separation of a single mind."

"You must put it in the matrix immediately!" Kwistocta exclaimed. "You're being stupid and endangering yourself, not to mention possibly contaminating your own personality."

Hyphanden put his hands behind his head and grinned. "Have confidence in me! It's not so difficult at this point to keep him separate, and I'm interested in what he might have to say."

Kwistocta crossed her arms. "I married Hyphanden, and I will lie with no other," she said. "Bear that in mind when you come to bed this evening."

"It's hardly like that," Hyphanden said, sobering. "I have only one body."

"And more than one person looking out of it," Kwistocta said.

Hyphanden gazed at her seriously for a minute, then pushed himself out of the chair and went to the kitchen, where he picked up the box and disappeared down the hallway. In a few minutes he came out, smiling, and put an arm around Kwistocta.

"Better, my love?" he asked.

She stared at him intensely for a minute. "Yes," she said. "Which mind was it?"

Hyphanden resettled himself in his chair and glanced from Rioletta to Kwistocta. "His name is Stelaphandon," he replied. "He is the one you used to guide you through the buildings. He is very accessible, more than happy to share what he can. He was thrilled to be released from the Crypt! He's been there for a very long time."

"Suspiciously accessible," Kwistocta said. "Was it he who convinced you to keep his mind within yours, or was it your own idea?"

Hyphanden looked a bit uncomfortable. "Truly, I don't know. Nor do I know why he was in the Crypt of Souls, or exactly who he was, yet."

"Yet?" Kwistocta said. "Are you planning on taking him out again?"

"Well, from time to time," Hyphanden said. "After all, that is the purpose of the matrix, or at least one purpose. I know he was imprisoned in the Crypt somewhere around the time of the Dispersal. I would like to know what he knows, not only his Skills, but also his information."

Kwistocta shook her head. Hyphanden turned to Rioletta.

"Well, Loremaster," he said. "Wouldn't you like to know? Don't you want to make your decisions based upon evidence, not stories?"

Rioletta shrugged uncomfortably. She wasn't used to being addressed by her specialty, rather than by her name. "The decisions we've been making for the last hundred years, based on what we do know, seem to have been working well," she pointed out. "We've created sustainable societies and communities, and we have what we need to live comfortable and healthy lives."

"But what if that's not true?" Hyphanden sat forward in his chair. "What if instead the decisions of the last hundred years have only brought you closer to some catastrophe? Or what if the decisions you make from here on out will turn your communities in a direction that will eventually lead to downfall and destruction?"

"Are you suggesting that's true?" Rioletta asked. "Are you saying this mind you've accessed is telling you we're headed for some catastrophe?"

Hyphanden shrugged. "No. I'm saying it's important that we know, and that we understand the truth behind the Dispersal. Otherwise, the possibility remains that our decisions, being founded on skewed or misinterpreted information, may be incorrect and harmful rather than beneficial. Do you admit this is true?"

"Of course. The more informed a decision, the better it is apt to be," Rioletta replied reluctantly.

"You see, Kwistocta, the Traditional Loremaster agrees," Hyphanden said with a smile.

"But I would not have you endanger yourself by accessing this mind for this information," Rioletta replied quickly.

"No," Hyphanden said. "But I can take this mind into mine for short periods without danger. I can put it back in the matrix I've created and access it when I wish. This is all I want to do."

Rioletta looked at Kwistocta, who stood by with arms crossed. Rioletta had a feeling Hyphanden would do as he wished; he was trying to justify his desires, rather than following a path to its logical conclusion.

"Anyway, we have many things to attend to today, and we can discuss this later," Hyphanden said. "Yesterday we were operating in crisis mode, but today the crisis has passed, and we must pick up the loose ends. Despite Rudon, we've accomplished what we set out to do, and that is encouraging. We are still in possession of the Key, and he cannot enter the Crypt without it, or without the necessary assembly of people, so we're safe on that front for now. We must make sure Duri is doing well and continue to support him, we must make sure Andor is healing and get her what she needs, and we should try and communicate with Marsavrina and Skadar, first because it must be very confusing for them, and second because I would very much like to know what happened with the Elder Council."

Nikal had come into the room as they spoke. "I agree," he said. "Does anyone know where the Twig Being is? I don't recall seeing it after a certain period last night."

"It's in the garden," Stolen said from the back door. "I planted it last night."

Hyphanden blinked several times. "Planted it?"

"Yes, well, I took it to the garden and showed it how to put roots into the ground for water and how to spread its leaves for

171

sunlight," Stolen said. "I don't know how else it will get nutrition; I didn't grow it a stomach or throat or even a mouth. I was rather surprised it came out with eyes. I have no idea how it manages to hear; I didn't grow it ears."

"Of course," Hyphanden nodded. "But you must be able to communicate with it in some form if you were able to show it how to do these things."

"Yes, although I don't know how to describe it," Stolen confirmed. "After all, it was once part of me. But I'm not at all sure I can translate what I feel from her into human words; her mind is very disordered and changes from moment to moment, as if it's slipping around, trying to find a good purchase on the substrate it has been provided with."

"You say *her*, and I presume you refer to Marsavrina. But how about Skadar? Can you also feel him within the body?" Hyphanden asked.

Stolen shrugged. "He is there and his thoughts run randomly through hers, but I am less comfortable touching his mind, and prefer Marsavrina. His thoughts are rapid and chaotic, even more than hers."

"Skadar was very young, but showed a great deal of promise. He was considered to have a mind well suited to interrogation and negotiation, as well as Loremastery. He was inducted at the age of eighteen, three years before the standard, with agreement of the full quorum of the Elder Council and Second Chosen. But I'm sure Marsavrina can tell us what we want to know," Hyphanden said. "Can you bring her in? None of the rest of us knows how to…un-plant it."

Stolen nodded and rose, but paused as Cardon, Creed, and Andor came in. Andor was up and walking, with her arm bound across her chest to support the multiple breaks.

"Andor! How are you this morning?" Rioletta exclaimed, jumping up.

Andor smiled. "Not bad. But I'm very hungry; the drugs I'm taking to help heal cause my body to use a lot of energy."

"Maybe you should learn how to plant yourself," Hyphanden said darkly. Andor looked at him blankly.

"We were just about to bring in the Twig Being to question it," Rioletta explained.

Hyphanden drummed his fingers on the arm of his chair. "But now that I consider it, I'm not sure it's fair to subject her to such questioning in front of us all. Some of what she has to say may be private or embarrassing. After all, we're not interrogating her; we want her to become comfortable with us. This experience has doubtless been traumatic enough, more than any of us could imagine. Perhaps Cardon and Stolen could go with her to some private location, and Cardon can tell the rest of us what he's discovered later."

Cardon looked around at them all in surprise. He was standing behind Rioletta's chair, outside of the group around the fireplace, nursing a cup of healing tea.

"It is you she knows the best of all, Cardon," Nikal agreed. "It is, after all, Marsavrina, the mother of your child, even if she does not look the same. It is your mind she sought out, and you who followed her call here to Hyolon, at great personal risk."

Cardon set the cup down on an end table without a word. Together he and Stolen went out towards the garden. Rioletta watched them through the large sliding-glass doors. When they paused she was able to pick out Marsavrina from the rest of the bushes between the garden and the orchard.

In just a few minutes, Cardon returned alone.

"What did you learn, Cardon?" Rioletta asked. "Do you know why the Younger Council enchanted their Elders?"

Cardon shook his head. "About all I could get out of her was that she recognizes me. I told her what had happened and assured her that Justah is safe in Andolith. But Stolen said her mind is still too disordered for him to be able to communicate with her reliably. She needs time, and I need time to get used to her as well." He sighed. "I have to admit that I find her alarming, if not repulsive. It's difficult to remember that the body before me harbors the mind of the woman who bore my child. I had convinced myself she was dead, and I have to turn my mind not only from the shock of seeing her like this, but the shock of finding her alive at all."

In a minute Stolen came back in as well. He sat down close to Rioletta and caught her eye. "There are Leaves on the wall," he said in a low tone. "The guards do not see them for what they are. Certainly there are Lefollah around here."

Rioletta felt a jolt of apprehension. "Is there something they want? I didn't feel them before."

"Nor I," Stolen said. "But I know they can follow me wherever I go, and pass messages very easily between separate groves. I expect they're still angry with me for escaping from the Twisted Trees, and will be even more upset that I've created a Twig Body; recall that I promised not to use the Skills I learned while I was with them. They won't see what we've done as being in any way acceptable."

"Will they dare come into the estate or the city?" Rioletta asked.

Stolen shook his head again. "I think not, at least not in their complete form, but they may send spies, and once we're out of the city in the woods, we'll be in their territory."

"I guess we'll have to cross that bridge when we come to it," Rioletta said. "For now, hopefully you are safe in the estate. Let me know what you perceive is happening with them."

There was a shout of greeting from the front door, and Cayon and Kerdahl came down the long flagstone hallway to the great-room, accompanied by Rath.

"I'm glad to see you've survived your mission," Rath said, clasping hands with everyone in turn. "But not unscathed. Where is Duri?"

"He's returned to the bachelor's estate, where he will stay," Hyphanden said. "Has Kerdahl told you what occurred?"

"That which he knows," Rath said, and turned to Andor. "Are there messages you wish to send, do you need more time to recover, or are you ready to return to Andolith?"

"Let's see what Cayon has to say, and I would guess Andor needs a few more days," Hyphanden said. "What have you found out, Cayon?"

"Several of us managed to enter the northwest part of the city unseen," Cayon said. "We took up a post on top of a building tall enough to give us a good view of the Council-house, with the help of distance-glasses. There are no Hyolonal to be seen around, and we took Mynador, who easily picks up the presence of other Sorcerers; she did not feel Rudon, nor did we see any rogue Outcasts."

"Is it possible we might be able to safely access the Council-house, then?" Hyphanden asked. "I dislike the idea of leaving Hyolonal bodies to rot in the heat in there. We will have need of the information in the libraries and store-houses."

"As for that, there will likely be little enough left of the bodies soon," Cayon said with a grimace. "The horse-creatures still guard the roof, and feed on the bodies of the Hyolonal."

"Ugh," Hyphanden said, looking at Cardon. "I didn't realize they would be so long-lived, or that they would be carnivorous."

"Neither did I," Cardon said. "Rudon taught me how to extend their lives until I could return them to the wall where I drew them, but I didn't know they'd take it upon themselves to find sustenance."

"And soon enough they'll be done with what they can find in the Council-house," Cayon said. "Then what will they do?"

"I'm not sure," Cardon said.

"No, but we can guess they won't be content to starve upon the roof of the Council-house," Hyphanden said. "If they manage to escape from it, I can foresee them rampaging through the city, looking for prey. An unpleasant situation. Cardon, can you not call them back to their place?"

"I called them to me on the roof, but I doubt I could call them from this far away, and if they did come, then they would be here, and I seem to have little control over them. In order to return them to the wall upon which I drew them, I would have to be there, at that wall, I believe. And it's possible I would need Rudon with me, since the two of us created them together."

"They will have little trouble leaving the Council-house when they wish," Cayon put in. "The front door stands open, although the pendulum still swings. When the horses are gone, I expect the Hyolonal will have a go at accessing it and salvaging what they can."

"Then I think we should make an attempt to secure it," Hyphanden said. "We should send a crew quickly, while the horses are still inside and there's no sign of Hyolonal. But I wonder what Rudon must have promised them to get them to band together; we've never seen that before. I doubt the opportunity to salvage the Council-house would have been enough."

"Who shall go?" asked Cayon. "Cardon obviously, if he is to return the horses to their place on the wall. I think no one else will be able to control his drawings. I will go; and we must have Sorcerers enough to overcome Rudon and any rogues he has with him if we encounter them. We should take physical guards who are able to maintain a larger view when Sorcerers are concentrating on a single target. We cannot accomplish everything through Skills."

"Of those here right now, Andor obviously cannot go. Neither will I call up Duri; he must spend time working on his own mind. Stolen should stay here with Marsavrina since he communicates best with her, and try to get her story; what we find out may be valuable. That leaves Cardon, who must certainly go; Creed, Rioletta, Nikal, me, and Kwistocta," Hyphanden said. "Others we can bring together from your crew."

"I volunteer to go as well," Rath said. "I have a few Skills, and other abilities."

"Agreed," said Hyphanden, "although it is dangerous, and I would not encourage you to go if you have any doubts."

"No doubts," Rath said. "I will find it interesting."

"Other than Cardon, I don't think any of us who went yesterday should go," Kwistocta said. "We are all tired. I assume someone will have to check the lower corridors, and that will bring us close to the Crypt. We do not know for sure that it's firmly closed, or that other minds released by Rudon aren't there somewhere. None of us should risk more mental assault. And some of us must stay here anyway, to guard against the possibility of Rudon's return."

"But only you and I are familiar enough with the Council-house to be able to find our way," Hyphanden argued.

"Then I will go," Kwistocta said. "You have taken greater assault than I. Please do not risk yourself again. You can stay and work on Protections for the estate; I have done what I can, and you may be able to add to it."

Hyphanden nodded slowly. "But in that case, Rioletta should also stay. She has more complete information than I about the events surrounding the liberation of the Elder Council, and could perhaps continue the conversation with Marsavrina in Cardon's absence."

"I have little wish to go, and will not be particularly valuable at this point anyway," Rioletta said. "I still have a knife I borrowed from Duri which I would like to return. I have no use for it."

"I'll take it," Kerdahl said. "I'll see him later at the bachelor's estate."

It was agreed that Cayon and Kerdahl, with a contingent of six other Outcast Sorcerers, and Rath, Creed, Nikal, Cardon, and Kwistocta would return to the Council-house. Several others would stay with Hyphanden, Rioletta, Stolen, and Marsavrina to provide protection for the estate.

Rioletta disliked seeing both Nikal and Cardon return to the Council-house, but there was little she could do other than clasp hands with both of them and warn them to be careful.

"Monitor me through your talisman," Nikal said. "We will be safe; it's not the same as yesterday. I will look forward to finding out more from Marsavrina later this evening when we return."

The group departed on horseback this time; they would move faster, and speed was now a bigger factor than stealth. The Hyolonal were aware that the Council-house was a focus of activity, and if they attacked in force, flight was the best option. Nevertheless, they took some precautions, using Concealment and muffling the horses' hoof sounds with Stealth.

After they had disappeared through the gate, Rioletta returned to the fireplace inside. But Stolen had retired to the garden to soak in the sun, Andor had gone to nap in her room, and she did not know where Hyphanden had gone.

Chapter Fifteen

Rioletta chose a book from one of the shelves in the great-room and sat down to peruse it. It was an old book, likely taken from the Council-house, or perhaps it had always lived in Trophandra's house. The dialect was archaic but not unreadable, especially with the use of Definition Skills. It was a small treatise explaining two different political views in a debate format; difficult without some background, but moderately interesting in a historical sense, and soon Rioletta was fairly absorbed in it.

She ignored a feeling that she was being watched for a while, but eventually her concentration was broken, and she looked up to find that Hyphanden had come quietly into the room and seated himself in another chair while she read. He sat with an arm on either armrest and a curious expression on his face, studying Rioletta carefully.

The expression on his face put her immediately on alert. She looked around quickly, but Stolen was nowhere to be seen. Hyphanden, seeing her glance, laughed out loud, but he did not move from the chair. Instead, he crossed one leg over the other and intertwined his fingers in his lap.

"Don't worry, we'll cause you no harm," he said. "There's no reason for alarm."

"We?" Rioletta asked carefully.

179

Hyphanden smiled again. "So, Loremaster, do you want to find out more about the reasons behind the Dispersal? Now is your opportunity. Will you go away from here having refused knowledge, aware that information exists which might guide you in your duties as decision-maker for your village?"

Rioletta said nothing. It was apparent that Hyphanden had once again picked up the mind of Stelaphandon, or possibly others.

"You are still suspicious," Hyphanden said. "I don't blame you. Let me show you something you might find interesting. I'll trade you. I'll give you access to information you want if you will hear me out."

Rioletta set her book aside. Hyphanden seemed to like bargaining for information, but she *was* curious. "All right, show me."

Hyphanden got up and went to a door in the wall of the hallway next to the kitchen. Rioletta had noticed the door before; Hyphanden and Kwistocta had entered it to retrieve wine, but had always closed it behind them. She had assumed it might be a pantry, given its location near the kitchen.

The door was apparently locked with several Skills, as it took Hyphanden a minute to open it. Rioletta followed him through into a small, dark room. It did indeed seem to be used for storage and there was a large wine-rack against one wall, but there was also a narrow staircase. They ascended to a second story, and from there the stair began to spiral, leading, Rioletta surmised, up into the turret she had seen from outside during her walks around the grounds.

At the top was another door, and behind it was a bright room with four windows open to each of the cardinal directions. The room was a library and study; all of the walls were lined with floor-to-ceiling bookcases, and even the small spaces alongside the windows were painted as though they were bookshelves. In the middle of the room there was a desk and chair, and nearer to one wall was an armchair and light.

Hyphanden waited for a minute while Rioletta walked around the room, looking out each window in turn. The view over the estate region was quite good, and Rioletta could see the layout of the orchards and gardens and the winding wall path.

"This was Trophandra's study," Hyphanden said when Rioletta turned to him. "We often credit Trophandra with being one of the leaders of the Dispersal, author of the Charter and Founder of Tabor. I am a direct descendant of Trophandra, and we have reason to believe this is her house. It took me and Rudon a long time to figure out the Protections and get in here when we first occupied this estate. All of these books belonged to Trophandra before the Dispersal. Some of them are her own writings. I've worked my way through most of them, but not all."

"So this is where you've gotten your information about the Dispersal and the times before it," Rioletta said.

"Here and elsewhere. There are still gaps in my knowledge; not everything has been written out explicitly, and some of it I have to guess at or interpret. Many books that are referenced by Trophandra are missing, along with other documents that might be useful. Some were destroyed, some were taken along, others have been looted or stolen by antique hunters. But I've found enough to begin to form some ideas about how and why the Dispersal actually happened, and to know that the Traditional story leaves a great deal out."

He went to one of the bookshelves and tipped a few volumes out, reading their jackets. Some appeared to have been handled more frequently, some were bound, and some appeared to be collections of loose paper in folders. He turned again to Rioletta.

"I'm willing to give you access to all of this," he said. "Many of the questions you must have formed in your mind by now could be answered here. I've even found references to those I believe to be your Lefollah, although there is more research I need to do on that front. But think of what you could learn here! I've spent years poring through these volumes, and now, with Stelaphandon to guide me, I'll be able to understand them even better!"

Rioletta ran her hand over the spines of the books on one of the shelves. The room smelled of old leather and paper and ink. The amount of information excited her, the new knowledge waiting upon the shelves.

Hyphanden clasped his hands behind his back and paced the room. Rioletta saw him shudder slightly; perhaps it was the influence of Stelaphandon. He continued to pace as he spoke to her, his voice taking on a different tone.

"Rioletta, didn't you ever wonder about some of the Technologies that were made Forbidden? Those that have no obvious major harm to people or to the environment? Or do you know of them?"

Rioletta watched him warily as he paced. "Of course I know them. I'm a Loremaster and have studied the Charter extensively, as well as the Papers appended to it. I could list you all of the Forbidden Skills, the Restricted Skills, and the Common Skills, as well as the Forbidden Technologies. And I could list you the Restricted Skills chosen for Andolith, and more."

Hyphanden/Stelaphandon nodded. "So. One of the Forbidden Skills is listed as 'permanent states of communication,' and one of the Forbidden Technologies is 'any device capable of remaining in constant communication with any other.' And the last Forbidden Skill listed is 'any Skill that controverts the individuality of the person.' How do the Traditionals explain these bans?"

"The ban on permanent states of communication is listed right after the Forbidden Mind-sharing techniques, and thus is interpreted as being an extension of Mind-sharing. It is not interpreted as being connected to the ban on devices that communicate with each other. And the final Forbidden Skill is interpreted as being a catchall, put there to anticipate other Skills that might be discovered in the future but that were not covered specifically in the Charter," Rioletta recited. This was familiar territory for her.

"What if all three of those were connected?" Hyphanden said. "What if the creators of the Charter intended those three bans to be taken together: you may not remain in constant communication with any other, using communication devices that maintain a constant interface, lest the individuality of the person be controverted?"

"If it was intended that way, I'm sure it would have been written that way," Rioletta said. "We assume that all the Forbidden Skills are Forbidden in and of themselves, as are the Technologies, not only in connection with one another. The preamble of each section, which uses the phrase, *in conjunction with*, is interpreted to mean that all of the following lists are valid, not that each is Forbidden only when used with the other."

"What if you're wrong in that interpretation?" Hyphanden paced in the small room. "Around the time of the Dispersal, there was political unrest as well as a growing knowledge about the state of the world. There's no dispute about that. But there was something else: constant communication."

He paused for a moment and cocked his head as though listening. Rioletta wondered if he was hearing Stelaphandon's voice inside his head. In a moment he resumed his pacing.

"On the face of it, that doesn't sound bad: how convenient it would be to be able to talk to anyone one wished to talk to, immediately, without having to employ a talisman or messenger! They had devices that constantly relayed information about events and moment-by-moment experiences. Coupled with certain Skills, people began to maintain a kind of constant Mind-sharing. The minds of large segments of the population began to vibrate together, to function more as one, with each separate mind contributing to the whole."

"It doesn't sound like something I'd personally want to be a part of, if indeed it happened," Rioletta said, "but I don't see the immediate harm in it, either."

"Neither did anyone else at the time," Hyphanden said, with a gesture Rioletta had never seen him use before. "But there were drawbacks to it. It became very easy to influence groups of people almost instantly, and to change that influence at will, even with false information. It was possible to track each person's preferences and desires, and to create messages to appeal directly to them. Think of the power of that!"

"I suppose with that kind of power, someone with evil intent could coerce large groups of people to do his bidding," Rioletta said. "Perhaps even raise armies and overthrow other societies."

"Yes!" Hyphanden turned abruptly to her. "Although people maintained an illusion of individuality, in truth they were addicted to this constant mental input and manipulated by those who saw the political or financial gain in it. This was the state of Hyolon and the other cities just prior to the Dispersal. This is why the Technologies and the Skills are Forbidden—in conjunction with each other, but not necessarily separately, as I have suspected."

"If this is so, why did the crafters of the Charter of Dispersal take such apparent care to conceal it from us?" Rioletta demanded. "Why not tell us up front not to engage in this behavior?"

"I'm not sure, but perhaps the idea was to conceal all information about such Technologies and Skills to make it more difficult for anyone in the future to rediscover them. It seems there was another reason as well, though."

Hyphanden stopped and ran a hand across his eyes. His voice trailed away, and he grimaced slightly.

Rioletta went to him and laid a hand on his shoulder. "Hyphanden, you had best put that mind away now," she said. "Kwistocta will be most upset if she comes home to find that you've accessed it."

"Yes," Hyphanden said, "but the chance to confirm what I've found, and know more, is something I cannot pass up. I believe I have enough evidence to support my view that Rudon used pre-Dispersal communication devices to control the Younger Council, and Stelaphandon is unique in his knowledge of the background reasons for the Dispersal and the reasons for the enumeration of the Forbidden Skills and Technologies. But I do not have full access to Stela's mind as of yet, or he is withholding information from me, one or the other." He paused. "There is time for me to study this, no rush. You will not tell Kwistocta?"

"No," Rioletta said hesitantly. "Not unless I see that you need help of some type."

"Then consider this library yours. As long as you stay here, you may access it. I'll show you how. Should you wish to spend more time here, in Hyolon, to study it, you'll be welcome."

"I want to go home to Andolith," Rioletta said. "Let's go down now, and you can put Stela away. We can talk about this later."

She escorted Hyphanden down the steep staircase and through into the kitchen. Hyphanden made his way down the hallway towards his chambers. At the door of his room he paused. "Stela says you are in possession of an amplifier for your talisman," he said. "It has pre-Dispersal Protections on it. Keep it; it may be useful." He turned abruptly and disappeared into his room.

Rioletta waited for a while, but he did not reappear. She hoped he had managed to replace the mind in the matrix; there was little she could do for him if he had not. Stelaphandon's revelations and Hyphanden's suspicions were disturbing, mainly because she had never been taught anything about them. If true, this was information that had been deliberately covered up, left out of the histories and study-books of the Traditional Sorcerers, for what reason she could not imagine.

The house was quiet in the heat, and she occupied herself by browsing through the books in the great-room, trying to ignore the books she now knew filled the turret overhead. She tried a couple of times to contact Nikal, but even with the amplifier she got nothing. The few times she thought she felt a response, on greater concentration it turned out to be the prickle she got when the Lefollah were about, which confirmed Stolen's suspicions.

In mid-afternoon, she heard the clatter of horses' hooves on the front drive, and opened the door to see the group returning. To her dismay, Creed led Nikal's horse, and Nikal sat in front of Rath, who was obviously assisting him.

As they rode up to the door, Nikal dismounted, with some help from Rath.

"I'm all right. Damn thing bit me," he said. His shirt was shredded to rags, and blood soaked the area over his ribcage. She helped him inside, where she sat him down on the settee in the great room and stripped his shirt off. It was not so much a bite as a scrape, for only one set of teeth, she assumed from one of the predatory horses, had made contact. Cayon had dressed the five long gashes temporarily with a bolster of cloth followed by a bandage wrapped around Nikal's body.

"Was anyone else hurt?" Rioletta asked as she examined the wounds, wishing for Cardon or even Rudon. Nikal raised his arm to give her a better view.

"No. Cardon called the horses, or whatever you want to call the vicious things, to the door of the Council-house when we got there. They came, all right, but one of them went directly for me. Cardon sent some of them back onto the wall, but I have to wonder why it picked me, of all people?"

"Nikal!" Rioletta said, shocked at his accusatory tone. "You're not insinuating that Cardon purposefully had it attack you?"

Nikal sighed. "No, not really. I'm just hurting. It was pretty horrifying. He drew them extra big, and you can see from the gashes

185

what size teeth they have. And they don't really respond to Skills, nor apparently can they be killed with regular physical force."

Cardon, Cayon, and the rest came into the room. Cardon went directly to Nikal.

"I'm truly sorry, Nikal," he said. "I had little control over them."

"Yes, well, at least some of them are back on the wall," Nikal said grudgingly. "Why'd you draw them so damn big?"

"I don't recall having drawn them that size," Cardon said. "I think they've grown."

Cayon opened a large bag on the floor and pulled out more bandaging and stitching materials. Nikal lay on his side on the settee, with his head in Rioletta's lap, as Cayon began to treat the wounds.

Andor and Stolen had also come into the room to greet the returning group. "Did you say *some* of them are back?" Andor asked Nikal.

"Unfortunately, yes, that's what he said," Cardon replied. "When I summoned them, only four appeared. I drew seven. The door was standing open; I have to assume three of them are roaming the city."

"That's better than all seven of them, anyway," Andor said.

Kwistocta looked around. "Where is Hyphanden?" she asked Rioletta.

"Taking a nap, I think," Rioletta answered, trying to concentrate on Nikal.

Kwistocta stared at her hard for a moment, but just then Hyphanden appeared from the hallway. Kwistocta turned her gaze to him.

"And whose mind did you access while we were gone?" she asked. "Was it Stelaphandon's, or did you try a new one?"

Hyphanden gave her a look of resigned frustration.

"I've been married to you for thirty years, I'm not a fool," Kwistocta said. "But that is a matter for later. Nikal is injured. I'll need to collect some more herbs from the garden for teas and poultices for both he and Andor."

"Cardon, tell us how it went," Andor said, seating herself on a stool near the fireplace.

Cardon drew back away from the settee, leaving Nikal's care to Cayon. He told the rest of them about their journey to the Council-house. The Hyolonal, he said, had not bothered them; they had seen a few in their respective territories, and those seemed to track and spy on them, but they made no move to attack. By the time they reached the Council-house, they were alone.

They could smell the Council-house blocks before reaching it. Pieces of Hyolonal bodies littered the ground around the building. The horses began to spook, so several of Cayon's crew had stayed back with them while the rest entered through the front door, avoiding the knife-edged pendulum.

"I immediately prepared to call the horses, which should perhaps be called something other than horses," Cardon told them. "Kwistocta and Cayon checked for residual Skills that might interfere with my recall, and it does appear that the animation Skill remains inside the Council-house. There were no objects moving around on a regular basis, but when Mynador put her hand on one of the desks, a letter-opener jumped up and tried to stab her fingers."

"It's not good," Cayon put in. "It seems all the objects that were affected by the animation rebound have some kind of vicious nature, and lie in wait for something to get close enough to attack."

"One reason that particular Skill was Forbidden, undoubtedly," Hyphanden remarked, with a glance at Rioletta.

"We had no choice but to go ahead with the recall, though," Cardon continued. "I summoned the horses and they arrived quickly, more quickly than I expected. I began to order them back onto the wall, but I could only control one at a time. They began to get frantic in the small space, and one of them attacked Nikal. Fortunately, I managed to stick it back to its spot before it did more damage."

Nikal grunted, and Cardon glanced at him. "Three of them did not answer my call. I cannot feel them, and don't know where they are. We went through the Council-house and cleaned up what we could. It was really a disgusting mess. The horses are incomplete scavengers."

"Every once in a while we encountered another object that seemed malevolent," Cayon continued. "We closed as many doors as we could and sealed them and other openings with Protections, so even if Rudon or others access it they'll have a hard time working their way through to the libraries and the Crypt. Finally we shut the front door, and Kwistocta placed a number of Protections on it. Only the Council-members will be able to open it now."

"But such was the case before," Hyphanden reminded them. "Rudon was a Council-member, and privy to all information we possess about Hyolon and the Council-house. But I doubt any other Council-member contemplates betrayal as he did."

"What else did you learn from Marsavrina while we were gone?" Cardon asked. "Do you know the reason for the Skill they Threw?"

Hyphanden shook his head. "No, she has been in the garden, where we thought it best not to disturb her. We will ask her more at another time."

Stolen nodded in agreement. "I have begun to show her how to grow her own leaves and twigs," he said. "Perhaps she can stabilize and increase her body and even grow features such as she wishes. Already she has put out some small new shoots for leaves."

Cardon looked disappointed, but after a moment's thought, he spoke up again. "Of course, there is also Malbec and Chasan. I'm not sure how complete their minds are, but could we not ask them as well?"

Hyphanden hesitated. "I don't want Duri accessing too much of their minds just yet. I want him to learn how to keep them completely separate from his own, otherwise he'll be plagued by bits of their thought patterns, and his own mind will be affected. But perhaps with a little help, he could discover just how fragmented their thoughts are. We'll call him over here tonight and have him join us after dinner. He should be included in what we do; he is inextricably linked to this group of people, like it or not."

"Didn't you say he already partitions part of his mind, and chooses not to access what he keeps in that part?" Creed asked. "Maybe you can also find out what's in there when you help him access Malbec and Chasan."

"No." Hyphanden shook his head. "It is none of our business. He must trust me and Kwistocta to do as we say and not intrude, or he will refuse our help and we will lose Malbec and Chasan, as well as any help Duri may be able to be as a messenger and tradesman in Tabor."

"What if it's something important to your decision-making? Didn't you say we should base our decisions on complete information?" Creed persisted.

Hyphanden snorted. "Very good, and I appreciate your cleverness. But this is a different situation, and all of us, even and including you, even and including Kwistocta and I from one another, have parts of our minds we choose not to reveal. When we reveal and share these parts, we lose our individuality, and become something other than what we are. I personally support the maintenance of these parts of our minds as separate and private; there is precedent for that in our society, so I suppose you can call me a Traditional!"

He laughed and glanced at Rioletta again. The reference was not lost on her, even though Hyphanden had curtailed his session with Stelaphandon.

"We will call Duri here tonight," Hyphanden continued, "and see what we might be able to learn from Malbec and Chasan, if anything. If we can retrieve what we want from them, it will take the burden off Stolen and Marsavrina."

Rioletta looked down at Nikal, who had fallen asleep due to the effects of pain-killing and calming medication, even as Cayon still worked on the gashes in his side. It was likely Andor would sleep again soon, too, but what they learned from Duri could later be passed on to them. With help from Kwistocta, Rioletta placed several pillows under Nikal's head and shoulders, and carefully moved from the settee. Then she went to help prepare an evening meal.

She sat to eat on a stool in the kitchen, and Cardon sat down next to her.

"How are you feeling now?" she asked.

"Good," Cardon said, pausing before a mouthful. "Better than I've felt in a long time, in fact. My mind is free from intrusion. I feel clearer and more rested with every hour that goes by, even if I haven't been sleeping or resting. I feel more energetic and have my appetite back. I regret what happened to Nikal today; there was nothing I could do."

"I know. I don't blame you," Rioletta said. "I'm glad you're feeling better; it will make things easier for you when we return to Andolith."

"Perhaps Cardon would prefer to stay here," Hyphanden suggested. He sat just to the side of them, in a large chair. "You know many of the Forbidden Skills now, Cardon; in most villages you'd be branded an Outcast. In fact, you have had some experiences many of the Outcasts here have not had, and you have shown yourself able to withstand a great deal more mental stress than I would have guessed and have learned new Skills quickly. I'm sure you'd be accepted into the Outcast community, if you wished it."

"No," Cardon said, shaking his head. "I've had nothing but bad experiences with the Forbidden Skills. I want nothing but to leave them alone and return to my horses, the real ones. Besides, my mother and daughter dwell in Andolith, and I would not abandon them. I think I can now be content with my duties there, at least for the time being! I won't want to travel again for a while."

"The option will remain open," Hyphanden said. "In a few years, things may change for you. Think too of the demands that have been placed upon your daughter. If her safety is at risk, consider our Protections."

He put aside the plate he'd been eating from, brought out the talisman on a chain he used to contact other members of the Outcast community, and spent a few minutes fingering it and concentrating. He looked up at the rest of those gathered in the sitting room.

"Duri will be here in a short while. Then perhaps we'll get some answers about the Younger Council."

With Nikal asleep, Rioletta decided to spend a few minutes wandering in the gardens and beneath the fruit trees before Duri arrived, settling her meal. As the heat began to abate and the insects shrilled from the encroaching woods beyond the wall, evening flowers opened in their beds, and a humid odor rose from the gardens. She walked slowly along the rows, identifying the plants in her mind, and thought she might eventually consult the book of the Crypt Key, which could prove useful as an identification book for Hyolon garden-plants. Of course, she could already identify Marsavrina, and she avoided her.

Presently she saw Kerdahl approaching. He continued to dress in the manner of the Tabor Sorcerers, she saw, with a high collar, unbuttoned in the heat. He had a formal appearance and somewhat reserved air. He stopped a few feet from her and bowed slightly, although he was not significantly younger than Rioletta.

She smiled encouragingly. His deference amused her. "What can I do for you, Kerdahl?"

Kerdahl looked around, as if to make sure he was not overheard, and took a step closer to her. "I wish to pass on a warning," he said seriously.

Rioletta stiffened, her amusement gone. "What do you mean?"

"I have been in contact with a young man whose name I do not wish to reveal," Kerdahl said quickly. "He is a true Outcast, unlike me, and has not joined the Outcast community, but is held as a rogue. A number of these rogues have fallen in league with Rudon. They support him in the hopes of gaining something for themselves, and in disdain of the Outcast community and the Council."

"This I understand," Rioletta said. "But what is the warning?"

"This man is a friend of mine, a contemporary," Kerdahl continued. "In fact, he is no rogue, but serves me as a source of information about their activities. Hyphanden does not know about him, nor do any of the Council; the fewer who know, the better."

"I see; he's a kind of spy," Rioletta said. "I gather he's discovered something of importance to us."

Kerdahl nodded. "He came to me this afternoon, or rather, he signaled me and I met him. He told me that Rudon has joined the rogues and seeks a particular book. I do not understand the reason, but it is said that the book is in your possession, that Hyphanden gave it to you in the Council-house where Rudon observed it. Does this make sense to you?"

Rioletta felt her heart rate rising. "Go on. I understand what you're talking about."

"He will do anything to get this book He feels it is some key to his own power, to a limitless increase in his Skills. So I warn you now: if you are in possession of the book, you would do well to divest yourself of it, and let that be known. It should be placed in a spot well-hidden and well-protected and known to few people, only those able to resist coercion and manipulation."

191

"What should I do with it?" Rioletta asked in alarm. Her large satchel suddenly felt obtrusive and obvious, and she glanced around involuntarily.

Kerdahl took a moment to answer. "It should not remain here at Hyphanden's estate. Apparently Rudon, when he was here before, set some Skill that makes it possible for him to access the estate even through Phando's Protections. You may know that it was he and Phando who originally entered this estate—the two of them broke the original Protections and set the new ones Phando uses today. Rudon is a breaker of such Skills even without prior preparation. Stay safe and do not let your friends fall victim to him."

"Thank you," Rioletta said. "I'll take your warning seriously. I don't want to jeopardize your friend, but is it possible he'll be able to pass on more information to you about Rudon's activities? Do you know where he is?"

"He may be able to pass on more information at some point, with some risk. Rudon hides somewhere in the city, but I do not know where. The city is quite large, as you have seen; more people once lived here than in all the Sydian and Tadian regions combined, many times over. There are many places for a few people to take up residence and remain unknown."

Kerdahl glanced up at the wall. "One more thing. I think it best if Hyphanden does not know about my contact with this rogue for the time being. Hyphanden is powerful and trustworthy; but I do not wish to be questioned by him. He is an Outcast who practices the Forbidden Skills, and I maintain my Traditional leaning as much as possible. I also do not wish to draw attention to myself and my activities, and any particular interest Hyphanden shows in me would certainly be noticed, especially if I were to be questioned by him or Kwistocta or another member of the Council."

"I understand," Rioletta said. "Please excuse me."

"Yes, and I will return to my post here, where I have a shift along the wall tonight, for Hyphanden has requested a few more days of sentries," Kerdahl said. Once again, he bowed slightly, turned on his heel, and strode through the garden.

Rioletta returned quickly to the house. In the bedroom she shared with Nikal, she removed the book from her satchel, where she had continued to keep it. She did not have any idea what to do with it, other than to get it off her person. For the time being, she placed it in one of the shelves of books in the room among a couple hundred others, where it was not obvious. As a further precaution, she removed the physical key from the back, and placed it in another location, inside a second book on another shelf. She realized she was now in a bind; she needed Hyphanden's advice, but she couldn't tell him how she'd come by the information without revealing Kerdahl and his source. And she wasn't sure how quickly they'd be able to move the book out of Hyolon or to a safer hiding place. She could only hope it would be fast enough.

Chapter Sixteen

Duri came over the back wall into the estate and through the back door, wearing his cocky grin and strutting slightly. He was apparently feeling quite well, previous injuries and mental shocks notwithstanding.

"Hey, look what I caught!" he announced as he came in, holding out his hand. In a firm grip, he held what appeared to be a leaf, struggling to escape, its points waving futilely.

"I figure it's an escapee from the Council-house or something," he said. "Though it seems an awful long way for it to have come this fast."

"It's not from the Council-house," Rioletta said with horror. "Put it back where you found it, Duri, quickly."

"Yes, yes!" Stolen agreed. "Put it outside the wall. Don't let it loose in here. Take it out now!"

"All right, all right!" Duri said. "I'll throw it out in the garden."

"No!" Rioletta and Stolen both said together. "It must go outside the Protection around the estate," Rioletta said. "Outside the wall!"

Duri gave them a strange look, but took the Leaf outside. Rioletta watched as he climbed the stile over the back wall, until she was satisfied he was placing the Leaf somewhere where it could not return.

Stolen watched as well. He looked very concerned. "Who knows what information that Leaf picked up in the short time it was in here?" he said to Rioletta. "Before this, they haven't gotten inside, only on the wall."

"Do you think Marsavrina is safe outside?" Rioletta asked him.

"Now I'm not sure," Stolen said. "I'll bring her in. Perhaps she'll want to hear Duri's story anyway, and add to it."

With Andor and Nikal both asleep and in their rooms for the evening, Hyphanden, Kwistocta, Rioletta, Creed, Cardon, Rath, Stolen, and Marsavrina/Skadar gathered in the sitting room to listen to Duri. Marsavrina stood in the corner near the fireplace; Rioletta wasn't sure if she was able to sit down. She intertwined the twigs of her fingers, to all appearances wringing her hands nervously, but her expression was impossible to read. Her eyes darted from one person to another, but her face comprised only of a jumble of sticks and leaves.

Hyphanden brought out some wine and set up the glasses on a side table. He had brought enough glasses for Marsavrina to have one, but she only looked at it, and he placed it near her on the mantle after a minute.

"Duri, how have you been managing with the two minds?" Kwistocta asked. "Have they been intruding into yours?"

Duri shook his head. "No, I'm not having any problem keeping them compartmentalized, and I haven't tried to access them by myself. Although I think I've caught a little bit of each of their personalities. It's not like an intrusion, but more like accessing a memory, as if I knew them and remembered what they were like. Chasan was more like the Traditional Vrinacs I've run into, maybe like Kerdahl: a little formal, but with a temper. A little closed, harder to reach. Malbec was different. I think he was friends with you, Cardon. He liked to drink more than Chasan, he liked to play games, maybe gamble. He seems a little more open, a little more apt to approach strangers, more relaxed."

"That's a pretty good portrayal of each of them," Cardon agreed. "I met Marsavrina first. But after I met the rest, it was Malbec I became the best friends with. He was the oldest and the most experienced, and he was easy to get to know and liked to show me what he'd learned. He was a bit of a braggart. Chasan was a little more distant, as you say, but he was very skillful. If you could get him to drink a little, he relaxed and could get very funny, very quick-witted. Skadar I never knew well. He was the youngest of them, just a boy, and he had an interest in other boys, so he often was out with his own friends apart from the rest of the Younger Council."

Cardon looked up at the Twig Being. She stared back at him wordlessly, with unwavering lidless eyes. A long moment passed between them, but finally Cardon broke his gaze. His eyes met Rioletta's as he turned away, and she saw a fleeting expression of dismay. She felt a flash of insight, as she often did when Cardon was nearby and experiencing strong emotions. For just a moment, she wondered if it might not have been better for the transfer into the stick body to have failed.

"Duri, I'd like to try to access some of the information from Malbec and Chasan," Kwistocta said. "It would require some Mind-sharing again, and I'm not convinced you could yet do it safely on your own."

"That potion again?" Duri grimaced. "It was unpleasant."

Kwistocta smiled. "No, I think we could do it without any Distraction. It will be a surface sharing, intended to keep you present and aware of yourself. You'll do most of the work, following the techniques we've been teaching you."

Duri nodded, and took a swallow of wine from the glass he was holding. "Hope this won't interfere, but it's good, and I haven't had a drink in a while," he said, putting the glass on a side table. "Seems like lately I've had a bit of a craving for good dry red wine. Perhaps that's Malbec's influence?"

"Perhaps," Kwistocta said. "If so, there may be more intrusion than you realize. I admit, I'm curious about how much of their minds survive."

Duri joined her on the settee and leaned back against her as he had before. Kwistocta put her chin on his shoulder. "Relax and open your mind to me and I'll help guide you if necessary. We'd like to ask Malbec a few questions."

Almost immediately, Duri nodded. "Go ahead."

"We're seeking information about the Skill the Younger Council Threw at the Elders. Why did they do it, and what did they think would happen? We need the truth now; there's no reason to conceal it, and no repercussions that can apply."

There was a long pause, but then Duri raised his eyebrows and cleared his throat. His voice took on a different timbre, slower and lower than his usual quality.

"The Skill was taught to them by Rudon; it's a Transmogrification, one of the highest orders of Shape-changing."

"That much we know," Kwistocta said. "We know Rudon retained contact with some of his relatives in Tabor after his Outcasting, and that he met Malbec when he traded antiques from Hyolon for spices and other goods in short supply here. Rudon shared some of what he received with the rest of the Council. But how was Malbec convinced to learn and do this thing?"

Duri paused again. With some hesitation, he continued. "Rudon offered to teach him certain Skills and described them in tempting terms. Malbec laughed his offer off at first, but the idea began to take hold in his mind. He met Rudon several times to broker trade for his relatives, but finally Malbec began to seek him out on his own."

"Rudon and Malbec are in some ways quite alike," Hyphanden said, leaning forward. "It makes sense that they'd be drawn to each other."

Duri nodded. "They enjoyed drinking and talking together, and Rudon began to teach some Skills to Malbec. Most of them were party tricks, amusements. This continued for quite some time, and Malbec taught some of his new Skills to others of the Younger Council. Slowly they became interested in learning more, because the ones to which they'd been exposed seemed harmless enough. And of course, several of them became interested in the Mind-sharing techniques."

Duri paused. Hyphanden poured more wine into the glasses. Rioletta held hers out; she was becoming quite used to drinking the Hyolon wine with every meal. She remembered Rudon's party tricks; they had certainly seemed harmless, only combinations of Restricted skills rather than Forbidden.

"I had some suspicion Rudon actively recruited the Younger Council, although he told me the Council had come seeking the knowledge themselves," Hyphanden said. "So Rudon always planned to use the Younger Council for some sort of revenge."

"Well, no, I don't think so," Duri replied. "At first I think...*Malbec* thinks Rudon just saw Malbec as someone fun, a younger Sorcerer to teach tricks to, someone to show off to, and a conduit to his relatives in Tabor. He never mentioned that he intended to get the whole Younger Council involved. But when that did happen, he told Malbec that he found it amusing that the Elder Council would be screwed out of an entire Council once again. For when they found out the Youngers were practicing the Forbidden Skills, as they surely would, they'd be forced to Outcast them, or relax their rules and seem hypocritical and biased. Of course, Malbec never believed they'd get caught."

"A typical conceit of those who practice the Forbidden Skills," Hyphanden said.

"Or perhaps just a conceit of the young," Rioletta added.

"Whichever. During the last year or so four of the Younger Council was well involved with the Forbidden Skills, and the other four peripherally so," Duri continued. "And then, somewhere along the way, Rudon found out about the Crypt of Souls."

"We all did," Hyphanden said. "Rudon knew what any of us knew. The existence of the Crypt has been known for many years, but it was only recently that references to it led me to find it in the Council-house, and further information led Kwistocta and I to figure out how to insert minds into it. Of course, we didn't have the Key to be able to open it until now."

"Opening the Crypt is very tempting," Duri said. "Rudon told Malbec about it. They realized there must be many powerful minds stored in there, ones who had practiced the Forbidden Skills before they were Forbidden. Obtaining access to those minds is indeed very, very tempting. And of course, all Outcasts are susceptible to the temptations of power and knowledge. That is how they became Outcasts in the first place."

Kwistocta looked pointedly at Hyphanden, but he avoided her gaze. "Find out from Malbec how they came to know the Skill and why they used it. It's a very powerful Skill, and the transformation of the Elders is the most complete Shape-shifting I've ever seen. Rudon must have known something the rest of us have not found out."

"As for that, I'm not sure how Rudon discovered how to control the Transmogrification Skill. He often wandered the city alone, or in the company of some of the Rogue Sorcerers who are not part of the community but with whom he established contact. He told Malbec about some of his journeys. It's likely he came upon documents he kept to himself, intending to use them for his own purposes."

"So it's possible he's been plotting for years," Hyphanden said. "I haven't trusted him for a long time."

Duri continued. "Rudon knew of a particular talisman that was displayed in the Tabor Council-house, an antique from Hyolon, which he believed to be the Key to the Crypt of Souls. He spoke to Malbec about it. During his time as a Sorcerer, before he was Outcast, that talisman had been removed from display. Rudon believed the Elder Council, or at least Stetsordahl, had discovered its true use and hidden it. If he could obtain it, he could access the Crypt himself, with the help of a few conspirators. This would require that he get access to the Elders and convince, or force, them to reveal the location of the talisman and release any Protections upon it."

"But it can't have been the Key, since we have it," Rioletta said. "I wonder what it was?"

"I don't know, but he believed it to be the Key. He convinced the Younger Council that when the coup came, they could protect the Elder Council from harm with a particular Skill he would teach them, the one you know of—a dangerous Transmogrification. The First Chosen would believe the Elders had escaped through the Council-house, and later the Younger Council could avoid Outcasting by supporting and pledging allegiance to the First Chosen, some of whom were close relatives and who might be sympathetic to them. Alternatively, those who wanted to join Rudon in opening the Crypt could do so, and in that they could be quickly transformed from acolytes to powerful Skill-users."

"Understandably tempting," Hyphanden said. "But I still don't understand how the Younger Council could have become powerful enough to successfully Throw this Skill. Knowing the procedure is not enough. You must have the experience to do it."

"Rudon distributed talismans to each of the Younger Council. These were devices he obtained during his travels. They were ancient technology, but also relied on a mental interface. They allowed almost instant communication and Mind-sharing far beyond what could have been accomplished otherwise. Rudon was able to add his Skill to theirs, and their power was concentrated as they all acted as one."

Hyphanden sat back, a look of triumph on his face. "I knew it. These devices not only existed, but it was possible to control the actions of others through them."

Nikal crossed his arms and shook his head slightly, as if disagreeing with Hyphanden's conclusion, but it was hard to dispute. Rioletta had not told anyone, even Nikal, about her conversation with Hyphanden in the turret. The idea was not as new to her as to the others, but this added credence to what he had told her. Despite her reluctance, she found that she now had to accept that some of Hyphanden's ideas, however far-fetched, might indeed be true.

"Of course, Rudon didn't risk himself. He stayed away and communicated from a distance," Duri said. "They were to bring the tapestries to him when they could, after the coup was complete and the Younger Council had sworn allegiance to the First Chosen, but before the First Chosen occupied the Council-house. The real purpose of this was not to protect the Elders from harm, but to find the talisman he sought. Of course that didn't occur; first, the Younger Council was immediately too ill to return to Tabor, and second, the Andolith Council stole the tapestries."

"So we rescued the Elder Council from Rudon, rather than from the First Chosen, even though we didn't know it," Rioletta said.

Hyphanden frowned. "The Elders most likely could have escaped on their own, and if they could not, I doubt that the First Chosen would have caused physical harm to them or even imprisoned them. Stripping them would have been political suicide. Most likely they would have been required to leave Tabor. The First Chosen would have had little fear of them following a successful coup."

"Of course the Younger Council also knew this," Duri agreed. "But Rudon used the devices to his advantage. The Mind-sharing they enabled was enjoyable and increased each person's power geometrically. But the problem was that they seemed to turn off the ability to process information for veracity."

"But like Rioletta, I wonder what that object Rudon believed to be the Key actually is," Hyphanden said. "I believe I remember the one he refers to."

"I don't know, nor did I ever find out where it was hidden," Duri said, speaking as though he was Malbec. "I only know that Rudon used us to our deaths."

Kwistocta noticed the change in Duri's presentation, and squeezed him hard. "Duri! Replace Malbec in the partition, and speak as yourself."

Duri closed his eyes, then grimaced. In a minute, he appeared to relax and opened his eyes, although a line of sweat appeared at his brow.

"Enough of this for now," Kwistocta said. "We have what we need. Malbec's memories were much more complete than I would have suspected."

"Cardon, are you satisfied?" Hyphanden asked.

Cardon nodded slowly. "I wish it were different. I had hoped to hear that the Younger Council's intentions were completely honorable. But I have to accept what Malbec remembers; at least I have an answer, even if it's not the one I wanted to hear."

He looked at Marsavrina. "I understand temptation. I was not immune to it. We played with something far more serious than we wished to admit. All of us paid the price."

Marsavrina gazed back at him, but she was unable to say a word, and she had not made any attempt to communicate in any other way. Rioletta wondered if the transfer had indeed been as successful as they had hoped; perhaps she would never be able to order her mind within the confines of the stick body. If not, what would become of her?

"Now I wonder what Rudon will do?" Hyphanden mused. "Obviously he knows what the Key is now. Whatever the talisman he originally sought is, it is not connected with the Crypt, and so he will likely focus on getting the book if he still plans to access the Crypt himself."

"I'm not sure the talisman isn't connected to the Crypt," Rioletta said. "There was that passage in the book that talked about a translator or index. Perhaps that's what he has."

Hyphanden nodded. "Of course. Rudon might have mistaken it for the actual Key; it could have been presented as a *key* in the sense of a guide or map."

"And the Elders of Tabor had it, and eventually discovered what it was, or they decided it was dangerous or useless. Whichever, they put it away," Kwistocta said.

"I suppose we could ask them what they thought it was and what they did with it," Rioletta said. "We have fairly regular contact with them."

Hyphanden snorted. "What are you going to do, tell them Hyphanden the Outcast would like to know what they did with the Index to the Crypt of Souls? Somehow I don't think that will get you very far."

"I suppose not," Rioletta admitted. "We would have to go about it some other way."

Kwistocta rose and went to the kitchen to make Duri a restorative, although Duri seemed more interested in finishing the wine he had put aside. When she came back, she turned the conversation to the Key. It was obvious that it had to be Protected in such a way that Rudon could not obtain it. The choices seemed to be to send it away from Hyolon to some other place where it could be secured and kept secret, or to keep it in Hyolon and rely on the Skills of the Outcast Council to Protect it. There seemed to be advantages and disadvantages to each approach. The group went back and forth without coming to a decision.

Duri, exhausted by the contact with Malbec's mind, nodded off on the settee. The rest of the group quietly moved away to allow him to sleep for a while. Rioletta went back to her room and found Nikal stirring, the last draught of healing tea beginning to wear off. She briefed him on what Duri had said and then left him to wash up and dress while she went to find Kwistocta.

"Kwistocta, I wonder if you might have some old clothing anywhere," Rioletta said. "I was thinking of giving some of it to Marsavrina. Perhaps with a little clothing, she'd take on a more human appearance, rather than appear as a jumble of sticks. It might make her feel more human, too, although I'm not sure what she actually feels."

Kwistocta nodded. "Of course. It's odd that none of the rest of us thought about it. We'll see what we can do."

She took Rioletta to a closet in the hallway and pulled out some boxes full of older clothing. Kwistocta was quite tall and the Twig Being very short and slender, so most of the clothing was not useable. However, there was a short cloak that would do, and an old tunic with a waist tie. They took the articles and went to find Marsavrina.

She was in the garden, but had not planted herself. Instead, she was sitting forlornly upon a stone bench by herself.

"Hello, Marsavrina," Rioletta said. "You and I are not acquainted, but we certainly know of one another. We thought you might like some clothing; it may make you feel more…human."

Marsavrina looked up at the clothing Kwistocta proffered and then stretched out a spindly hand to finger the fabric. Together they managed to fit the tunic over her leafy head and tie it around the branches that made up her torso. It was long enough on her to resemble a short dress. They threw the cloak around her shoulders and fastened it at the throat. Altogether, it gave her a more solid look.

"We'll be able to fashion clothing that fits you better. There are some people in the community that create fine clothing," Kwistocta said, standing back to observe Marsavrina. "But this will have to do for now. Let's go back in and we'll see what everyone else thinks."

"Yes, please join us," Rioletta said. "You are part of this community now, and welcome here."

Nikal and Andor both joined the group in the great-room, and Duri awoke from his nap.

"Now that we've done what we came to do, we should really get back to Andolith as soon as possible," Creed said. "We've been gone a long time. I think we should go as soon as Andor and Nikal can safely travel; I'd like to get Andor back to her own home to heal."

"But travel may not be safe," Rioletta said. "We will have to avoid Tabor. Once we get around the town and can blend with travelers on the road to the Ford we should be all right, but we'll have to skirt Tabor through the woods first, and that may be hard on Andor and Nikal."

"That's not something to worry about," Rath said. "I have friends near here, and we'll be able to stay with them. We can travel slowly and go light, knowing we'll have lodging for the evening."

"That's helpful," Rioletta nodded. "But there's yet one more problem to deal with: Stolen and I are aware of Lefollah in the area, and they have definitely been watching the estate. It's likely they're after Stolen, and may seek to recapture him."

"That problem may also be easily solved," Stolen said quietly. "As you say, it's most likely the Lefollah are interested in me alone, to punish me for creating the Twig Body of Marsavrina. If I was not with your group, the Lefollah would not bother you."

No one answered for a moment, so Stolen nervously went on. "I have thought I might stay here in Hyolon," he said. "With permission of Hyphanden and the others, of course. Marsavrina must stay, and it seems I may be important in ensuring her survival and helping with communication."

"Of course you can stay," Hyphanden said. "I'm sure you'll be easily accepted into the community here."

Stolen turned to address Rioletta directly. "I don't think I'll ever truly be accepted in Andolith. Of course I'm very, very grateful to you, Rioletta, for releasing me from the Twisted Trees, and to the rest of Andolith for providing me with housing and teaching me how to be human. I sincerely regret what I did as a young man, and understand enough now that I would never do such a thing again. But I feel an undercurrent of suspicion. It will not be forgotten that at one time I abducted a young girl. This is a thing I don't think can be overcome."

"You were forgiven long ago," Rioletta said. As she said it, she realized it was true. It had been a long time since she had blamed Stolen for her childhood abduction.

"Cardon, of course I'll return the horse and tack I've used; I can go about on foot here," Stolen continued.

"Forget about the horse and tack. It's yours," Cardon said. "The horse has grown fond of you, anyway, and you can't pretend he'd be as happy with me."

Rioletta leaned towards Stolen and took his hands. "Stolen, I'm sorry you feel that the residents of Andolith don't trust you. I think maybe in time they would, and you know I've forgiven you, and I'm quite comfortable around you now. You had no idea what you were doing when you were young, but since we've come to know each other, you've protected me and my friends, and proved invaluable in all sorts of situations. You'll always be welcome in Andolith as far as I'm concerned, and I hope to see you there in the future."

Cardon stood up and clasped hands with Stolen with a smile. "I'll miss you and your help with the horses," he said, with a hand on Stolen's shoulder. "I expect to see you riding at the Polebray every summer; with a little practice, you should be able to pick up at least part of the purse every time."

"Let's share the rest of this bottle and welcome Stolen to Hyolon," Hyphanden said, picking up one of the wine bottles from where it stood on the floor. "You're a quick study, Stolen, and we're happy to have you here." He poured the wine into the glasses that were extended towards him, and the group drank to Stolen's health before heading to their rooms for the night.

Chapter Seventeen

Rioletta crawled out of bed early the next morning. Nikal slept soundly, but she had been restless, and she finally gave up and dressed and went out to the kitchen. There she found Kwistocta in the early morning light, sitting at the large kitchen table near the glass doors out into the back garden, sipping a cup of tea.

"May I join you?" Rioletta asked, after pouring hot water into her own cup.

"Please," Kwistocta said, indicating a chair. "I'd like to talk to you anyway."

After a long silence, Kwistocta, who continued to look out the window, began to speak again.

"Are you truly concerned about the quality of the information you use to make decisions for your village?"

Rioletta considered. "Yes, I am, in some ways. I take my responsibility very seriously. My decisions can't be sound if they aren't based on sound and complete knowledge. Our interpretation of the Charter has guided us well for the last hundred years. Our lives are quite good, and following the Traditional path has kept us in that state."

She paused and took a sip of her tea. What she had just said, she realized, was Traditional dogma. And while she had learned it so well that she could repeat it without thought, she could no longer accept it as completely as she once had.

"But I was abducted by Stolen; I later rediscovered the Lefollah; and that, as well as Cardon's contact with the Younger Council and the coup of the First Chosen, seems to have led me down a path I could not have anticipated a few years ago. I have been exposed to things I didn't know existed. As a child, my stories weren't believed, and as an adult, what I've discovered has often been dismissed by my own Council. But I can't in good conscience return to Andolith and ignore what I know, and make my decisions as if that knowledge was inconsequential."

"Do you believe the minds in the Crypt of Souls, and the ones we have here, might contain information vital to your decision-making?"

Rioletta let out a long breath. If she was going to reveal and discuss her doubts, then an Outcast with no allegiance to a Traditional Council was probably the safest person to talk to. "I don't know. I think there's a possibility they do. There have been hints already that the Charter either is not what it appears to be, in that it was purposefully created to deceive us or conceal information, or that it has been misinterpreted. If so, don't you think it's important for us to know, so as to avoid the same mistakes in the future?"

"Not if following the Charter specifically protects you from making those same mistakes that led to the Dispersal," Kwistocta said. "But I'm hardly one to speak; I have not followed the Charter. I have practiced the Forbidden Skills, and far be it from me to keep such knowledge from one who wishes to know it."

"I have very little desire to use any of the Forbidden Skills, other than the minor Mind-sharing I do with Nikal," Rioletta said.

"But the knowledge you seek, if it's not in the Charter, is Forbidden. And you seek it--you've admitted it. I can only ask you this: please do not encourage Hyphanden to seek it through the mind of Stelaphandon. It is dangerous and damaging, and I fear what it might do to him."

Rioletta met Kwistocta's eyes. "I won't encourage it, but I have no power to stop him, either. He is tempted, in the same way Rudon was tempted."

208

"No!" Kwistocta exclaimed. "Not in the same way. Rudon seeks power and control; he wishes to influence others to increase his own prestige and comfort. Hyphanden is tempted, it's true. He may say he has grown and is not subject to temptation as he was when he was a young man, but in many ways he is that same boy. But he seeks knowledge for knowledge's sake!"

"I'm sorry," Rioletta said. "I didn't mean to suggest that Hyphanden is really similar to Rudon."

Kwistocta took a few deliberate sips of her tea. "No, I'm sure you don't really think that. He is not like Rudon. But I admit he is tempted, and I do fear what might happen to his mind if he continues to access the minds of those in the Crypt of Souls, especially if he does so indiscriminately, without knowing who he contacts."

"I'm not sure I can help," Rioletta said. "But I promise I won't encourage him, if he should ask again."

"That's all I can ask," Kwistocta said with a sigh. "You will visit us here again?"

Rioletta raised her eyebrows. "I wasn't planning on it...I hadn't thought about it."

"But you will want to know what else has been discovered about the Dispersal," Kwistocta said with certainty in her voice. "You won't be satisfied to return to Andolith and never know more. And Hyphanden would enjoy knowing that what he's discovered is being used. You will be welcome; don't fear to come. There are few enough Loremasters in the Outcast community. Most of us fall into different specialties, and I don't begrudge Hyphanden the opportunity to converse with one of like mind."

"I'll remember that, and I thank you for your hospitality," Rioletta said. She had not considered very far into the future. At the moment she was only concerned with getting home, and with making sure Nikal was well enough to get to his own home.

When everyone had assembled in the sitting room later that morning, including Duri, who had spent the night, and breakfast was over, Rath spoke up.

"We should begin to think about traveling, and make plans. Andor, when do you think you'll be able to ride?"

"I can ride now," Andor said staunchly. "The splinting helps a great deal, and the medication I've been given is helping me heal and keeping the pain down. And I'd be willing to push myself to get home. We've been gone a long time."

Cardon, Rioletta, and Creed were all ready to go at any time, and with Stolen staying at Hyolon, it remained only to determine how to get Nikal home safely.

Nikal shrugged. "I'll be stiff from the stitching, but nothing is broken. With some help mounting, I'm sure I can ride by myself."

"I thought perhaps you'd ride with us to the house of my friends, north of Tabor," Rath said. "They can escort you from there to Dobor. I'm sure they'd be willing. Or you can call for Adla or another to come and ride back with you."

Nikal conceded. "Then we'll ride together to your friends' house. They'll not mind a few unexpected guests?"

"Hardly unexpected," Rath laughed. "I've been staying with them, and told them to expect travelers. It's a small place, but we'll manage."

After some discussion, the group agreed to leave the following morning. Cardon and Stolen went out to the stable to check the horses and tack. Kwistocta took Andor to the garden to gather herbs to make healing talismans so Andor would have some knowledge of her own treatment. Nikal and Duri relaxed in the sitting room, and soon were engaged in conversation, so Rioletta left them alone.

She encountered Hyphanden in the hallway leading to their room. "Hyphanden, what have you decided about the book?" she asked. "We must make a plan before tomorrow, if we are to leave."

Hyphanden considered. "It's your book," he said. "It was purchased for you by Nikal and it was gifted to you. You discovered its secrets. I have no right to take it from you, and anyway, I think that for the time being, it would be safer away from Hyolon. I have no need to use it; there are seven minds within the matrix here, if I should choose to access them. Rudon is crafty and Skilled, and it's possible he might be able to gain access to this estate. If he did, it's likely he could find and take the book no matter how I hid or Protected it. He is very good at reading Skills, as you've seen, and then undoing them. So I think it best that you take it with you. It will be safe enough in Andolith for the time being."

Rioletta was relieved that Hyphanden had decided by himself that his estate was not the appropriate place for the book;

that would put Kwistocta's mind a little more at ease, and fit with Kerdahl's warning. On the other hand, Rudon might be watching for them to leave, and might try to take the book from them when they were away from Hyolon. Without the Outcasts, they would be unable to escape or prevail over Rudon, particularly if he brought other rogue Sorcerers with him. But they could hardly have the Outcasts riding with them; that would be too obvious, and the Outcasts could be arrested once outside Hyolon.

Rioletta hesitated. "Hyphanden, I have been given some information from someone, whose identity I won't reveal, who is in contact with a rogue Sorcerer in Rudon's company. That rogue acts as a spy, and I do not wish to endanger him or his contact here. He could provide valuable information for you in the future."

"Not if I don't know who to contact to find out this information," Hyphanden said. "So you have managed to find out more about Rudon than even I, the Leader of the Outcast Council!"

"I was only approached because I was in possession of the Key," Rioletta said. "In the future, I suspect the bearer of this information will turn to you, particularly if you make it known that you will not press him closely."

"Hmm," Hyphanden mused, with a slight smile. "So this person is likely a Traditional, one who fears me and my Forbidden Skills. But no matter. I will not coerce you to tell me who it is, and I'll bide my time."

"It's possible I might be able to pass a rumor through him if we can come up with a story," Rioletta said. "Propaganda, or disinformation. That way Rudon will be looking elsewhere when we leave. This is a Skill of Andolith, after all: Misdirection, Ruse, Deception."

"Ah, the Council of Thieves," Hyphanden smiled. Then he sobered and his eyes grew dark. "But although I think the book should leave, and we have no use for it until we learn further how to control the Crypt and rescue the minds within it, I would certainly like to have a look at the Index, as you have called it: the talisman Rudon mistook for the key. You have contact with the old Tabor Elder Council. Although we joked about it before, if the opportunity arises, can you not find out what happened to it?"

"I'm not sure how I'd do that, and I'm not a contemporary of the Elder Council of Tabor," Rioletta reminded him. "Most contact with them is through Ladon. But describe it for me, and I'll keep it in mind."

"I recall it as a translucent stone with a lavender or pale pink color, diamond-shaped and about two inches on a side. It was somewhat flattened, like an amulet, with beveled and smoothed edges," Hyphanden gestured as he talked, forming the shape of the stone with his fingers. "It belonged to Stetsordahl. For a while he displayed it in a small alcove in his study, standing on end in a holder, with several other talismans, antiques he enjoyed collecting. Whether he ever knew what it was or not, I don't have any idea. It's likely in the hands of the First Chosen, now. But it would be most useful, if it is what we think it is."

"All right," Rioletta agreed. "I promise nothing, though."

"No?" Hyphanden smiled slightly. "You will not promise to return here, to discover more information? Stelaphandon finds you…interesting." He put a hand on the wall, blocking her exit.

Rioletta studied him with some apprehension. "Are you sharing your mind with Stelaphandon?" she asked.

"No." Hyphanden relaxed and shook his head. "I have only been synthesizing what I learned from him. Some of it only becomes clear with time. But we must plan what we are going to do to distract Rudon tomorrow and the tale you are going to pass on. Let's go see what ideas the others might have."

Rioletta followed Hyphanden back into the sitting room, where she sat down close to Nikal. The details of their plan would have to be exact, if they were to escape from Rudon, and she felt the relief of going home turn to apprehension.

Hyphanden called the rest of the group together. "Here's what I suggest," he began. "Tomorrow morning, Rath, Creed, Andor, Cardon, Rioletta, and Nikal will set out down to the gate of the estate, then turn and make their way through the old streets towards the greensward, and from there northeast towards the grave of the Younger Council. At the same time, Stolen, Duri, Kerdahl, and several others from the bachelor's estate will leave via the back wall."

"Who will have the book?" Rioletta asked nervously.

"You will, but don't worry. I think we'll set up enough of a distraction that you'll be relatively safe. Of course, there's some risk."

"I think there's greater risk leaving it here in close proximity to Rudon and the Crypt," Nikal said. "I'm willing to take the chance."

"So am I, of course," Rioletta said, although she realized she would be taking the greater risk if she was the one carrying the book.

All right," Hyphanden said. "Just behind the Andolith group, Kwistocta and I will ride out with Cayon, Mynador, and several others. We'll make our way into the city center and head for the old Security House. I hope this will be seen as a move to hide the book; the Security House itself is well Protected, and it leads led to secret passages through the city, which Rudon is aware of. Rudon's attention will be split three ways, and he would either have to split his followers, or make a decision about which group he'll confront."

"You think it's more likely he'll confront you?" Nikal asked.

"I think so. I doubt he'll suspect that I'd entrust the book to a group of minimally-skilled Sorcerers or allow it to leave Hyolon. He might also suspect that I've given it to the bachelors to get it out of my estate, which I know to be compromised. Hopefully the Andolith group will be gone before he discovers that we haven't taken anything to the Security House, nor was anything secreted in the bachelors' estate."

There was a long silence while the group considered the plan. Finally Nikal spoke up. "Well, I think that's the best we can do. Rioletta, are you sure you're ready for this?"

Rioletta nodded her agreement, as she thought her lips might be too dry to speak. An encounter with Rudon would be terrifying. But she couldn't think of a better plan. On the other hand, she had hoped to be rid of the book; what would she do with it when, and if, they made it to Andolith?

After they had agreed how to proceed, Rioletta left the estate and traveled apprehensively along the wall by herself to the bachelor's quarters, where she found Kerdahl.

"Kerdahl, would it be possible for you to pass on to your friend that the five Andolith residents, plus Nikal, will be leaving tomorrow morning, headed north, to locate and mark the resting place of the Younger Council?"

"I'll try," Kerdahl said. "I gather this is a deception of some sort, but I won't ask the details of the plan unless Hyphanden decides to include me."

"If you can, please also pass on that the book will be transferred to the bachelor's estate temporarily, to get it out of Hyphanden's estate, and that the Security House is being considered as an appropriate storage facility."

Kerdahl went over the details with her several times. When he was satisfied, he brought her partway back to Hyphanden's estate along the wall and then branched off by himself, fingering his communication talisman. Rioletta watched him for a while, hoping he would be able to contact his friend. The disinformation would be a vital part of their plan.

The following morning, they rose early, packed what they needed, and readied the horses. They came out of the city through a disused metal gate and into the woods of the greensward, following a roadway described to them by Hyphanden. The old path wound close below the city wall. Rioletta felt a prickle of adrenalin; looking up, she saw the bachelors' group, with Stolen and Duri and Kerdahl, come into view. The outside of the wall, within the ivy, fairly crawled with motion, and Rioletta suddenly realized the movement was hundreds of Leaves. They crawled steadily up the wall towards the top lip and Stolen, now outside the Protection of Hyphanden's estate. And in fact she saw that the trees standing just below the wall, on the top of the rise, their upper branches just reaching the rim, were not trees at all: they were Lefollah.

She stood in her stirrups and screamed Stolen's name, hoping he would hear and understand. Creed, Cardon, and Rath all drew their machetes as she did so, alarmed by her voice. But it was too late; even as she cried out, and Stolen stopped and looked down at her, a slender branch whipped out from the top of one of the Lefollah, struck Stolen in the hip, and toppled him off the wall, his machete falling free and away from him as he plummeted towards the ground.

Cat-like, Stolen twisted in midair and clawed at the ivy and limbs wrapping the wall. A shower of Leaves dislodged and fell with him. He hit the ground at the bottom of the wall hard, but the entanglement of the vines had slowed his fall. Stunned, he crouched against the wall, looking about for his machete.

His companions on top were powerless to help him. At Kerdahl's direction, they ran towards an offshoot of the wall that would bring them closer to the ground.

The forest around Stolen came alive; there were many Lefollah hidden there, and as one they began to move, their limbs stretching to reach him, their branches raining down to create many Twig Beings.

The Lefollah were tall and long-limbed, with many elongated branches and tendrils, and the Twig Beings, after a minute of assembly, quickly began to run up the slope towards Stolen. Rath, Creed, and Cardon had pulled their mounts up short, but they sat stunned, unsure what to do. The rise to the base of the wall was too steep to ride up, but none of them dismounted to run among the Lefollah on foot. It seemed likely to Rioletta that they would be bowled over or crushed, or perhaps entangled by the tendrils.

Stolen came to his senses and saw the Lefollah coming. He jumped up, looked up the wall, and seeing he could not climb it, elected to run. He leapt down the rise, taking the only route he could that was relatively free of Lefollah, but that route took him away from the Andolith Sorcerers and out into an open part of the greensward. The Lefollah swung around in place, and the entire grove, including the Twig Beings and the tree-like shells with their spindly roots and long branches, began to move after him.

Stolen was much faster than the Lefollah, now that he was running on a relatively flat area. But there were weeds and shrubs blocking his path, and he had no place to go, even if he outstripped them.

"Come on!" Creed shouted to Cardon and Rath. "Ride after him! We'll pick him up, and then we'll fight these things if we have to!"

The three of them spurred their horses to action and aimed to pass in front of Stolen, avoiding the oncoming Lefollah. Neither Andor nor Nikal could ride with any speed, and Rioletta was not a good enough rider to join them; they could only watch. And as they did so, they saw a horrible change come over the Lefollah.

With the crack of breaking branches, the Lefollah threw aside their outer shells of bark and limbs. Their leaves and branches fell away, and they split open from one end to the other, and smaller, faster beings leapt out, long of trunk and limb, naked and distorted, and sped after Stolen with growing speed.

Stolen had reached an area of old gardens and fields; between him and the riders rose a tall stone fence. Creed's big horse balked suddenly, and he was thrown forward over its withers, although he managed to catch himself well enough to land on his feet beside its neck. Rath pulled her horse up sharply. She rode a short, stocky mare, and it would not make the jump. But Cardon's leggy Mahquant horse did not hesitate or miss a step: it flew over the wall in a long leap, landed solidly on the other side, and Cardon turned it sharply, yelling to encourage it to greater speed.

The others could only watch as the bare Lefollah sped by, increasing their speed to match that of the horse, and Cardon gained on Stolen. He would have to pull up; he was not strong enough to pull Stolen to the saddle at a run. Creed remounted, and he and Rath galloped up along the fence, seeking a way through. There was a narrow gateway, the old gate long since salvaged, and they guided their horses through and spurred them into a gallop again, racing behind the Lefollah.

As Cardon reached Stolen, he pulled up sharply. Stolen leapt up, climbing bodily up Cardon's leg and stirrup, with Cardon grasping his arm. He swung a leg over the saddle behind Cardon, and they were off again within seconds, fleeing the oncoming Lefollah.

Creed and Rath rode close together, circling around the side of the Lefollah, swinging their machetes. The Lefollah turned away from the riders, then suddenly dispersed, running in all directions at once. Within seconds, they had disappeared completely into the trees on either side of the field. Creed and Rath continued hacking at the Twig Beings and Leaves that crowded around them, but it made no difference if parts were chopped off the Twigs; they continued milling around, poking the horses with sharp fingers until they bucked and threatened to throw their riders off.

As suddenly as they had assembled, the Twigs collapsed onto the ground and the Leaves crawled rapidly off like giant spiders. Cardon pulled up and Creed and Rath turned in their saddles. All of them looked wildly from side to side, but there was no sign of the Lefollah other than their discarded skins of bark lying between them and the wall.

Carefully, Cardon, Creed, and Rath cantered back to where Rioletta waited with Nikal and Andor.

"I don't like this," Cardon said. "I'd rather see them. I feel like they might jump out at us from all sides at any minute."

"Agreed," Creed said. He held onto his machete.

A moment later, Kerdahl, Duri, and several others came running along the bottom of the wall, having found a way down. Kerdahl pulled up panting as he saw Stolen behind Cardon.

"Stolen! I thought we'd lost you! I've never seen those things," Kerdahl said. "What do they want with you?"

"I escaped from their punishment, and then built the Twig Body for Marsavrina and Skadar," Stolen said. "They don't take kindly to one of their own controverting their law, or revealing their Skills to the outside world."

"But you're not one of them," Kerdahl said.

"No," Stolen agreed. "And I would say they've broken their agreement to keep themselves secret, having revealed themselves this way. These are not Lefollah of my grove, but others, doing the bidding of those of the north woods. My grove could not move like that; these have had more infusions into their bloodline, of one type or another."

Rioletta shuddered as Mynador's comments about those who brokered children came suddenly back to her mind.

"We must get Stolen back into the city and within some kind of Protection," Cardon said. "Let's not delay. Does the bachelor estate have Protections on it that will keep these things out?"

Kerdahl nodded. "It has the standard Protections of all the estates, and we can add more. Come; there is a spur of the wall this way, where we can regain the top. We'll hasten to the estate, and be on the lookout as we go. Stolen, are you hurt?"

Stolen examined his hands and arms, where he had sustained cuts and bruises from the vines. "I have some minor injuries, but I can go along on my own," he said. "Let's go now, before the Lefollah return and collect their skins, or make some attack. They are easily dissuaded by chopping weapons such as machetes when they're out of their bark, but once inside they are well protected, and you could chop their Twig Bodies to pieces with no consequence."

The group rode quickly around the base of the rise upon which the wall was set, following Kerdahl and the others on foot. At the spur wall, Stolen slid off from behind Cardon.

"Now you must continue towards the grave of the Younger Council," Kerdahl said. "We have not seen Rudon, unless this is some manifestation of his."

"I think it's separate. The Lefollah wouldn't be likely to join forces with him for reward or power," Rioletta said. "Stolen, please take care. How are we to know what happens here, whether everyone is safe?"

"I'll bear a message, or send one," Duri called to them from where they were ascending the wall. "That's what I'm here for! Look for me!"

"Easy enough," Rath said in a low tone. "I'll always know where he is, if he carries his mapping device." She clapped the one on her belt.

Cardon turned his horse, and the rest followed him. They passed the discarded bark skins again, but no one stopped to examine them. There was still no sign of the Lefollah who had been within them, and soon they had crossed the greensward and were traveling through the woods to the northeast.

"Rioletta, can you tell if there are Lefollah around?" Cardon asked.

"If I concentrate, yes, I think I should be able to tell," Rioletta said. "And right now I don't feel them. I think we've left them behind, at least for the time being."

"Good," Cardon said. "I can't believe you used to go talk to them alone in the woods. They are some frightening beings."

"They didn't present themselves that way when I spoke with them," Rioletta said. "And remember, Stolen was imprisoned because of what he did to me, or what they perceived he did to me. They swore to protect me to make up for it."

"You mean they attacked Stolen out of some misguided attempt to protect you?" Rath asked.

Rioletta shrugged. "Perhaps. I can't say for sure. They have tried before to regain Stolen, whether to re-imprison him or to use him to enrich their bloodline, as they originally intended, I do not know. But in my view Stolen is a human being, and doesn't belong to them. As such, he's deserving of all of our protection."

Andor rode up beside them. "At one point, I disagreed," she said to Rath. "I thought releasing Stolen was a poor idea, and that he was dangerous. But he has done nothing but good for us, and I admit I'll miss him in Andolith. Although he's never developed much of a sense of humor…perhaps that will come in time."

The group began to relax as they continued, and the remnants of adrenalin drained away. Finally they arrived at the old farm where the remains of the Younger Council lay, and silence fell over them as they entered the grove.

"Well, Cardon, do you hear anything now?" Creed asked in a low tone.

Cardon shook his head. "No, but I'm not sure how to feel. I know the body of the mother of my child lies here in death, but the mind survives. Do I mourn for the death of the body, or rejoice that her mind lives on? I'm not convinced we did her a favor, placing her mind in that being we created. It must be horrible to look at yourself in the mirror and see that."

They rode more slowly after the grove, following Rath as she marked the way with small reflective metal pins pushed into the bark of trees. "Maybe I'll stick a pin into a Lefollah?" she joked.

They stopped for lunch near a small, clear-running brook; afterwards they continued in a more easterly direction. The forest began to open up into familiar oak woodland and the going was easier. Occasionally they rode along hilltops or the sides of rises where they could see out over the trees and catch a glimpse of Tabor to the south.

In late afternoon they began to cross beaten paths and wide trails, and then came into an area of small houses with large gardens and small vineyards. The houses were neat, mostly made of stone and oak logs, and similar in construction to each other.

"A community of guards," Rath said. "Many of those who patrol the streets of Tabor live here. Their vocation is the protection of people and property, and they serve the Security Council, which is separate and apart from the Sorcerers' Councils to avoid corruption and influence. Thus their political views are less fanatical than some others."

She led them down a small side street to a stone house shaded heavily by huge oaks. They dismounted, Creed lifting Andor down and Nikal dismounting with some help on a short wall alongside the garden. They took the horses in to a small neat barn, and then Rath led them to the house to meet the occupants.

Chapter Eighteen

The house was inhabited by two women, Betar and Luridos, who welcomed the party inside. Betar was just returning from work; she still wore a stiff leather vest with the yellow sash of a guard and a wide leather belt adorned with various holsters. With Rath's help, they prepared a good meal with fresh poultry and pasta from Tabor, wine, and vegetables from their garden. After dinner, Rath helped move several mattresses in to the main room. The women opened the doors, one on either side of the main room, to allow an evening breeze to cool the house. The back door led out to a fenced garden, with several fruit trees providing shade.

Although Creed was on alert, watching for any sign that they'd been followed, the rest of them spent a pleasant evening sipping more wine, of which the two women had a wide variety they were eager to show off. Rioletta enjoyed discussing the various herbs they grew in their kitchen garden; she had a mind to try to grow mustard in Andolith. Cardon practiced his Healing Skills by tending first to Nikal, who had removed his shirts and bandages to allow his wounds to air, and then to Andor. Andor removed her swathes, which bound her arm to her chest, and relaxed with only the splints on; she claimed that the pain was much abated. They were joined by two dogs and several cats, as well, and the small house was quite full by the time they began to drop off to sleep.

221

Rath slept on the couch, while the rest of them occupied the mattresses, close together on the floor.

In the morning they dallied a bit, partly because they all realized Nikal would not be continuing on with them. Betar would take a message to Tabor and send it on to Adla in Dobor through a messenger service; Nikal would stay with the two guards until Adla arrived to ride home with him, in case he needed help or care along the way. The group of travelers relaxed in the main room, sipping second cups of tea, watching the dogs trot busily in and out of the garden and the cats creep around the fireplace.

"I never expected to be gone this long when first we left for the Polebray," Rioletta said. "I wonder what's been going on at home?"

"There was to be another meeting with the Elder Council of Tabor right about now," Andor reminded her. "That will have come and gone without our input, not that we would have done much but listen, anyway."

"I'm looking forward to seeing my daughter," Cardon said. "I hope she's been all right staying with Lida."

"I expect Alaxas has taken up the slack," Creed said, speaking of his eldest sister, who had three children of her own. "Justah gets on well enough with her youngest."

Nikal stretched, carefully raising the arm on his wounded side. "Cardon, you ought to consider marrying," he said casually. "Give the little girl a stable home, maybe produce a few more kids to teach your horse business to. You can do it now that you're not a Council-member anymore. There ought to be a few young women in Andolith who'd be happy enough with the proposition."

Andor suppressed a smile, and Cardon returned an uncomfortable look; of course Nikal was aware of Cardon and Rioletta's past relationship, and it would be to his own advantage if Cardon was married and unavailable, especially now that he was healthy again and regaining his strength.

"Nikal, when are you going to come up to Andolith?" Andor asked, changing the subject. "Seems to me Rioletta's spent a lot of time in the Tadian; it's your turn to come to the Sydian."

Nikal smiled. "I expect I'll have all sorts of duties and responsibilities waiting for me when I get back to Dobor, having been gone this long. But you're right, and when I've put things in order, I'll take a ride up that way. Perhaps this fall during the harvest. Everyone's busy at that time, and there's less work for Sorcerers and Councils to do."

When the group was finally packed and loaded to leave, Rioletta spent a few minutes alone with Nikal. This was the longest time she'd spent with him, and she regretted leaving, but each had duties, and the parting must be done.

"Don't forget the talisman," Nikal said. "Answer me when you feel me call. The more time we spend together, the stronger it will get, and the easier it will be to communicate."

When Rioletta had mounted, the party, now reduced to five, turned east towards the Tadian River. They planned to skirt Tabor, then travel up to the ford and cross there with other travelers and tradesmen. Once across the Tadian, they would make for Matbor, and from there it was a long half-day's ride home to Andolith.

Rath was familiar with this part of the Riola, and all the rest had been through the area as well. Andor seemed fairly comfortable and strong, and they rode well, arriving at the ford in mid-afternoon. They crossed the bridge with several other lone riders, and after a brief break in the shade of the oaks on the east side, continued on towards Matbor. From the Tadian east, the land began to rise; the oaks became larger and older, and the temperature began to drop slowly. Past Matbor the rise continued until the elevation and soil properties excluded the oaks and the forest turned to pines. Andolith was at this intersection of forest types, also a snowline, where the deeper snows of the north moderated. There, the temperature would be a full ten degrees lower than in the Tadian.

They took a room in Matbor that evening, arriving some time after the main dinner rush, when the eating establishments were being cleaned and closed for the evening but dark had not yet fallen. As they turned their horses over to the stable-hands, Andor noticed a large black horse being carefully groomed in the stable-yard.

"That looks like the horse ridden by Stetsordahl Vrinal of the Elder Council of Tabor," she commented.

Cardon looked closely at the horse. "I'm sure you're right. The meeting you mentioned last night was to take place in Matbor; perhaps some of the Elder Council are still here."

"If that's so, we should at least acknowledge them and pay them a visit for diplomatic reasons," Andor said. "But I admit, I'm very tired and don't feel much like doing it."

"I'll go," Rioletta said. "I'm the only other member of the Council here, and I'm not too tired. Besides, I have an interest in talking to Stetsordahl. I'll freshen up first and then go."

Rioletta washed and changed her clothes, then made her way downstairs to the lobby near the eating establishment, where she asked after Stetsordahl. The clerk told her he had remained in his room for the evening, but declined to tell her which room it was, instead sending a boy up the stairs with a message. Rioletta waited at the desk, and soon the messenger returned with an invitation to visit. She followed the boy up a flight of stairs to the floor where the larger suites were held aside for important personages, and was let into a suite behind a heavy door.

Stetsordahl was the eldest member of the Council, a man well past middle age, white-haired and showing some bowing of the back, although he was still quite active. His motions were quick and decisive, sometimes almost violent, and he had a reputation for quick temper. He was a Traditional who had broken with Andolith during the days when the Andolith Council was led by Mosse Amwiska, but after her death and the rescue of the Council by the Andolith Sorcerers, he had mellowed towards them, and Ladon had worked diligently to establish a relationship with Stetsor and the others of the Council.

"Ah, Rioletta, of the Younger Council of Andolith," he greeted her. Rioletta smiled; she was not sure he remembered her, but of course the boy had told him who she was, and that she wished audience. "You were not present at the meeting. Ladon told me you and Andor Acaladon were delayed."

He motioned to a chair nearby, and Rioletta took it. There was a boy there as well, probably not past his teens, but Rioletta was not introduced. She assumed he was there to provide services for Stetsor, as a valet of sorts; Stetsor often mentored young boys who showed promise as Sorcerers and took them along on trips to introduce them to the art of negotiation.

"I'm sorry we couldn't be here for the meeting," she began. "We are now on our way back to Andolith. We hope to arrive tomorrow. Andor is with me, but unfortunately she has been injured, and although we expect her to make a full recovery, we rode long today and she needs rest and medical care."

"That's too bad," Stetsordahl said. "She has a gift for negotiation and can support an opinion without angering those with whom she disagrees. I hope she will be well."

"She sends her regrets. I came myself both to greet you and express my apologies for missing the meeting, and also to pass on some information I think you will want to know. I would not have you hear it elsewhere first."

Stetsordahl relaxed back in his chair and crossed one leg over the other. "That's very considerate of you," he said with a slight smile. Rioletta reminded herself not to equivocate with Stetsor; she was not a negotiator, like Andor, and Stetsor had a reputation for being able to read the truth beneath the words. He had not achieved the position of Leader of the Tabor Council by chance.

Rioletta began, abbreviating the tale somewhat. She told him they had received information concerning the Younger Council while they were at the Polebray. They had gone to the location of their temporary burial intending to mark the location so their relatives could find them. They had traveled secretly, fearing the First Chosen. They had also hoped to find information concerning their motives in imprisoning the Elder Council.

"Indeed," Stetsordahl said, raising his eyebrows. "I should like to know what motivated the Younger Council myself. My anger at them has abated somewhat, and I agree that their bodies should be properly disposed and their families given closure, but I still begrudge them the Skill that cost us the Council-house and nearly our lives."

Rioletta nodded. "I understand. While there, I met a young man I believe to be your grandson and namesake, Stetsordahl."

Stetsordahl smiled broadly. "I heard he fled to the Ruined City rather than pledge allegiance to the First Chosen. It's a shame he must consort with the Outcasts, but he fought bravely, so I've heard, and will not give up his values. But how did you come to meet him? Is he well?"

"He is well. His life in the Ruined City is not as bad as might be imagined; in fact, he has all he needs, including a community, many of whom are not true Outcasts either. When we were at the resting place of the Younger Council, we met two Outcasts, who later brought Stetsor to us," Rioletta said, avoiding mention of entering the city itself. "Perhaps you remember them: Hyphanden and Kwistocta."

"Hyphanden!" Stetsordahl spat, sitting forward in his chair. Then his expression softened. "Of course I remember him. Highly Skilled, he was, and highly intelligent. He picked up anything he was taught more quickly than anyone else I've ever seen. Surely he could have eventually led the Council as a whole; he was Leader of the First Chosen for a period of time."

"Then you will not be surprised to know that he is Leader of the Outcast Council," Rioletta said.

Stetsordahl laughed shortly. "Yes and no. His mind was undisciplined and he ran wild; he sought out all information, any information, any Skills, any knowledge, and absorbed it all. Unfortunately Phando was tempted by the Forbidden Skills. This is a failure of those of us who are most suited to be Sorcerers, and indeed all of the Skilled: our minds are weak, in a strange way, and we are easily tempted, especially by Mind-sharing techniques. The most Skilled among us, it seems, are often the weakest."

He shook his head, remembering. "It's perhaps the hardest thing I've ever done, to cast him out; I did it personally, and the only way I could do it was to bring myself to anger. I was forced to order Kwistocta Outcast as well. She followed him, for they had been bound together since childhood. Without him, I think she could have gone on to become a powerful and valuable Council-member, but I could not make exception."

"She remains with him," Rioletta told him. "She is also well. I can see you were very fond of them. It must have been difficult for you to cast them out."

Stetsor nodded. "I called Phando in to my study and told him he must go, leave the city immediately. But he refused to leave at first, and tried to argue with me. I closed myself to his arguments, for he was very persuasive. I told him I would imprison him and Strip his Skills if he did not leave, and I would put a warrant on his head. But I gave him this chance to flee the city. Still he argued against me and stood his ground; he was not afraid of me. Finally I took up a staff and struck him physically, which shocked him; he took Tocta, and they fled to the Ruined City without the Stripping of their Skills. I have heard little of him since, though some rumors

226

reach me. He was a leader always; people followed him and trusted him, despite his transgressions."

"And they follow him still," Rioletta said, fascinated by Hyphanden's history. "He has created a community much like any other village, where the Outcasts live fine and orderly lives. Both have the respect of their community, and they have continued to learn and grow."

"I must admit I'm glad he has made his own way," Stetsordahl said. "But tell me what he said to you."

"We talked about many things," Rioletta said. "He remembered you with respect, if not fondness. He recalled details about you, after all this time. Once he noticed this talisman I wear…" Rioletta pulled out her black pendant, "…and asked me if I was a collector of them. I said I had collected a good many talismans, and he told me that you, too, are a collector of talismans. He remembered some specific ones, in fact: he described a diamond-shaped lavender one you used to display. He believed it to be an antique from Hyolon; he told me to tell you, should I meet you, that he often comes upon such things, and would be happy to trade for them!"

"Ha!" Stetsordahl snorted. "I won't trade with an Outcast, much as I regret having lost Phando. But I know the one he talks about, and he's right: it did come from Hyolon. But it is less of a talisman than a storage device. It appears to have a list of names printed in it, if one is adept enough Loremaster to access them."

"I suppose all of those are now in the hands of the First Chosen. It is too bad," Rioletta said.

"Oh, no. We made an agreement a few months ago for representatives to enter the Council-house and remove our personal belongings. I have all of my possessions at West Ford, including my collection of talismans. I will show you them some time, if you come to West Ford."

"I would be very interested," Rioletta said. "But let me tell you more of what Hyphanden revealed. He told us about another Sorcerer Outcast, one they call a Rogue. This Sorcerer first contacted, recruited, and tutored the Younger Council in the Forbidden Skills, and it was he who taught them the fatal Skill they Threw at you."

Rioletta gave him a short version of the way the Younger Council had been manipulated, and told him a little about the devices Hyphanden suspected had been used to concentrate their Skills and bring about consensus. She assured him that while they were not blameless in their practice of the Forbidden Skills, their motive was at least not altogether evil.

"Who is this other Outcast with whom they had contact?" Stetsordahl asked, scowling.

"His name is Rorudon," Rioletta said.

Stetsordahl started up. "Rudon! I should have known! I was not so sorry to Outcast *him*! He showed great promise: he was highly Skilled, but undisciplined and arrogant. He angered me without me having to bring myself to it; it came naturally. And he was too much of a fool to leave when given the chance. I imprisoned him and had his Skills Stripped. But he was stronger than I realized, and we did not successfully Strip all his Skills. He was able to keep them separate in his mind, and then he fled, although we believed his own resistance might have damaged his mind. So he wished revenge against me?"

"Yes, and now he has also betrayed the Outcast Council, and Hyphanden feels he is dangerous. Beware any messengers from Rudon!"

"I would not accept any message from Rudon," Stetsordahl said. "And I appreciate your information, although I'm dismayed you had to have contact with the Outcasts to obtain it." He looked suspiciously at Rioletta. "You don't practice the Forbidden Skills, do you?"

"No!" Rioletta said. "Nor did I learn any while in the company of Hyphanden. I am a Traditional, as an Andolith Sorcerer."

"Andolith has done well this past one hundred years, or ninety-seven since its inception," Stetsordahl mused. "Ladon is somewhat more liberal than Mosse was, but we get on better. He is a negotiator, and Mosse was not! Anyway, I look forward to further cooperation between our Councils."

Rioletta stood and clasped hands with Stetsordahl. "I have traveled far today, and must return to my companions, but I thank you for your time," she said. "If I can be of any further assistance in obtaining information about the Younger Council, or Stetsordahl the Younger or any of the others who shelter there, please let me know."

Stetsordahl smiled. "Oh, and I'll be certain to keep that talisman safe," he said casually. "I suspect you had a reason for mentioning it other than small-talk. I will not let it fall into the hands of Rudon, whatever it is. Should you choose to tell me what it means, please know you will be welcome at my residence in West Ford."

Rioletta flushed and bowed her head. "There's a reason you became the Leader of the Elder Council," she replied. "The talisman is not particularly important, only a useful thing. Perhaps I will be able to tell you what I believe it to be at some point, but it will require a much longer story!"

"All right! Until we meet again, then!" Stetsordahl said, releasing her hand.

Rioletta returned down the stairway to the lobby, and then up the second stair to their room. Creed and Rath were preparing a meal from food they had brought as well as some Rath had obtained from downstairs.

"How is old Stetsordahl?" Andor asked sleepily.

"Well enough. I managed to keep on his good side, and got out before I rubbed him the wrong way," Rioletta said. "He now knows something about the death of the Younger Council, although I abbreviated the tale a good deal and skipped certain parts."

Later that night, Rioletta lay on one of the beds awake in the dark. There were only two beds and a cot in the room; she had agreed to share one of the beds with Cardon, and she trusted he would not do anything inconvenient. Rath had taken the cot, and Creed breathed deeply from the other bed, nearer the window.

Her mind turned to the talisman in the possession of Stetsordahl. If Hyphanden was going to continue to access the seven minds in his possession, as it seemed he was determined to do, it would be important for him to have background information about who each one of them was, in order to avoid manipulation or accessing a damaged or dangerous mind. If possible, she would get that information, or the talisman itself, for him. And if he did continue with his research into the causes behind the Dispersal, she wanted to know his results. Partly it was because she was a Loremaster and a Sorcerer, and needed accurate information, as she had claimed; but partly, she had to admit, it was simply because she was curious.

Chapter Nineteen

Rioletta spent the first few days back in Andolith cleaning the dust from her possessions, resting, and answering as few questions as she could without seeming rude. But she knew there were Council duties to be taken care of, so eventually she visited Ladon at the Council-house.

Ladon crossed his arms and sat back in the big wooden chair he had claimed for his own in the inner chamber of the Council-house. Rioletta pulled her own chair up to the large, solid table, inlaid with a map of the Sydian region, and leaned on her elbows.

"I'm glad to see you back and well-enough rested to resume your duties," Ladon said. "You were overlong in Hyolon. In fact, a single day in that place is too long."

"I realize you're not happy that we ended up in Hyolon, in the company of the Outcast Sorcerers," Rioletta said, "but at the time it seemed we didn't have much choice."

"Of course, I wasn't there, but from what I've heard from your compatriots, I tend to think different decisions could have been made. You've put me in an awkward spot. What do I tell the citizens of Andolith? That two of their Younger Council have been consorting with the Outcasts?"

Rioletta looked down. "It's up to you," she said. "I suppose those we govern deserve to know the truth."

231

Ladon considered her for a long moment. "In some cases, it's better that those we govern don't know the whole truth. Without the details, it may only serve to trouble them."

Rioletta met his eyes. "That seems to have been a popular opinion in the past, given the way the Charter was crafted."

Ladon grunted. "Remember that what you think you've learned about the Charter came through Outcasts. I expect you to abide by the decision this Council makes regarding the story of what you've been doing for the last month."

"Of course," Rioletta said. She sat back and clasped her hands in her lap. The idea of concealing where she had been from the rest of the population seemed wrong to her, but she wasn't ready to gainsay Ladon or the rest of the Elder Council.

"There are other matters to discuss," Ladon said in a lighter tone. "While you were gone, the Elder Council chose several promising young folk to be trained and inducted to complete the Councils and allow a quorum. One of these is Kestrella, Creed's younger sister. She has just reached the age of eighteen and will thus be ready for induction within a few years. I expect you to work closely with her. It's possible she may show Skill as a Loremaster."

"I'd be happy to," Rioletta said. Kestrella was as easy-going as Creed and would make a fine addition to the Younger Council.

"Good," Ladon said. "We'll meet as an entire Council for the first time since spring this evening, and we'll hammer out the details of how we'll filter your story. I'll see you tonight."

Rioletta went away unsatisfied from the conversation. It left her wondering exactly what had been filtered out by other, older Councils. Rudon's comments about the Special Skills of the Inner Circles echoed in her ears.

All the remaining members of the Younger and Elder Councils met that evening after dinner. Morcah and Pateret had already heard most of the story, but Ladon had Andor and Rioletta tell the assembly everything from the start to make sure all of them had all the details.

"Certainly it's unwise to tell the entire populace that two of our Younger Council have been living with the Outcasts and even following their advice," Amidon said after Rioletta and Andor had finished their tale. "It would only serve to create a feeling of distrust."

"It was an unfortunate decision," Boradon agreed. "Certainly some other solution could have been devised."

Rioletta shot Andor a glance, and saw the scowl forming on her face.

"What's done is done," Ladon said. "I agree it was unfortunate, but the issue before us now is to decide what, exactly, we will allow to be known. I think we have a ready solution. Rath of Luth introduced our group of travelers to two Tabor security guards who sheltered them during their journey home."

"Ah, security guards are generally required to be politically neutral," Amidon said. "Few would find it unusual that our travelers spent a month staying with friends of Rath of Luth."

"Exactly," Ladon said. "Are we agreed that this will be the story?"

Ladon, Amidon, and Boradon agreed quickly, and Morcah was eventually persuaded that this story would be the best for the stability of the community. With a majority reached, Ladon continued.

"There's another matter I'd like to discuss. The Elder Council is not near retirement, but with only three of us, and me involved in duties that take me away from Andolith regularly, I feel the need to expand the role of the Younger Council, with an eye towards moving some members into the Elder Council in the future"

Ladon eyed each of the Younger Council in turn, then focused on Pateret and Morcah. "I would move Pateret, and Morcah into positions with expanded duties. Morcah I would like to see become the Leader of the Council in the future, because I think he has the ability to do so. He has a large family here and has shown little inclination to travel, and he is very good with policy and of a stable personality. And Pateret would make a good second to Morcah. "

Morcah flushed visibly. It had been assumed by the Younger Council that Morcah would someday become the Leader, but this was the first time Ladon had specifically confirmed it. Ladon turned to Andor and Rioletta, who sat close together.

"Andor, I would not move you. You have enough to do with the duties you already have, and those take you away from Andolith too much for you to spend enough time managing the village. You, Rioletta, I would move into an Advisory position; we now have no

233

Loremaster on the Elder Council. But perhaps you have more interest than I've noticed in a leadership position. I don't mean to exclude you."

"No," Rioletta said truthfully. "I'm more interested in continuing my research as a Loremaster, and in providing solid input into the decisions that must be made. My temperament is not that of a Council-leader. In fact, I think perhaps you should reconsider moving me into a position of more responsibility. I would like your leave to travel a bit more often, to explore some information I encountered during this journey. I feel it might affect how I make my decisions."

Rioletta had not revealed her conversations with Hyphanden to Ladon. Now he frowned at her, and studied her face intently.

"I don't want you to get involved with the Outcasts," Ladon said firmly. "Your experience with them was good, I admit, and I was surprised to hear how well they live and how healthy most of them appear to be. Nevertheless, they practice now, and have practiced in the past, Skills that our society has chosen to Forbid, because of the damage they can do to mind and body. They themselves chose to abandon our communities. They are subject to temptation, to violence, to distraction, and they chose these ways rather than to contribute to the orderly progression of our villages into an infinite future."

Rioletta looked down at her hands in her lap. She was not sure this was true, but she would not contradict Ladon, especially in front of the rest of the Council.

"I do not agree with or accept them," Ladon continued. "I have made allowances for Cardon because it appeared to me he truly repented of what he did, that he was led into it through his affection for the mother of his child, and he has promised not to practice what he learned. But do not mistake that considered allowance for tolerance. Any knowledge garnered from them is suspect."

Ladon paused and Rioletta shifted uncomfortably. Out of the corner of her eye, she could see that Andor had crossed her arms and continued to glower.

"Your desire for information is admirable, but don't confuse knowledge with sound decision-making," Ladon continued. "Decisions can be made in the absence of complete knowledge, and can still be sound and good. Complete knowledge is not possible;

there's always some doubt, some future event that cannot be foreseen. I want you to concentrate on using the knowledge you have and can gain from studying the Charter of Dispersal, rather than on adding facts that may or may not simplify the issues."

"Then you will forbid me from seeking further knowledge from sources outside this village?" Rioletta challenged.

Ladon sat back and was silent for a minute, studying her. "I do not forbid it," he finally said. "If this is what you truly want and you are convinced seeking this knowledge is within the bounds of what we permit, and you truly believe it will serve to move Andolith into the future soundly, I do not forbid it. After all, you were led along this path by Amwiska. You were told to seek information outside the village, and I cannot blame you if you have followed that to its logical conclusion. But there are certain aspects of such seeking I will forbid. I must know exactly what you are doing and where you are going, and from whom you seek such information and how you obtain it. If I find you have concealed any of these things from me, my trust in you will be damaged, and your decisions will be suspect."

Rioletta nodded, although she resented his close control. "I understand, Ladon. Please don't misunderstand me; your leadership has been sound, the training and education I've received has been thorough and complete, and Andolith has existed for the last ninety-seven years because of such leadership and through the Traditional interpretation of the Charter. I don't seek to question these things, or you; I seek only to add to it. Many other villages have existed for as long as we have, and they, sometimes, interpret the Charter differently, and operate using different principles. It does not make them unsuccessful."

"No," Ladon admitted. "That is true, and besides, I have sworn to myself not to isolate Andolith and to allow for the input of information from outside sources, unlike Mosse. I apologize for mistrusting you. I only want you to be careful, and remain aware of your sources. The loss of Cardon from the Council was more painful for me than you might realize; he is my kin, and it hurt me to see him fall into ways that damaged him. But you are not Cardon, and certainly your contact with the Lefollah, and the Outcasts, has changed you and changed the way we view our world. That cannot be undone."

"There's no need to apologize," Rioletta replied. "You are protective of me and the rest of the Younger Council, and that's a good thing, not something to be sorry for. But you're right: the Lefollah have changed me. Besides, there is Justah to think of. We made a promise to the Lefollah, and it's important we find out as much as possible about them before the time comes when they'll come to collect on that bargain."

"We'll see how we can manage this seeking of yours, then," Ladon said with a half-smile. "I trust Nikal of Dobor. He has a good reputation, and if you are in his company, I'll not feel as uncomfortable."

Rioletta unconsciously fingered the pendant at her neck. "I can travel with Andor, too, and I hope you'll come to trust Cardon once again, if not as a Sorcerer than as a traveling companion and horseman. Kestrella will need to be introduced to our allies and oriented to traveling routes. But there is one other thing we must consider."

"Yes, the book," Ladon said. "Another matter for the Council. I've hidden it here in the Council-house, but that's not sufficient in the long term."

"Certainly by now Rudon understands that Hyphanden didn't take it to the Security House in Hyolon and that it wasn't taken to the bachelor's estate either," Andor said. "He must by now have deduced that it's been removed from the city, and he'd guess Rioletta brought it here to Andolith."

"Without consulting with outside Sorcerers, and thus possibly revealing our concern, there are few Protections I'm able to place on it," Ladon said. "I'm not Skilled at Protections in particular. I suggest we place it underneath one of the wind machines for now, in the gear-house, with mechanical and other Protections such as the Council can devise as well as Concealments, which we are better at. That will keep it far enough from Andolith itself that someone seeking for Protections in the village area will not be able to detect them. And we should consider moving it out of this region, although where we would put it I'm not sure. I'm of a mind to destroy it, myself."

"But that would destroy any hope the minds within the matrix have of being anything but imprisoned. I admit that their minds should likely have died with their bodies, but since they didn't, should we take it upon ourselves to complete those executions?"

"No," Ladon said. "I would *like* to destroy it, but I will not. But the matrix should not be used again; it is unnatural and dangerous. We will do our best to keep the book safe until some point in the future when we can hope a solution can be found for this dilemma."

Andor and Rioletta left the Council-house together when the meeting was adjourned.

"Old Ladon's pretty shrewd," Andor admitted. "He always seems to know more than I give him credit for."

"Yes, but I feel like he's singling me out for mistrust," Rioletta complained.

"Give him some time. Maybe he'll mellow over the winter. It's still a shock to him that we spent all that time with the Outcasts."

"I hope so," Rioletta said. "I have no intention of restricting myself to reading only what I can get here in Andolith. There are important questions I need to answer for my own peace of mind, and if I have to look elsewhere for that information, I will."

"I'm sure we can smuggle you in some documents from elsewhere," Andor said. "Be agreeable with Ladon and don't rouse his suspicions."

"You're better at being agreeable than I am," Rioletta said, "but I'll try. Thanks for your support."

Andor left her near the sundial, and Rioletta made her way home alone through the dark village.

One afternoon, a lone rider entered the village from the Matbor road, his horse's hooves skittering the early-fallen acorns. Rioletta heard the horse-hooves and came around from the back of her house, where she was preparing the kitchen garden for winter.

"Duri!" she exclaimed as the rider swung down to the ground. "Welcome! What news?"

"As for that, I'm not so sure all will welcome me here," he said, with his characteristic grin. "There's plenty of news. I'd rather not tell it multiple times, though."

"Of course. Please, come in and have a drink. I'll tie your horse up in the shade in the back; we can unpack him later and bring him down to the paddocks. I'm sure I can round up Andor and

Cardon in just a minute. Creed is out hunting, I saw him and Morcah slip off this morning at dawn."

"No loss as far as I'm concerned," Duri said. "Thanks for the drink. I can unsaddle my horse while you're gone to get Andor and Cardon."

Rioletta left Duri alone at her house while she hurried to the Council-house for Andor and to Charnia's clinic for Cardon. Both of them dropped what they were doing and followed her back to her house eagerly.

"I'm anxious for news about how the diversion went," Andor said. "I hope all are all right and no one was hurt."

"Duri seemed cheerful enough, but that's not unusual," Rioletta said. "Certainly he doesn't appear to have been damaged himself."

"You shouldn't have left him alone at your house," Cardon said. Rioletta turned as she walked to look at him.

"Why not? He's not a thief, as far as I know, despite having been born here."

Cardon shrugged. "Just something that came to my mind. He wouldn't mind knowing where the book is, I suspect."

"Well, it's not at my house, so he can look all he likes," Rioletta said. "Besides, I don't care if Hyphanden and those who have used the book know where it is."

"Perhaps not, but the fewer who know, the better," Cardon said. "Don't give Duri information you don't want spread around to others. I don't trust him."

"Just what you've learned from Creed, I expect," Rioletta said, but Andor shook her head.

"Remember that Cardon has Mind-shared, and his mind is open due to the potions he took," she said. "He may be getting something that you and I can't feel."

They had paused not far from Rioletta's house. "All right," she said. "I'd like to send a message back to Hyphanden, but perhaps it will have to wait, or I'll have to figure out some code. Let's see what he has to say, anyway."

They entered Rioletta's house, and settled into chairs in the main room, where Duri sat sipping a beer Rioletta had left him with. She brought out more, filled the glasses, and turned a kitchen chair around into the room for herself.

238

"So what happened after we left, Duri?" Andor said. "Last I saw you, you were running up the wall with Stolen."

Duri swirled the beer and happily launched into a story about what had happened following their departure from Hyolon. Rudon had chosen to follow Hyphanden and his group, which consisted of Kwistocta, Cayon, Mynador, and several others, all Sorcerers of one type or another. That group had taken off quickly towards the Security House with many obvious Protections around them. Rudon had waited until they were well within the city to attack. He had been accompanied by a good-sized group of Hyolonal, who served as a distraction while Rudon and a number of rogues Threw all manner of Skills. They were hard pressed to counter what he Threw at them, Skill for Skill. The Hyolonal worried them at the edges and tried to stick their horses, but suddenly Cardon's serpent-horses had showed up.

"Maybe they were attracted by the sound, I don't know; funny thing is, they've grown," Duri said.

"That's what you said, Cardon, after one of them bit Nikal," Rioletta remembered. "I didn't think animations could change size."

"Well, I've seen them myself since, and they are huge," Duri said. "Anyway, the Hyolonal scattered as soon as they showed up, and the serpent-horses went for Rudon's crew. They're almost impervious to any Skills. Phando's group managed to escape and fled back to the estates. By the time Rudon and his gang regrouped, you were well away from the area, and we were back in the bachelors' estate with Stolen. Some of us rode out to assist. Phando and the others were on their way back by that time, but they encountered a group of Hyolonal just as we found them. The Hyolonal made a kind of half-hearted attempt at us, but all that happened was that Mynador managed to capture a Hyolonal kid, probably fifteen or sixteen years old. They took him back to the estate. He has the look of a Vrinac, and no one is sure what he was doing with the Hyolonal. Mynador keeps him at her estate for now, hoping to glean some information from him."

"Good news, then," Cardon said. "I'm pleased the serpent-horses came in handy. I was upset that I couldn't find them or call them in. I suppose they might go for the Hyolonal because they developed a taste for them in the Council-house."

"That's disgusting, if true, Cardon," Andor said with a grimace. "What's been happening since?"

Duri shrugged. "Things as usual, I guess you could say." He told them about the special precautions they were all taking when moving about the city and the special details they'd developed to keep an eye out for Rudon or his crew. Stolen had managed to move back and forth between the bachelors' estate and Hyphanden's estate through the streets, rather than on the wall, several times, but the Lefollah had not been seen. Stolen had told them he couldn't feel any Lefollah about anymore, and the Leaves had departed.

"Marsavrina has been growing. She's filled out quite a bit, you'd be surprised. She's managed to grow the sticks Stolen made for her larger, and she's been able to form them into limbs that look more human in shape and are more flexible. She's taken to wearing more clothing and looks a lot like a person made of wood now. Although if you touch her, it doesn't feel like wood; it feels like thick skin. She's grown a face, too, ears and all, although she still can't speak. And thankfully she's grown some eyelids and at least gives the appearance of blinking. That lidless stare was a little creepy."

"You'll take a few belongings of Stolen's back with you, won't you?" Rioletta asked. "He had only a few things that he left here, but he would probably appreciate having them back, as he has little enough of his own."

"Of course," Duri said. "He sends his greetings, and says the horse Cardon gave him is in fine shape. Phando and Tocta send their greetings as well."

"You've gotten quite familiar with them," Andor teased, "calling them by their nicknames and all."

Duri smiled smugly, and Rioletta refilled his glass with beer. "Well, it's a small community, you know. Have you any messages you want me to take back, along with Stolen's gear?"

Rioletta smiled. "You'll be staying for at least a night, won't you? So no hurry; we'll tell you anything we want to pass on before you go. But for tonight, let's take this as an excuse to celebrate. We're happy to hear everyone is all right in Hyolon. And if I recall, while there's a lot of good wine in Hyolon, there didn't seem to be any beer."

"No," Duri said, swishing his around in his glass again. "I do enjoy a well-brewed beer every once in a while, too. More than wine, really, although it goes in waves."

"Well, have some more, there's plenty," Rioletta said. "Tell us more about what your life is like in Hyolon now and what's happening with Malbec and Chasan. Let's get some dinner, too. I've nothing else to do this afternoon other than listen to news from outside."

"Me either," Andor said, catching Rioletta's eye as she stepped to Duri's side to refill a pitcher from a small cask. "Go on, Duri, talk to us."

Duri was more than willing to hold court, and settled in to describing his life and the politics of the Outcast community, then moved on to descriptions of the city and the districts and how he'd learned to navigate through the streets and avoid the Hyolonal. Through sessions with Kwistocta, he'd learned to access the memories of Malbec and Chasan as he wished. Rioletta continued to refill his glass; Cardon, Andor, and Rioletta drank more conservatively, and listened carefully.

"They treat you like a Sorcerer there, it seems," Rioletta commented. "You've learned some Skills?"

Duri nodded sleepily. "Yes, the basics, and a few more. I can use talismans for communication, Monitor. I've learned a few Reading Skills, and Cardon, I can animate objects as well!"

"I wasn't aware many people taught that Skill," Cardon said. "I learned it directly from Rudon."

"Me, too," Duri said, then opened his eyes wide and grinned. "That is, I learned it from someone who learned it from Rudon: Malbec. One of the advantages of accessing their minds is that I also know the Skills that are intact in their memories. Very useful."

Rioletta exchanged a quick glance with Andor. She wasn't sure if Duri was lying, and had actually learned it from Rudon, or if he had in fact been able to access Malbec's mind well enough to extract and use Sorcerer-level Skills. Duri wasn't trained as a Sorcerer, and the thought of him using not only Sorcerer-level, but *Forbidden* Skills, was somewhat alarming.

After Duri fell asleep in his chair, Rioletta walked Andor and Cardon outside, where night had fallen hours before.

"Well, nothing definitive," Andor said. "I wouldn't be surprised if he's had contact with Rudon, though. Be careful with what messages you give to him to pass along to Hyphanden. Now I have to go home. Creed will be wondering where I've got to and why I've been drinking beer without him."

"Are you sure you'll be all right with him sleeping in your house?" Cardon asked.

"Yes, Cardon, he's out cold, and besides, I can take care of myself, thank you," Rioletta replied. "Don't worry."

Cardon disappeared into the dark towards his house, and Rioletta returned to her own and turned down the lights. She left Duri sleeping in the chair and retired to her bedroom.

In the morning, Duri appeared a bit worse for wear. Rioletta made him breakfast and gave him some pain medication, and eventually he began to wake up and become more himself.

"I need to visit my relatives, I suppose, before I leave," Duri said. "I haven't had any contact with them for a while; it'll be awkward. But since I'm here, I guess I'll do it. Have you thought of anything you want to pass on to anyone at Hyolon?"

"Only my greetings, and the hope that I'll either see them here in Andolith, or be able to meet them elsewhere in the future. My sincere thanks to Hyphanden and Kwistocta for their help. A special thanks to Kerdahl, as well, and tell Stetsor I saw his grandfather and we had a nice talk. You can tell Hyphanden that Stetsordahl the Elder remembers him fondly, with no malice, and wishes him well. I promised Stetsordahl I'd give him more news of Hyphanden and Kwistocta when I could, and it seems I may have the opportunity to visit him in West Ford."

Duri shrugged. "I can pass that on easily enough. Thanks for the food and the beer, though I had enough of it to last me for a while. Oh, and one thing I almost forgot: Hyphanden sent this for you. A gift, he said, an antique from Hyolon he thought you'd like."

Duri reached in a vest pocket and pulled out a small talisman, which he dropped into Rioletta's hand. It was stone, like most talismans, but carved intricately into a tiny dog, curled with its head over its feet, and with a carved collar with a hole in it so it could be hung as a pendant.

"It's charming!" Rioletta exclaimed. "Thank him for me! I'll certainly enjoy it. Ride safely, and bring us news again some time."

242

Duri scrutinized her face as she put the talisman on a shelf in the main room, and she wondered if he'd tried to decipher any Skills placed on it on his way to Andolith. She wouldn't try it herself until he was gone, but she undoubtedly had more Skills than he did, and might be able to unlock it more efficiently. It could even have been coded for her alone, and no one else would be able to access it.

It was that evening before she had a chance to relax alone in her house and examine the talisman more closely. After a few tries, she felt a kind of vibration from it, but she was unable to decipher exactly what it meant or what function it performed. It was perhaps a communication talisman like the black glass pendant. She'd have to work at it, but meanwhile she placed it on the shelf with a good view of her room, in case Hyphanden could use it as a Viewing stone. She did not begrudge him that; his contact with the outside world was limited, and if he wished to expand his horizons, she was happy to oblige. The little dog's sleepy, jeweled, life-like eyes peered down at her as she went about cleaning up, and every once in a while she gave it a glance.

Chapter Twenty

A few days after Duri left, several members of the Tabor Elder Council arrived in Andolith. Stetsordahl was accompanied by Lindordahl Vrinal and Syravrina, as well as several young acolytes. Rioletta saw them as they passed her house enroute to the Council-house, where Ladon welcomed them. She hurried to follow, as Stetsor's arrival undoubtedly was a matter of state and thus business for both Councils. Amidon and Boradon soon arrived, and the other members of Andolith's Younger Council were called. Lindor greeted the Younger Council enthusiastically; he was the youngest of the Tabor Council, and closer in age to Andor and Morcah. The back rooms of the Council-house were turned out and prepared for occupancy to allow Stetsor and his group to stay comfortably.

Stetsor had business with Ladon, but afterwards he found Rioletta.

"Come and talk with me," he requested, and Rioletta left the rest of the Council and walked with him towards the sun-dial in the center of the village.

Stetsor slipped an arm around her shoulders and patted her in an almost fatherly way. "I have a gift for you," he said. "Or for Hyphanden; you may do with it as you see fit."

He slipped a hand into one of vest pockets and removed an object wrapped in soft cloth, which he placed in Rioletta's hand. It

245

was heavy, and fit neatly in her palm. Out of sight of the rest of the Council, Rioletta stopped and carefully opened the wrappings. A flat diamond-shaped stone, less than an inch thick, lay upon her palm; although translucent in the sun, it appeared deep lavender, grading to pink around the edges. The sides were beveled and the corners rounded, so it felt smooth in the hand; it seemed to weigh more than it should.

"Stetsor, are you sure this is the right decision?" Rioletta asked quietly after a moment.

"Young lady, I'm never sure my decisions are correct until long after I've made them," he said with a smile. "In some cases I've never found out. Who can tell how the things we do will affect the far future? I've decided to give this talisman to you, and that is as it will be."

"Thank you," Rioletta said, wrapping the talisman carefully back up in the cloth. "I can only tell you that it's an index, but that you already knew. It's a source of information that I hope will help someone make safer decisions."

"And I can truthfully tell any emissary of Rudon's that I don't have it," Stetsor said. "Not that I fear him or his minions. But if there is to be some contest of wills between Hyphanden and Rudon, as I suspect from the little you've revealed to me, I would prefer that the victory go to Phando. Hyolon as controlled by Rudon could be a dangerous place, not only for its inhabitants, but also for those of Tabor."

"I hope such a conflict never occurs," Rioletta said.

"So do I. Now, let's return you to your friends, and I am in need of a drink and rest."

The two walked slowly back through the village to the Council-house. Ladon looked at Rioletta curiously as they returned, but he did not question her regarding what business she might have with Stetsor. Rioletta kept the talisman in her satchel and later took it to her house, where she placed it carefully in a cabinet in the back. She was glad Duri had left before Stetsor's arrival; she was sure the talisman could be perceived by one searching for such a thing.

Nikal arrived the following week for a short visit. He brought a pack-horse loaded with glass goods, some of which he sold and a few of which he gave away. His side was well healed, with only five long brown scars to mark the places where the serpent-horse's teeth had scraped him. He had remained with Betar and Luridos for two days after Rioletta and the Andolith group left; then Adla had arrived and ridden with him back to Dobor. She'd continued to treat his wounds, and once home where he was able to rest, he had healed quickly.

The nights were chilly, with the first frosts on the ground in the morning, so in the evening the Younger Council and a few others from the village gathered in the Council-house in front of a fire and listened to news from Dobor while they shared beer and food. Nikal spent part of his time during the next few days with Pateret, as he'd convinced his Council he needed to go to Andolith to examine Pateret's family's gear transfer cases and blade configurations in their wind machines, and see how Andolith's water-turbine worked. Dobor was not likely to get a water-turbine, as there was no suitable running water nearby, but they did use wind machines and sun-plates, and were willing to share technology. Sun-plates and other sun-heaters generally used glass, so they were in less use in Andolith than the wind and water machines.

Nikal brought greenhouse plans, as well. Dobor had many greenhouses, which they could build because of their access to glass. An interest in greenhouses would increase Dobor's trade potential with Andolith; Rath had one at her place in Luth, although it was patched and incomplete. Nikal had agreed to bring enough glass from Dobor in the spring to build a demonstration greenhouse in the communal garden.

Alone at night, Rioletta told Nikal about Duri's visit, the attack on Hyphanden's party, and their suspicions about Duri. Nikal was quite interested, but he was also less concerned.

"Duri has two other partial minds on board," he said. "I doubt Cardon could tell from a distance whether Duri had duplicitous plans, or was simply of more than one mind, so to speak. He brought the news and messages from Hyolon at some risk to himself, I would suspect; anyone who caught him and realized what he is would likely take him to Tabor for examination and possible imprisonment. After all, he now practices both the Forbidden Skills and Technologies, so he is a double threat. Cardon worries over much."

"And you discount him overmuch," Rioletta countered. "Cardon was once a Sorcerer, and retains all his Skills."

"You defend him, as you always do," Nikal snapped. "You still have feelings for him."

"I defend him the way you would defend Adla if I said something you felt was unfair about her," Rioletta rejoined. "There is nothing more to it."

"Fair enough," Nikal said. "I'm sorry; I don't know Cardon as well as you, and I've never known him as a functional Sorcerer, so you may be right."

"There's no reason to worry about Cardon, Nikal," Rioletta said. "Our lives have moved in different directions. And Ladon has given me leave to investigate some of the information I learned during our journey to Hyolon, within bounds and reason. I have something to show you."

She went into the back room and retrieved the Index talisman, still wrapped in its cloth. She placed it carefully on the table in front of Nikal.

"Take a look."

Nikal unwrapped the talisman and picked it up. He examined it curiously from all sides.

"It's the Index, Nikal. Stetsordahl gave it to me. This is what we were missing: a way to identify who is in the matrix of the Crypt of Souls, when they were placed in there, and why; perhaps even details about their lives."

"This would allow the opener of the Crypt to pick and choose which mind to remove, and to be prepared for the kind of information and personality he'd encounter," Nikal said. "It would be most useful for Hyphanden. He could determine whose minds he holds in his estate, and make better decisions as to what to do with them in the long run."

"Or whether or not to access them," Rioletta pointed out.

"I hope he won't consider doing that," Nikal said. "It's dangerous, even for one as accomplished as he is. Kwistocta dislikes the idea of it, and she has had considerable experience, both with the minds of Chasan and Skadar, and the minds she involuntarily took on in the Crypt. I trust her judgment on this."

"But the information he could gain could be valuable; perhaps he could learn Skills to use against Rudon if Rudon makes trouble for them. Perhaps he could discover information valuable to all of us."

"If so, it would probably be Forbidden knowledge, so it would never reach us," Nikal said. "I would not give him a tool to use if this is what he intends."

"The decision about how to use it is his alone," Rioletta said. "Once we give it to him, we won't be able to control what he does."

Nikal considered for a minute, turning the talisman over in his hand. "Do you trust him and Kwistocta, the rest of the Outcast Council, enough to give them this piece of the secret of the Crypt of Souls? Do you truly want to put more power in the hands of the Outcasts?"

"If you had asked me that this spring, I would have been horrified," Rioletta replied. "But I've discovered a great deal in the time since then. Things are not as I imagined in the Ruined City, nor do the Forbidden Skills appear to be quite as I have been taught. My inclination is to send this to Hyphanden and to put it in his hands to deal with. Who better to deal with the issues of Hyolon than he?"

"All right," Nikal said. "But how are we to get it to him? I don't think much of trying to contact Duri in Tabor, and giving it into his hands."

"No, that's not a good way to do it," Rioletta agreed. "We must send it with someone we trust a great deal, or bring it ourselves."

"Then it seems you'll have to visit the Tadian again," Nikal said with a smile. "We'll pay a visit to Hyphanden and Kwistocta and bring them this gift. We can go this winter, if you can get away; it's warmer around Hyolon than it is here, and it will be a nice break from the snow for you. In the meantime, what do we do with it? It's likely Rudon is still searching for it, as well as the book. I would hate to have both of them here in Andolith, drawing attention."

"Do you want to take it to Dobor?" Rioletta asked.

Nikal re-wrapped the Index. "I can find a place for it for a short while. But I'd like to see Rudon's face when he finds out Hyphanden has access to both the Index and the Key, as he surely will eventually!"

Rioletta took the Index to store it until Nikal left. As she passed the shelf upon which she'd put the little dog talisman, the gift from Hyphanden, she noticed that its half-lidded eyes almost seemed to glow in the light of the lamps. The dog had a content look upon its muzzle, and she could almost have sworn its sleepy eyes winked as she went by.

About the author:

K.A. Krisko is the author of fantasy fiction novels, mysteries, and non-fiction and literary short stories. She grew up living in national parks, where her father worked as a ranger. Her mother, a William and Mary graduate in English Literature, encouraged her to write, read, and recite poetry competitively. Her father took her on star walks and taught her about lightning. Later she became a ranger herself, and worked in parks from Texas to California. She now lives in northern Colorado with her two Australian Cattle Dogs. She enjoys walking and hiking with her dogs, canine scentwork, DIY around the house, and reading and writing.

Join me at:
kakrisko.com

Other works by K.A. Krisko:

Novels:

Stolen (Book One of the Stolen Trilogy)
Crypt of Souls (Book Two of the Stolen Trilogy)
Hyphanden's Box (Book Three of the Stolen Trilogy)
The Stolenworld Companion
Cornerstone: Raising Rook (Book One, Cornerstone)
Cornerstone: The Delving (Book Two, Cornerstone)
AFTERThought (A Derange Mystery)

Short Stories:

The Snow Deer and Other Stories (short story anthology)
Finding Mandel (in Of Words and Water 2014)
The Name of the Dog (in Of Words and Water 2014)
The Natural Seize (in Of Words and Water 2013)
One Wet Dog (in Happy Endings II & on Amazon)
Almost A Dog (in Happy Endings I)
The Possessed RV (in American Blue: Real Stories by Real Cops)
Mother Bear (in Wisdom of Our Mothers)

www.ingramcontent.com/pod-product-compliance
Lightning Source LLC
Chambersburg PA
CBHW061609170626
46811CB00001B/365